# MOVING TARGET

A PORTER NOVEL

R.A. MCGEE

*To The Original RAM*

*What I wouldn't give to play one more round with you. I'd drag those eighteen holes out for days...*

LIKE FREE BOOKS?

Check in at the end of the book to see how you can get R.A. McGee's starter library, for free!

# ONE

PIMA WONDERED where the men took the drugs when they were done making them. She wasn't dumb; she knew people would pay a lot of money for the stuff in the big containers below. Her town had plenty of people who wanted the drugs.

Not Pima.

She loved to stay near the creek, hidden in her tree, and watch. Watch the men below as they went back and forth, planting big water bottles in the creek bed, retrieving the yellow rocks when they were done, and sometimes taking breaks to smoke some of their goods.

The woods were filled with a sickly-sweet smell when they did, and Pima would hold her breath as the smoke climbed high into her tree.

Pima would often take pictures of the men with the phone her parents had just given her. It was for emergencies, they'd said. She told herself it was okay to use the phone for pictures. That one day, she'd show the pictures to her father, and he could figure out who the men were and stop them. Pima hadn't quite managed to show him the pictures stashed on the phone yet, because that would put an end to her secret place and the fun she had when she snuck away.

It wasn't a complete secret, of course. Scarlett knew. She'd come with Pima many times before, pedaling their bicycles over the hill, cutting across two farm fields and taking a secret way into the little valley where they'd hide in the trees and watch the men for hours.

But Scarlett had band practice today, and couldn't get out of it. Mr. Rutherford could be a ballbuster.

The men were more active than normal today, so Pima had to be extra quiet as she listened in on their conversation below.

"Did you plant that last base?" the man with the red hat said.

"Not yet, Seth. Give me a minute."

"What's the problem? Get your ass moving. You being so slow is costing me money."

"I'm tired," the big man said.

Pima had seen these two the most. Seth, the wiry one, always kept his hat low and Pima had never been close enough to see his face, but she knew it wouldn't be good to look at. The one he was treating like a pack mule was Dusty.

He was big.

Actually, *big* didn't cover it. She'd never stood next to him, but from her tree he looked like a giant. Or at least an ogre. He had big arms covered with tattoos and a square head with no hair.

"Tired? Hell, I thought you was some kinda athlete. You should be able to do this all day, you lazy asshole."

"I'm not lazy, Seth, I just need a break. I been pulling these jugs all day. I'm tired. Maybe if you'd let me get right, I could work a little harder," Dusty said.

"What'd I tell you? No more 'til we get done. We got too much to do."

Dusty mumbled to himself.

"Besides, never get high on your own supply."

Dusty looked at Seth, his face scrunched up. "What's that mean?"

"Ain't you ever listened to Biggie Smalls?"

"Is he a rapper? I don't do rap."

Seth shook his head. "You need to expand your horizons. He had a song called 'Ten Crack Commandments.' One of them was, 'Never get high on your own supply.' Because then you make dumb decisions and waste time. And my money."

"But you smoke all the time."

"Yeah, it's my shit," Seth said. "I can do what I want."

"Isn't Richie in charge? I thought it was his."

Seth stood and drained out the last of his beer, adding the can to the growing pile at his feet. "All you need to know is I'm your boss. Got a problem with that?"

"No, Seth."

Pima watched the two men arrange the big water jugs and put plastic piping in them.

"You got any of that music?"

Seth opened another beer. "What music?"

"That Big guy," Dusty said.

"In the truck."

"Can I listen to some?"

"Yeah, man, when we're done. Now get your big ass to work."

"Okay, Seth."

Pima watched as Dusty grabbed three of the big bottles—like from the watercooler at her dad's office—picked them up, and carried them off to the side of the creek that ran through the small valley the men hid their stash in.

After Dusty clambered down into the creek, digging out space and stuffing the jugs into it, Seth stood on uneasy feet.

Pima thought several times that he would fall over, but he caught his balance and slowly walked over to the tree she was hiding in. She was still as a statue, perfectly hidden in the mass of branches despite the fact that half the leaves had fallen off for the year.

Seth leaned against the tree, then reached for the front of his pants, unzipping and loosing himself.

Pima looked close, then squeezed her eyes shut.

It wasn't that she hadn't seen one of those before. The internet was a weird place; she'd seen more than she wanted to. It wasn't that she wasn't interested in them, either. She dreamed of the day she'd meet a boy who wasn't an immature idiot so she could see what all the fuss was about.

But she definitely wasn't interested in Seth's.

Eyes closed, Pima counted to a hundred. That way, Seth would be done peeing and there would be no chance of seeing *it* again. Around seventy-five, she felt a pang of hunger in her stomach, and her mind drifted off to what her mom was making for dinner. She was pretty sure it was Taco Tuesday.

The sound of Seth's stream on the crunchy leaves stopped, but Pima gave it another minute or so just to be sure, then peeked below her.

Seth was still at the base of her tree, except now he was looking right up at her, his bloodshot eyes locked onto her.

"Huh. I thought you was dead or something, all in that tree not moving."

Pima's breath caught in her chest. She didn't say anything, instead remaining perfectly still.

"Girl, I ain't that drunk. I see you there. Get down here."

Pima didn't answer. Her breath returned, except now it was fast—faster than she could control—and she was getting lightheaded.

"You won't come down, huh? That's okay. When I hunt

coons, they won't come down either. I got something for that." Seth pulled out a revolver, big and shiny in his grip. He aimed it at Pima with unsteady hands, wavering back and forth.

Pima wanted to turn away, to not see the big gun, but her eyes were drawn to it. She couldn't even blink. She watched as Seth swayed back and forth before leaning a little too far back on the uneven ground and falling on his ass.

"Dammit," he said as he pulled himself to his feet. "I shouldn't shoot you anyway. You might have some info, huh? I want to know who you're spying for." He stuffed his pistol back into his waistband. "Maybe I can't shoot, but I can damn sure climb up there and get your ass."

With that, he cracked his knuckles and circled the bottom of the tree's thick trunk. Pima lost sight of him as he moved to the back, then found him again as he circled back around.

"You gotta be a damn monkey to climb this thing," he said.

Pima's knuckles were white as she gripped the branch she sat on. She watched as Seth hoisted himself up onto the first branch, then the next, and the next.

"Go away!" she screamed. "Leave me alone."

"Don't think so, girlie." Seth climbed a bit more, then paused and looked around. "You seen some stuff you shouldn't have."

Seth pulled himself up to the next limb and Pima moved. She slid closer to the tree trunk, her foot too close to her pursuer for comfort. She picked her way down the tree, staying opposite of Seth, keeping the big trunk in between them.

Pima was much smaller, more nimble—and sober—and she moved quickly through the branches. She moved down until she was out of limbs to climb. Her favorite way down, the best way down, was on the other side of the tree. The side Seth was on.

Instead, she looked down at a ten-foot drop to the damp forest floor.

"I'll be right there," Seth said.

Pima couldn't see him, but heard him as he lumbered through the branches. She lay on her stomach, then wiggled back until her weight was supported by her arms. Then she slid back just enough so she could hang.

She stayed like that for several seconds, feet dangling above the earth until her grip started to slip. She counted to three and let go.

The ground rushed up to meet her and then Pima tasted dirt and copper in her mouth. She wiped her face and looked down at her blood-streaked hand.

Pima looked from her hand back to the tree. Above her, Seth was starting to pick his way down the tree, so she pulled herself to her feet and ran as fast as her legs could carry her. She pumped her arms up and down, trying to remember the things she'd learned in track practice the previous spring.

Somewhere behind her, Seth roared something she couldn't make out. She didn't stop to think about it. Ahead was the grove of thickets where she'd hidden her bike. It was just in sight, and growing closer with every stride.

Her hair trailed behind her in the breeze and the taste and smell of blood was replaced by the smell of an Appalachian fall, trees and all. She reached the thicket and threw off the extra branches she'd left on top of her bike, slinging her leg over and balancing on the pedals.

Using her momentum to push the bike forward, Pima heard Seth roar again and turned to take a peek, sure the man was right on her heels.

He wasn't. He'd just made it down the tree and was pointing at her, running after her.

Pima turned back around and rode face-first into the biggest fist she'd ever seen.

It knocked her up into the air, and she crashed into the dirt, her bike rolling away on its own. She couldn't open her eyes, so she clawed at the dirt, pulling herself along, trying to get away from Seth. She wondered how he'd caught up to her so fast.

She forced her eyes open and looked straight up at Dusty, the giant. He was so much larger on the ground than he had looked from her safe tree.

Pima coughed and sputtered. "Hel... Help me. Please."

Dusty reached down and wrapped one hand around her throat and began to squeeze. Pima had never felt anything like it before. It was like she was trapped at the bottom of the world's deepest pool and everything was crushing down on her.

She clawed and scratched at him, unable to reach his face, instead digging her nails into his forearms. He didn't seem to mind. As everything started to turn black, Pima was struck by how bad Dusty's teeth were, and how he had no eyebrows.

The last thing she heard as she blacked out was Seth screaming, "Don't kill her! Don't kill her."

And Pima Newton remembered nothing else.

# TWO

THE WOMAN in the tiny skirt leaned over the pool table, unsteady on her heels, which were higher than anyone with sense would wear. It was the third time she'd done it in the last ten minutes, smiling at Porter each time.

He'd tried to avoid eye contact, instead focusing on the large screen above her table. Last week's fights were on, a repeat, but the place was too loud for him to hear the commentary. He tried to keep his eyes on the television, but the lime-green set of panties was tough to ignore.

Instead, he swirled the finger of vodka around his plastic cup, hoping to be spared emphysema from the secondhand smoke. He leaned back in his chair; the front door was a better place to keep his eyes.

"You need a refill?" a waitress said. Her T-shirt was emblazoned with a logo of an alley cat wearing a leather vest and riding a motorcycle.

"I'm good. Just waiting for someone," Porter said, loud enough to be heard over the crackle of the music from oversized speakers.

"It's okay to drink alone," the waitress said. "You don't have to lie to feel good about yourself." She turned, off to try to hustle the next patron for a drink order and tip.

The place was small, barely fifty feet from the front to the back door. Even though daylight streamed in through the glass door, it was like night on the inside.

Porter went back to swirling his booze. A legitimate look at the television screen again resulted in an inadvertent look at green panties. This time, one of the pair of leather-vest-clad men with the woman was staring him down.

Porter had noticed their colors as soon as he walked in. It had been a while since it was his job to know the various motorcycle clubs and what their patches meant, but this one was pretty basic. There was a logo of several mountain peaks, with what appeared to be blood poured over them. The big patch at the bottom, called a rocker, read "Peaks MC."

On the front of the vests, the men had a myriad of patches, the most notable being the white diamond which read "1%."

The term had come from a misquoted article saying that ninety-nine percent of motorcycle riders were good law-abiding citizens. The other one percent were proud of their outsider status and cared very little what anyone else thought of them. Porter was sure that one-percenters hadn't done an about-face and suddenly decided to walk the straight and narrow. It was trouble he didn't need.

He looked away from the pool table.

The front door opened and a man stepped in, backlit by the sun. It was impossible to see clearly, but Porter nevertheless recognized the man's stocky silhouette and waved him over.

He tried not to notice the man's limp as he moved, a big hitch in his step as he navigated the bar floor.

Porter stood and embraced the man when he made it to the table. The hug was awkward—he towered over the man—but genuine. None of the half-hugs that tough guys usually gave each other.

"Nice mustache," Porter said as he examined the man's face. Porter used to tell him that he looked like a cartoon character, the human version of the bulldog that always kicked Tom's ass to help Jerry out. New to his appearance was a thick handlebar mustache, which suited him fine.

"Me? What about that beard? You lose your razor?"

"I'm not as pretty as you are, Joe. I have to hide some of this ugly mug."

The men laughed.

Joe tapped Porter's drink. "Plastic cups? You like the finer things in life now?"

"I was going to eat, but I figured I'd pass on the *E. coli*," Porter said. "Besides, you picked the place; don't blame me for the drinkware."

"I figured it was as nice a place as any to catch up."

"Really?" Porter waved his hand around. "Just give it a minute to let the smell catch up to you. Your house—that would be a nice place to catch up. This is a shithole."

"Thing is... I don't have it anymore. When Heather left, she took half of everything, so I had to sell the place off."

Porter raised his eyebrows. "What?"

"I don't blame her. She stayed home all those years taking care of the house. She deserves something, you know? It just means I had to downsize a bunch. No biggie."

Porter swirled the vodka in his glass. "I didn't know about that."

Joe nodded his head. "It's okay, kid; it's been a while. I don't expect you to keep up with an old man."

"Stop it." Porter looked toward the fight again, another glance across the pool table. This time the girl was sitting in her chair, a cross look on her face. The man who'd mean-mugged

Porter was talking to a much larger friend, clad in the same colors.

"Enough of my sob story—what about you? You married way up, you know that, right? You'd never find another woman to keep you in line."

"Me and Trish got divorced."

Joe grimaced. "Damn, kid, I'm sorry to hear that. It's okay, I never liked her anyway."

"Liar," Porter said.

"Yeah, I'm lying. She was amazing. I'm guessing she left you?" Joe said.

"Of course," Porter said.

"Sometimes it just doesn't work out. Like me and Heather. I never even seen it coming. One day, bang, here's my papers. But it's okay. I've got the job and I've got Amanda, and that's all I need."

Porter nodded. "How old is Amanda now? When I left, she was in high school."

"She's great, kid. Just got out of grad school, believe it or not. She does something with computers I don't even understand. Not sure where she gets her brains from, but it ain't me."

"Grad school? Good for her. Maybe I'll buy her a drink to celebrate," Porter said with a small smile, sure of the reaction he'd get.

"Not only no, but hell no. My daughter's too good for you, Porter. She deserves better than knuckle-draggers like us," Joe said. "She needs... an architect or a lawyer or something like that. Not you."

"Now you're just trying to hurt my feelings," Porter said, standing up and moving his chair back.

"What, you leaving? I just got here."

Porter patted the older man on his back. "Relax, I gotta piss. Unless you want to hold it for me, give me a minute."

He moved down a nearly dark hallway until he saw a wooden door with a plywood patch over it. He stepped into the restroom and was assaulted by the smell of urine. He held his breath as he did his business, careful not to get his Chuck Taylors in the small puddle of piss underneath the urinal.

The door swung open and the man with the Peaks MC vest came in. The smell of urine was overpowered by the odor of stale beer. Now that he was closer, Porter could see the man's small, stringy goatee and the motorcycle chain he wore for a necklace. The bright light of the bathroom also revealed eyes that were impossibly dilated, and the man's pasty skin stood in stark contrast to Porter's mocha complexion.

Porter flushed and moved to the sink. The man replaced him at the urinal. "You think I don't see what the hell you're doing?"

"What's that?" Porter said, looking at the man via the mirror.

"You're dogging my girl and I don't like that shit."

Porter turned around as the man finished up. The patch on the front of his vest read "Joker." "I'm just watching the fights. I can't help it if her ass is up in the air. Maybe you should take it up with her."

Joker smiled and ground his teeth. "I'll reprimand her later. Right now, I'm checking you."

Porter shrugged. "Reprimand? Check? I don't speak biker. If you can't speak English, I think we're done." Porter moved to the door, but Joker blocked the way with his arm.

"You be sure you hear what I'm telling you, boy."

Porter had six inches and a hundred pounds on the man. "I'm going to let the 'boy' thing slide. This is North Carolina and maybe you've never learned better. But if you don't move your arm, I'm going to rip it off and slap your girl on the ass with it. *Then* I'll be hitting on her."

Joker blinked at Porter several times, then slid out of the way.

"Good choice," Porter said and slung the door open, slamming it into the stunned Joker.

Porter walked down the hallway and back to the table to find that Joe had slid his chair next to his.

"Hey," Joe said as Porter sat back at the table. "I didn't mean any offense about Trish or anything. You kids were a good couple."

"The best," Porter said.

"What happened?"

"We just... we just grew apart," Porter said, pushing aside memories he didn't want to think about. "It didn't work out. Change the subject."

Joe nodded. "You got it, kid." He looked around then motioned Porter in. "So the thing I called you about. You interested?"

"I drove ten hours, didn't I?"

"Good, good. I have a file to give you, out in the car. I figured it would be better not to meet at the office, you know?"

"Are you ashamed of me? We used to go everywhere together and now you won't even show me off to your work friends, will you?"

Joe laughed. "Something like that."

Porter leaned in. "I get it. Better if we keep this thing under wraps."

"Good. So here's the short version." Joe looked around one more time. "Mike Newton's kid went missing."

"Who?"

"Mike Newton," Joe said.

Porter shook his head.

"Come on, you remember him, right? We hit a couple of houses with him back in the day?"

"Doesn't ring a bell," Porter said.

"Whatever. He's one of the good ones. Not one of us, you know, but still a solid guy," Joe said.

"What happened?"

"No one knows. The girl was here one day and then she never came home from school," Joe said.

"How old is she?"

"Thirteen," Joe said.

"Runaway." Porter took a sip of his vodka.

"Not this kid," Joe said. "Not Pima."

"What kind of name is Pima?"

"How the hell do I know?" Joe said. "What does it matter?"

Porter frowned. "What have you guys done so far?"

As Joe started to list a myriad of steps and procedures, movement drew Porter's eye. Joker and his much larger friend had left the pool table and were walking toward them. Porter sighed and leaned back in his chair.

Joe stopped talking. "What? Am I boring you?"

"You'll see—"

"Hey, asshole," Joker said.

"There it is," Porter said to Joe.

"You hit me with that door," the biker said. "I don't appreciate that shit."

"You should have moved," Porter said. "Only an idiot stands in the middle of a doorway."

Joker's friend had a patch on that read "Priest." He wasn't as big as Porter, but was no small man, and Porter could see a knife strapped to his belt. "Maybe I don't like you touching my boy."

"Priest? Your name is Priest? You know you can't find a church. Do you even know how to spell *church*?"

The man stepped closer, but stopped short when Joe slammed his fist into the tabletop. In his other hand was a shiny badge, impossible not to make out, even in the gloom of the bar.

"I bet you can spell this, can't you? FBI? Real easy, only three letters. So, unless you want me to get involved, I suggest you and your entire dumb-ass wagon train get the hell out of here."

Joker and Priest looked at each other, then at the badge Joe held.

"Well?" The mustachioed bulldog had come to his feet and was leaning toward the two interlopers.

The men backed off, muttering things under their breath. They grabbed green-panty girl and were out the front door in moments.

"'Dumb-ass wagon train'?" Porter said. "What the hell does that even mean?"

# THREE

"GIVE ME A BREAK, kid. I'm trying." Joe slid his badge away and settled into his seat again. "Used to be, I'd have dragged those idiots out back and tuned them up myself."

"I know. I've seen you."

"It's just—time catches up, you know? I'm mandatory in a few months, then they're gonna push me out the door."

Federal agents had a strict age cap on their career. Anyone still on the job at age fifty-seven was summarily handed retirement papers. Do not pass go, do not work any longer. Thanks for giving us the better part of your life, now go away.

"That's probably best. You don't need to be chasing people down at your age," Porter said.

"Your time's coming. What are you now, twenty-three, twenty-four?" Joe said with a smirk. "Hell, you even old enough to drink the stuff in that cup?"

Joe knew full well how old Porter was. It had been almost a decade and a half since Porter had been a new agent with the Department of Homeland Security. He'd been the youngest guy on a multi-agency task force that Joe commanded, which was composed of several federal, state, and local law-enforcement entities.

He was the best boss Porter had ever worked for.

Porter'd been green and new, and Joe had taken the time to show him everything: the right way to do things, as well as the most effective. Often, those were two *very* different approaches.

"Hell, my time's here," Porter said. "I feel everything creaking in the morning when I get up."

"Cry me a river, kid. You still have your momma's breast milk on your breath."

"That's better than having your mom's breast milk on my breath," Porter said with a smile.

Joe laughed and smacked Porter on the arm. "The job, it just isn't what it used to be. When you worked for me, what did we do? Real work. Gangs and drugs and perverts—real criminals. Now everything is bitcoins and computers. White-collar bullshit. Even this weekend, we caught a big load of meth out by the coast, but it was so boring. Traffic stop by the troopers, then they called us to take over. Everything's different."

Porter nodded.

"Hell, you aren't even in anymore. When you were on my task force, I thought you'd do the job until you keeled over and died."

"I'm happier," Porter said.

"Really?"

He thought for a moment. "Leaving was a good thing. Working for myself pays better. Speaking of which..."

"Right, Pima." Joe looked around, then leaned in toward Porter. "Like I was saying before we got interrupted by the Sons of Idiocy, she's gone, and we could use some help."

"Your guys couldn't find her? That's what you do."

"Nope. I've had almost fifty guys out there combing the area and none of them can find shit. It's disappointing."

"Why do you think I'll do better?" Porter said.

Joe narrowed his eyes. "Please. You've got a pretty good track record of finding these kids. Not to mention, sometimes my hands are... restrained."

"And I don't have those restraints," Porter said matter-of-factly.

"Bingo," Joe said.

Porter rubbed his face. The drive had left him a bit tired; he had hit the road as soon as he'd heard from Joe, despite the unreasonable hour. "How much did you say the reward was?"

"A shitload," Joe said. "We set up one of those fund-me sites. Got to seventy-five grand in one day. If somebody finds Pima, they get it all. That somebody might as well be you."

"Might as well," Porter said. "Here's the thing. It might look like I just haphazardly find these kids, but I usually pick my cases very selectively. I like to make sure I give myself a decent chance of getting the job done. I'm not sure about Pinya."

"Pima," Joe said

"Whatever. What if I say no?" Porter said.

"Then you say no. I can't force you to do anything. I just figured, with the line of work you're in now, this was a match made in heaven. Nice check, spend a little time in North Carolina again. Plus, you got me helping you. It'll be like the old days," Joe said.

"Like hell it will," Porter said.

Joe frowned. "Why not?"

"There's a reason we met at a bar and not your office. I was joking earlier, but I get it. You have to keep out of this. People can't find out the FBI is leaking information to a regular dick-head off the street."

"But you aren't a regular dickhead," Joe said. "You're a special dickhead."

"To you. To everyone else, I'm just Joe Schmuckatello. If I

help, you aren't coming with me. You're staying right here," Porter said.

Joe looked hurt. "What do you mean? I'm solid. I'd never tell anyone anything, you know that."

"I do know that. I also know that if people find out, they could try to hang you for it. Just the fact that you're telling me this is a fireable offense, isn't it? An ongoing investigation is privileged information. You want to get fired a month before you get that fat pension?"

Joe shook his head.

"Then it is what it is. Give me the file and I'll look it over. If I help, you aren't getting the full story about what's going on. You'll have to trust me. Those are my terms. Can you handle that?"

"Yeah, fine. Just try to keep me in the loop a little, okay? I can get you info if you need it."

Porter stood and fished a couple of bills out of his pocket, enough for his drink and a tip, and gestured to Joe. "Let's go get your file."

The men walked out of the dark tavern into the bright light of the day. Porter blinked the sun out of his eyes. Joe pushed him to the right. "I'm parked around back."

Shielding his eyes, Porter followed Joe around the small building to the back parking lot. He watched his friend limp the entire way.

Joe popped the trunk of an Impala, shiny and new.

"G-ride?" Porter said.

"Yep."

"They'd love it if they knew you were at a bar in it," Porter said.

"What are they gonna do, fire me?" Joe said. "By the time the paperwork goes through, I'll be sitting around with my feet up, smoking a Macanudo."

He unlocked a big, flat safe in his trunk and handed a manila file to Porter. "This is everything I got on the case. Who my guys talked to, who they didn't. When Pima left the house that morning, her usual routine, everything. If the answer is anywhere, it's in there."

Porter thumbed through it and shook his head. "Love all this paperwork."

"We're the FBI, what do you expect?"

"I'll check it out and let you know," Porter said.

Joe got into his sedan and paused for a moment. "Hey, Porter?"

Porter looked up from the file.

"Thanks for coming up."

"Anything for you, old man."

"I'm not that old," Joe said, firing up the new car and driving away, leaving Porter in the parking lot.

Lost in thought, Porter thumbed the file as he walked the blacktop to his car, an older model GMC Yukon. It was a holdover from a time when both he and his ex-wife had great jobs and no debt. The blue paint of the four-door Yukon had faded over time, but Porter loved it because both him and all his stuff fit comfortably inside.

Back at his car, he fished his key fob out, but before he could open the door, a motorcycle revved its throttle. He looked up to see two bikes rolling toward him. He sighed and opened the driver's side door, set the file Joe had given him on the seat, and then shut the door.

He slipped his keys into his pocket and turned toward the two men.

They cut their engines. "You probably should have got in that car," Joker said. The girl from the pool table was sitting on the back of his bike, smoking a cigarette.

"But then I wouldn't get to talk to you," Porter said.

Priest stepped off his bike, the sunlight revealing crudely inked tattoos on his arms. "We can talk, but you ain't gonna like what I have to say."

"Try me," Porter said, leaning against his truck.

Joker heeled his kickstand down and swung his leg off, like a soldier dismounting horseback. "Where's your FBI friend, huh?"

"He said he was going to your mom's house," Porter said with a smile. "Something about cleaning her pipes. I warned him not to—I mean, everybody's heard about your mom—but he said he was the man for the job."

Joker's eyes went wide and he charged the last ten feet between him and Porter. Porter saw the haymaker coming a mile away, and moved his head to the side, letting Joker's hand bang into the door jamb.

The biker stepped back, howled with pain, and tucked his hand into his armpit, hopping around like he was on a pogo stick.

"Ouch," Porter said.

Priest was moving toward Porter, who stepped up to meet him. A small knife blade glinted in the sunlight as Priest moved it in short, controlled strokes. "I'll gut you, you son of a bitch."

Porter held his hands up, bouncing slightly on the balls of his feet, circling to get his back away from the Yukon. Priest moved from slashing to stabbing as Porter backed away. A big lunge left him off balance. Porter caught the biker's wrist with his right hand and slammed his forearm into the biker's elbow.

There was an audible crack as the joint gave way. With his arm now bent the wrong direction, Priest tried to pull away from Porter, but it was no use. Porter grabbed him by the back of the head and slammed half a dozen knees into his face.

Priest collapsed to the ground.

Porter looked over at Joker, who was still howling. He

smashed his right hand into the man's chin and knocked him out. Joker lost his feet and his head smacked against the asphalt.

Porter looked at the two men, then at the girl on the back of the bike. Her mouth was wide open and Porter watched the cigarette fall from her lips. "Get off the bike."

She stared at Porter. "But you... but... but..."

He reached his hand out and helped her off Joker's bike. "Be careful with those stupid heels."

She obeyed, carefully dismounting the motorcycle.

"What's your name?" Porter said.

"T-Tammy."

"Tammy, do you have a light?" Porter said.

"Huh?"

"A light. Do you have a light?" Porter said.

Tammy reached into her bra and pulled out a disposable Bic, handing it to Porter. "You're not gonna light them on fire, are you?"

"What? No, don't be stupid," he said. "Still, you may want to step back a little."

She moved backward, away from Porter and the motorcycles. He stepped over to the one Joker had gotten off of; unfamiliar as he was with bikes, he still recognized the Harley Davidson logo. He unscrewed the gas cap and pushed the big hog over. He did the same to Priest's bike, watching as the streams of gasoline intermingled on the blacktop of the parking lot.

Then he touched the Bic to the gasoline. He didn't even have to get too close—the gas vapors were flammable and caught first, transferring the flame to the actual puddles. The fire crept along the gasoline and into the gas tanks, until both of the pricey motorcycles were on fire.

The heat grew overwhelming and Porter stepped back. He slid the Bic into his pocket and jumped into his truck.

Tammy followed, giving a wide berth to the flaming motorcycles, and knocked on the window. "Hey, how about a ride?"

"I'm sure there's someone else you can call," Porter said. "I'll bet your Rolodex is full."

"Rolo-what?"

"Never mind," Porter said.

"You can't just leave me out here," Tammy said.

"Watch me."

"But I want to go with you," she said, switching to her best sultry voice. "Besides, I like black guys."

"You're out of luck. I'm only half."

"It's okay, I like Spanish guys, too."

Porter laughed as he rolled up the window, and was still shaking his head as he stomped the gas and left Tammy, the engulfed motorcycles, and the unconscious one-percenters in his rearview mirror.

# FOUR

PORTER STEPPED OFF THE ELEVATOR, hand squeezed tight around the handle of his duffle bag. He trudged through the lobby, over the shiny tile floor, and back to the front desk, ignoring the aches in his back and legs. He leaned on the counter, coming face-to-face with the thin man with the golf-ball-sized earrings weighing down his lobes.

"Problem?"

Porter held his clenched fist out in front of him, then opened it, letting a snapped room card fall to the counter. The man with the earrings, whose shiny nametag read "Clarence," looked down at the pieces.

"What's this?"

Porter dropped his duffle bag, then looked at the younger man. "How about I ask a question?"

Clarence scrunched up his face.

"What part of 'non-smoking' didn't you understand?" Porter said.

"I'm not sure what you mean."

"Are you just playing dumb, or is this a full-time thing for you?" Porter said.

Clarence's mouth opened, then shut.

Porter continued. "I got here, what, an hour ago? I had to wait for you to check in the person in front of me. No problem, I'm not special, I'll wait my turn. Then you took a phone call and disappeared for damn near half an hour. I'm patient; I get it. All I asked for was a non-smoking room. And you give me that shit."

"All our rooms are non-smoking."

"Then why does five-twenty-five smell like a cigar bar?"

Clarence looked at Porter, then tapped away on his keyboard. "That's all I got, pal."

"'Pal'? Okay, 'buddy,' here's the thing. I got up way earlier than I'd have liked and drove halfway up the Eastern seaboard. All I want to do is sleep somewhere that doesn't smell like a chain smoker's asshole. Can you make that happen or not?"

There was a small ding from the smartphone next to the hotel employee. He eyed the phone, then eyed Porter.

"Don't do it," Porter said.

Clarence snaked his hand out and grabbed his phone, turning it over to text.

Porter laughed to himself. "So, you aren't giving me a new room?"

"One second," Clarence said, fingers blazing away at the keyboard of the phone.

Porter reached over the counter and engulfed the man's phone, hands still attached. He squeezed. "It's been a second, Clarence."

"Ouch."

"Ouch? You have earrings the size of grapefruits and you say 'ouch?' You know what? I'll handle this myself. You can't be the most important person around here. Where's your boss?"

"We don't need to call hi—"

Porter pulled the man's hand toward him, dragging

Clarence halfway across the counter. "Sure we do." He let go of Clarence and looked at the wide Formica counter in front of him. At the end was a flip-up door, like a bar would have. Porter pushed it up and stepped behind the counter.

There was an elevated platform that the whole thing stood on. While they were talking, Porter and Clarence had been nose-to-nose. Now that he stood on the platform, Porter looked down at the hotel employee.

"You can't be back here. It's for employees only."

Porter watched Clarence briefly think about trying to bar his way, and then think better of it.

"Smart move, Clarence."

Porter walked down the hallway behind the counter. "Hey, boss? Boss, where you at?"

The hallway was narrow, and Porter's shoulders almost touched the sides. There were several empty offices, their blinds open, lights off. Down at the end of the hallway sat a lone office, metal blinds down and twisted shut. Faint lines of light leaked through the sides.

Porter's Chuck Taylors squeaked along the shiny linoleum as he walked toward the far door. "Hey, boss? I have a question."

He tried the handle. It was locked, so he knocked. "Is Clarence's boss in there? I have a question about hiring standards."

From behind the door, there was a faint rustling. "Just a minute," came a muffled reply.

Porter kept knocking. "Hello?"

"I said wait a damn minute."

Porter didn't let up, slamming his fist into the door over and over again.

The door swung open. A red-faced man answered, looking down at his belt buckle as he tried to fasten it. "Clarence, would you wait one fu—"

The man looked up at Porter and stopped talking. He dropped his belt, letting it hang from his waist. "Can... can I help you?"

"I would love some help. Mind if I come in?" Porter said, stepping past the man and into his office.

The manager stammered as Porter went by.

In the corner, by the window with the closed blinds, Porter saw a pretty woman with red hair pulling down her pencil skirt. He looked back at the manager. "Getting some cardio in?"

The woman began to blush, smoothing out the wrinkles on her blouse.

"Just... ah... just get me those profit and loss statements when you get a chance, Cynthia. Thanks," the manager said, standing straight and adjusting his tie.

Cynthia nodded and skinnied past Porter to get to the door. She broke into an awkward jog once she hit the doorway.

Porter sat heavily in the chair opposite the manager's. He took a quick look around and saw golf trophies and award plaques made out to James Huggins, a desk full of paperwork, and a small television in the corner. Most interestingly, he saw several photos of a handsome group of children, posing with their father and a mother who was decidedly not an attractive redhead.

The manager shut the door behind Cynthia and walked around his desk, gave one last sweep of his hand to check the status of his belt and fly, then sat down.

"What can I do for you, Mr...?"

"Porter."

"Mr. Porter, what can I do for you?"

"Just Porter."

"Okay, just Porter. What can I help you with?" the manager said, the red flush in his cheeks draining away.

Porter gave a quick rundown of the interaction with Clarence. The manager put on an overly sympathetic air.

"We have had problems with Clarence in the past. I assure you, I'll speak to him about this incident."

"I don't care what you do, Jim. Just give me a room that doesn't smell like a forest fire."

"I can make that happen," Jim the manager said, firing up his own desktop and tapping away noisily on the keyboard. "Just give me a couple minutes."

"That's mighty white of you," Porter said with a smirk. He reached across Jim's desk and picked up a picture. The entire smiling brood was posed in front of a ship's railing. "Have fun on your cruise?"

Jim stopped typing and took the picture away from Porter. "We had a great time."

"I'll tell you what—why don't you give me the type of room you'd let your family stay in if they were spending the night?" Porter said.

"I'm sorry?"

"Your kids? Wife? What kind of room would you put them up in? If you give me that one, I'll know I'm getting the all-star treatment."

Jim cleared his throat and went back to typing. "I would put my kids up in our best suite. Top floor, jacuzzi tub and all the amenities."

"Wow. So generous," Porter said. "How could I say no? I mean, if it's good enough for the Huggins family, it should be good enough for me."

Jim the manager worked feverishly, typing away on his computer. When he was done, an ancient printer whirred to life behind him, spitting out a piece of paper with all the proper information on it. "I was just thinking, my kids would get a comped room if they stayed. Only right I treat you the same."

"I like free," Porter said.

Jim handed Porter the new reservation printout. "All you have to do is see Clarence and he'll get you your new room key."

"You know, I'm not a big fan of Clarence. Maybe you should go and get it for me."

Jim chewed his lip, then stood and stepped out of the room. In less than a minute, he was back, holding a folded envelope with two room keys. "I trust your stay will be enjoyable."

"It better be, or I'm going to look you up again," Porter said.

Jim forced a smile. "Mr. Porter?"

"What'd I say?"

"Porter... one thing about my kids. They are excellent at keeping secrets. You follow my meaning?"

Porter took the key and smiled, leaving the manager hanging as he turned to seek out his new room.

# FIVE

THE SUITE DIDN'T DISAPPOINT.

Porter guessed it was nearly a quarter of the entire top floor, with absurdly expensive flooring and a bed that must have been larger than a king.

He pushed back the curtain to look at the city's skyline. While not as nostalgic as New York or as recognizable as the Sears building in Chicago, he had always liked the view of Charlotte. Despite having lived there for some time when he was younger, the only thing he could pick out was the Bank of America Stadium. He wondered if there would be a chance to catch a Panthers game while he was in town.

A long shower later, Porter felt almost human again. The aches and pains of the car ride had been washed away by enough hot water to sink the Titanic.

He took another look at the skyline and the late-afternoon sun washing over it, and set an alarm on his phone.

Sleep took him immediately.

* * *

HE WAS ROUSTED by a Johnny Cash song blaring through the shrill speaker on the bottom of his phone. Something about killing people just to watch them die.

He turned the alarm and pushed himself to his feet.

Porter had heard the song a hundred times, but it seemed like it was in another language. The power nap hadn't worked, and now he felt worse than before, his eyes almost glued shut.

He hit the shower again, hotter than he preferred, his skin actually pink in spots from the heat. As much as he hated staying in hotels, at least he didn't have to worry about paying the water bill. There was an added bonus of as many clean towels as he could get his hands on.

The towels were laid out on the floor, protection against whatever funk could be on it. The cream-colored tiles looked clean, cleaner than most of the places he stayed, but the thought of getting some sub-Saharan parasite between his toes before he put his socks on turned his stomach.

Porter dressed quickly, finishing his outfit with his favorite pair of Chucks and slipping his Glock 17 into his waistband. The pistol was larger than most would find comfortable, but for a guy his size, it fit like a glove. He was happy that North Carolina and Florida honored each other's concealed carry handgun permits.

He'd hate to have to break the law.

A quick elevator ride later and Porter was again in the lobby, which was empty save for Clarence talking away on his cell phone. He turned around when he saw Porter, who waved at the young man.

He stepped out into the crisp fall air. If there was anything that could get him to leave Florida for good, it would be the fact that the weather was atrocious and the heat was unbearable. A place with all four seasons had its appeal.

Porter fired up the Yukon. Although it was nearing a decade

in use, it still ran like a top. He dropped the shifter into drive and pulled out of the parking lot.

It had been twelve years since he'd worked in Charlotte. He hadn't kept up with the city in the interim, but he knew that if he was going to look through Joe's file, he'd need some brain food.

Fortunately, his favorite pizza joint was right where he'd left it, a bit older and more worn, but standing as a beacon of familiarity. He ordered his favorite and in minutes the big box was ready for take-out. Porter stepped to an empty table, stuffed a slice into his mouth, and closed the box lid, taking the rest to go.

Porter hopped into the Yukon and ran smack into one of the things that was very different from what he remembered: traffic.

He sat in the stop-and-go affair for nearly thirty minutes, trying to relax.

Stuck in traffic, his takeout pizza rapidly growing colder, Porter drummed his fingers along the steering wheel to "All Along the Watchtower." Before he could make a fool of himself with an air guitar solo, his phone rang. He let the call filter through the car's speaker.

"Yeah."

"What's going on?"

"I'm sitting in traffic. You?"

"Just got done with the worst client. In school, they always talk about a mythical person who's a decade behind on their taxes and comes into your office with everything in a shoebox and dumps it on you. I met that person today."

"Ross?" Porter said.

"What?"

"I didn't actually want to know that boring shit. I was just being polite."

"And you wonder why you're single," Ross said.

Porter laughed.

"How did the meeting go with your old boss?"

"It went. Some kid disappeared," Porter said, trying to cut into a lane of traffic.

"You're gonna help... Joe, right? That's his name?"

"I don't know. I mean, I should."

"Yeah, you should. Guy takes a bullet for you and you won't go and look into a missing kid for him? That's shitty," Ross said.

"What happened last time I did someone a favor? You were there; tell me. I'll wait."

"What happened, you big asshole, is you found the kid."

"I got shot," Porter said.

"So?"

Porter frowned. "Maybe I will."

"How much is the reward?"

"Seventy-five thousand."

"So what's the problem?"

Porter checked his rearview mirror and pulled all the way into the lane. "I don't know. It's weird—the kid, she's like thirteen. She's probably stoned on the couch at her boyfriend's house. Older kids always have a habit of just being somewhere they aren't supposed to be."

"Who cares? Find her high at her boyfriend's house. You're still getting the same check."

"You just want your cut of the money."

"My cut? My cut? When did I start taking a cut? That's news to me. I know I invest your money. I know I grow your money. I don't remember ever getting a cut," Ross said.

"If my best friend charges me for financial advice, what's the world coming to?"

"Don't worry. One of these days I'm just going to sell your house or something. I'll get mine."

"I'm sure you will," Porter said, eyeing the sign for his exit.

"Go help those people. Find the runaway, make a nice payday. What else are you doing?"

"When you're right, you're right."

"Glad you admitted it. And Porter?"

"Yeah?"

"Try not to be an asshole, okay?"

The phone clicked off, and the speakers were filled with Jimi Hendrix again.

Porter's Yukon bumped along the surface street until he turned into the parking lot of his hotel. He grabbed the cold pizza box and the file Joe had given him and walked into the lobby.

Clarence had been replaced at the front desk by someone who was much blonder and decidedly better-looking. She wasn't on the phone, and looked up and smiled at Porter when he walked by.

He briefly thought about heading to the front desk to chat, but wasn't sure how effective a greasy pizza box would be at picking up women. Instead, he rode the elevator to his fancy suite and locked the door behind him.

Porter spent the next several hours poring over every piece of paper in Joe's file. As much as he liked to rag on the FBI, their agents had been thorough. There was a record of everyone they'd interviewed in the short time since Pima Newton had gone missing. They'd partnered with the probation officers to roust all the registered sex offenders and grill them. They'd gone through Pima's school, asking every kid they could find if they knew anything that could help. They'd gone door to door in the neighborhood, asking if anyone had seen anything unusual.

In the end, they had nothing.

When his patience was as gone as his pizza, Porter showered and lay on the bed, staring at the ceiling. His mind raced with the possibilities. Where was the girl? Who was she with?

Why hadn't the FBI turned anything up? As much as he wanted to stay out of it, there was this small itch in the back of his head. The itch that wouldn't let him stop thinking about the case. The one that played to his ego and told him he could do something the FBI couldn't.

In the end, he wasn't sure why he'd even pretended he had a choice. Joe Palermo had asked for a favor. It was as simple as that. Besides, he could use a little late-fall air in the mountains. Everything always seemed so peaceful out there; maybe he could have a break. A mini-vacation. He'd been going after so many cases lately he thought he'd never stop. If Pima was hiding at her boyfriend's house, or had run away with her bestie, it could be a big payday for a small effort. Then he could relax a bit.

A little downtime would do him good.

# SIX

WAKING without an alarm the next morning, Porter trudged his way into the bathroom and abused the North Carolina water table again. When he was done, he packed all his things neatly in his duffle bag, and slipped his pistol into his waistband as he left his upgraded suite for the last time.

The pretty blonde at the front was gone, replaced by Jim the manager. He looked up, caught Porter's eye, then quickly looked away. Porter made a beeline for the man. "Pretty nice suite you guys have."

"Thank you, sir. We pride ourselves on the rooms."

"Sure you do. Where's my buddy Clarence?"

"Clarence... didn't come into work today. I think he took a sick day."

"Damn. I wanted to tell him goodbye."

"I'll pass the message on," Jim said.

"Good. Mind if I give *you* a message?"

Jim raised his eyebrows.

"Stop being a dick."

"I'm sorry?" Jim said.

"You know what I mean. You have kids, man; find a little

respect. Your wife let you put your tiny little dick inside her and knock her up, the least you can do is cool it with your secretary."

Jim shrugged. "She's the accountant."

Porter shook his head and turned from the counter, walking through the sliding doors and into the bright sunlight. He shielded his eyes and walked toward his Yukon, becoming aware of a faint scratching noise as he did. He squinted and looked left.

"Clarence?"

The young man with the gauged-out earrings had a screwdriver and was going to town on a Cadillac sedan.

"I thought you were off today."

"Off? That asshole fired me. Couldn't have called me and told me—waited until I came all the way into this piece of shit," Clarence said.

"That's too bad," Porter said. "Don't worry. A guy with your customer-service skills, I'll bet you land on your feet."

Porter's eyes finally adjusted to the outdoors. Clarence stood up, punctuating his words with a shake of the screwdriver. "This is your fault."

"Me? What the hell did I do?"

"You caught him with Cynthia, that's what pissed him off. Now I got no job. I wish I knew which car was yours. I'd have started in on that one first," Clarence said.

"This seems like something you need to work out with your boss."

"I don't have a boss, dickhead. I told you, I got fired. This seems like something I need to work out with you."

Porter turned around and looked at the young man. "You're kidding me, right?"

"I'm serious as cancer."

Porter raised his eyebrows. "Look, Clarence, I can appreciate you feeling some kind of way, but you need to use that squishy little ball in between your ears for something besides a pincushion."

Clarence took a step toward Porter. "How about I use you as a pincushion?"

"Unbelievable," Porter said. "Everybody in Charlotte has lost their mind."

Clarence didn't answer, instead holding the screwdriver out in front of him like a knife.

"Tell you what, what if I pay you for the day? Will that get me off your shit list?"

"What?"

"What did you make—five, six bucks an hour?"

"Eleven fifty," Clarence said. "A buck more for overnights."

"Okay, so... damn, I'm bad at math. Let's say you worked an overnight. That's a hundred bucks, right?"

"I think so," Clarence said.

Porter pulled out his wallet and held up a c-note. He took a couple steps toward the skinny young man, who shuffled back a bit. "Do you want it or not?"

Clarence stepped forward and reached out for the bill. When he did, Porter caught him by the wrist. Applying a little bit of pressure, Porter made Clarence drop the screwdriver.

"Listen, I'm going to give you this. But you need to learn a couple lessons. First, don't mess with a guy who can stomp you into paste. This isn't high school, there aren't trophies for the losers. Get your head out of your ass."

"Oww, oww, oww," Clarence whined.

"Second, go find a trade or something. I can tell you aren't a college guy, but the world needs electricians, too. That's noble work, got it?"

Clarence didn't answer.

"I said, 'got it'?" Porter said, and squeezed a bit tighter.

"Yes, yes, yes. I got it, man, damn."

"Good." Porter let go and gave the young man the bill. Clarence took it carefully and stepped back a couple of steps.

Porter got into his Yukon and rolled his window down as he pulled up next to Clarence.

He was staring at the hundred-dollar bill as Porter spoke up.

"And Clarence," Porter said. The young man looked up at him.

"Don't spend it all on weed."

# SEVEN

THE SIGHTS from the highway had been changing as he drove. First, there was the city proper, with its traffic and pedestrians. Then, he hit the urban sprawl. The overflow, people wanting to be near the city, but unwilling to live too close. The strip malls and box stores and drive-throughs.

Then the urban sprawls gave way to more and more green space, with mountains rising dramatically in the distance. Porter's mind was running in the background: how would he find Pima? Where would he start?

His ringing phone pulled him from his thoughts.

"Yeah."

"Hey kid. How'd you sleep?"

"Great. Wasn't hard with a belly full of pizza."

"I can't believe you still eat like that," Joe said. "I'd be four hundred pounds if I did."

"It's catching up to me," Porter said. While no one would accuse him of being fat, he could tell he was getting soft around the edges. Too much time in hotel rooms and on the road, not enough time in the gym.

"Sure it is. So... I was wondering if you had a chance to think about our conversation yesterday."

"I did, Joe, and I think I'm going to have to pass. It just doesn't seem like my thing, you know?"

There was silence on the other end of the phone.

A smile crept over Porter's face.

"Well... okay. If you'd rather pass, I understand. Not fair of me to ask you to get involved."

"It's not that, it's just... I'm not sure I need the seventy-five grand, you know? I'm already pretty flush with cash."

There was another silence on the phone.

"Seriously, I swim in that shit like Scrooge McDuck. Why work anymore?" Porter said.

"You're screwing with me."

"Of course I am."

"You're an asshole," Joe said.

"Maybe so," Porter said, staring at the mountains as they grew closer.

"This is good. This is really good. You get out there and shake things up, maybe see what falls out."

"Tell me more about this guy, Newton," Porter said. "An FBI agent can't find his own daughter, what's up with that?"

"That's not fair. You know we won't let him investigate—it's a conflict of interest. I ordered him to stay out of it no matter what. Not to mention, he's not anywhere near the headspace to handle that. The guy's been a mess the last few days. I don't even recognize him when we talk on the phone," Joe said.

"I'm heading out there now," Porter said. "I can't promise anything, but I'll give it a shot."

"I'll tell Mike you're coming."

"Don't."

"Why not? Unless... you're trying to catch him off guard? You think he might have done something?"

"The only person I know for sure didn't take Pima is me. That leaves a lot of other people who could have done it."

"Fine, but once you meet him, you'll realize how crazy that sounds. Tell him to call me when you show up. I'll need to vouch for you."

"What the story you're gonna give him? We're supposed to keep me under wraps," Porter said.

"No story. I told you, Mike is solid. He's not going to say anything. He just wants his kid to come back. It'll be quiet."

"Okay, as long as you remember your pension is on the line."

"I said he's cool, kid. Stop breaking my balls," Joe said.

"I don't want anything to do with your old balls," Porter said.

The speakers in Porter's car went silent for a few moments. "Thanks for doing this."

"I haven't done anything yet."

"Well, I owe you one," Joe said.

"Don't get disappointed if I can't find the kid, Joe. I don't want you to think I'm the great white hope or anything."

"I'd never call you the great white hope. You're more of a great brown hope. What's the word for that? Mulatto? The great mulatto hope?"

"Not enough people say *mulatto* anymore. Apparently it's racist now," Porter said.

Joe's end of the phone went dead quiet for a moment. "Shit, is it racist? I'm sorry, kid, I didn't mean anything by it. You know me, I'm not like that."

Porter laughed. "I know. But I'm going to use your guilt to make sure you think we're even."

"Says you. You don't get to tell me we're even. If I owe you, then I owe you. A little guilt won't stop that," Joe said.

Porter thought for a moment. "Want to make it up to me?

You could set me up with Amanda," he said. "I think I'd make a great son-in-law."

"I don't owe you that much," Joe said, and hung up the phone.

Porter laughed to himself, turning the Yukon west on I40, leaving Asheville in his rearview mirror.

It was the largest city in western North Carolina, and Porter had worked there several times. With its college and progressive base, Asheville liked to think of itself as North Carolina's Austin, or San Francisco east. What that really meant was that in addition to artists and academics, there were plenty of hippies, hipsters, and panhandlers.

Porter shuddered at the thought.

Asheville firmly in his rearview mirror, he was deeper into the mountains than he'd ever gone, and had to rely on his GPS to show him the way.

It wasn't long until the mountains he'd seen in the distance were all around him, rising beyond his view, sunlight shining over the tops of the peaks.

The GPS told him it was time to get off the highway and Porter obliged, following the instructions laid out by the machine. The small road he was on dead-ended in a large, gated entryway, with a guard shack in the center of two wrought iron fences.

Wanting to still surprise the Newtons by showing up unannounced but concerned the man in the glass-walled guardhouse wouldn't let him in, Porter stopped behind a yellow line and rolled his window down. He thought of a story to spin to the guard, something to say to let him by.

In the end, it wasn't necessary. An old man ambled up to the window.

"Hi. My name's—"

The ancient guardsman mashed an out-of-view button and waved Porter on.

"Guess good help is hard to find," Porter muttered to himself.

He pulled in slowly, the entry road turning into an intersection with a golf course beyond. Porter turned right, following the GPS. The homes in the neighborhood were impressive, the architecture and landscaping right at home in their mountain location.

Expensive cars passed on the other side of the small road, every driver with a wave for him. He wasn't a car guy, but it was obvious that his Yukon didn't fit in.

He wasn't surprised that the Newtons lived in such a nice neighborhood. The salary for a government job was set by the agency, but there were variances for cost of living. While Mike Newton's salary might not get him too far in, say, New York or Chicago, it seemed to be taking him plenty far in the mountains of North Carolina.

Two final turns, past a racquetball court and the neighborhood clubhouse, and Porter saw the house he was looking for on the left. Even without the GPS, he would have known he was in the right spot.

Underneath the mailbox hung a small flag that read "Newton." A large sticker with the letter "N" on it had been applied to the garage door. With two cars in the driveway, Porter pulled past the mailbox, half on the grass.

He walked over to the sidewalk, taking in the two-story structure as he did. The house had a warm-colored stone mortared to the front of it, and the rest was a dark wood. Part of the façade was covered in irregular, wooden shingles. Porter thought they were called shaker, but he wasn't sure.

He wasn't much for design.

There was a bike in the middle of the sidewalk, a little boy's, with baseball cards stuck in the spokes of the tires. The smell of new mulch from the flower beds hit Porter's nose, and he saw several fat bumblebees dancing among the flowers.

He stood in front of the large double door with its glass insert and pushed the doorbell. From somewhere inside came the rhythmic chiming of the doorbell, continuing for several moments before the door cracked open and a short man with dark hair and bags under his eyes answered.

"Thanks, but we don't want any," he said, then shut the door in Porter's face.

# EIGHT

PORTER STARED at the door for a few seconds, then rang the bell again. After several more seconds, the man answered again. He looked at Porter with tired eyes. "This isn't a great time."

"Are you Mike?"

The man looked confused, then scrunched his face up at Porter. "Who... I mean..."

"Mike, my name's Porter. Joe Palermo sent me to check in with you. Can I come in for a few minutes?"

Mike Newton opened the door a bit wider and cocked his head at Porter. "Joe sent you? You here to run the office? I can get you a key. I have it..." The man trailed off and patted his pockets.

"I'm not FBI. I really think I should come in for a minute," Porter said.

Mike stared at Porter, an unblinking thousand-yard stare.

Porter had made his bones deciding if people were putting him on. Lying, being deceptive—these were all things he was great at sniffing out. There was no subterfuge in Mike Newton. The man was stunned and damn near catatonic. A small hand appeared around the edge of the door. It was pulled wider and there was a woman standing there, smaller than Mike, with black hair and vivid blue eyes. She slid herself under Mike's arm, pulling it around her shoulders.

"I'm Terri."

"Mrs. Newton? I'm Porter. Joe Pa—"

"I heard, Mr. Porter. Please come in." Terri pushed the door the rest of the way open, then gave Mike a tap on the shoulder.

Her husband looked around, then spoke up. "Yes, yes—please come in."

Terri led her husband away. Porter shut the door behind them and locked it.

He followed the Newtons through the hardwood foyer, past an open kitchen with an island in the middle of the floor, and into the comfortable living room with its enormous leather sectional.

"Please," Terri said, "have a seat, Mr. Porter."

"Just Porter is fine," he said, sitting gently on the edge of the sectional. The Newtons sat opposite him.

"Okay, Porter, then."

Mike sat on the edge, his hands clasped in front of him. Terri looked at him for a few moments, then back to Porter. "You're here because of Joe?"

"He's an old friend. He gave me a bit of insight into what you guys were dealing with out here, and asked if I might be able to help."

"Insight?" Terri said. "It sounds clinical when you say it like that."

"I mean no disrespect. Can I ask you a few questions?"

"I... I mean, sure... I'm just not sure what it is you expect to be able to do. We've been looking for Pima for days."

"I realize that, but if you'd just humor me, I'd appreciate it."

Mike Newton stood to his feet, knocking his wife's hand

from his thigh. "Joe sent you?" he said, as if everything was finally clicking. "I need to call him. I need to call him."

With that, Mike disappeared through the living room and slammed the door to a room behind him.

Terri leaned back and watched her husband as he went.

"He's having a tough time," Porter said.

Mrs. Newton looked at him, squinting one eye. "His little girl disappeared. Wouldn't you be struggling?"

"I imagine so," Porter said.

"You don't have kids?"

"No."

"Never wanted any?" Terri said.

Porter didn't answer, unsure what to say. Wanting children and having them were two different things.

There was a nearly minute-long pause in the conversation before Porter started talking again. "You seem to be holding up well."

"It's amazing what Valium and a good night's sleep can do for you. I figure somebody needs to keep their shit together."

Porter nodded, glancing at the view from the patio window. The sun was topping the peaks now, and further below, the foothills were warmed in bright light.

"Mike's run himself ragged. They won't let him help with the investigation. He won't sleep; he just sits there, phone in his lap. Like he expects Pima to call him out of the blue or something."

"Would she?" Porter said.

"Call us? Of course. She's not a bad kid, she doesn't run away. If she's not here, something is wrong. My question is, why does Joe Palermo think you can help?"

"Just a long shot."

Terri nodded her head back and forth. "Fair enough. A long shot is better than no shot at all."

"Can you tell me what's happened so far?" Porter knew what he'd read in the file, but he wanted to hear it from the family. Maybe they'd have something new to tell, or an idea that the FBI hadn't seized on already.

"Bless them, everyone's been looking so hard, but they don't have anything. They asked everyone they could think of; nobody's seen anything. If we were in some city, they could check traffic cameras, I guess. Try to see if they could get a peek of her somewhere. Not here. There isn't any of that. The sheriff told me sometimes people just stay gone. What kind of shit is that to say to someone?" Terri's voice cracked and Porter watched her eyes fill with tears. Masterfully, she composed herself, pushing aside the emotions.

Porter imagined she'd had plenty of practice the last few days.

"So that's the word from the sheriff? I'd expect them to know more locally than the feds. They don't have anything?"

"They haven't done anything. At first, they didn't want to look into it yet. Said they had limited manpower and figured Pima would turn up in a few days. 'Most missing kids her age are runaways,' they told us. Mike flipped his lid, and threatened the sheriff. Told him if he didn't get his ass in gear, he'd have the Department of Justice come in and investigate every little thing about the sheriff's office." Terri leaned forward and rubbed her hands over her face.

"I'm sure that went over well."

"Swimmingly."

Porter glanced around, seeing the pictures and mementos of an average family. "What about your son?"

"Bryce? What about him?"

"They talk to him?"

"Sure, but he doesn't know anything. He can only help as

much as he can. He'd do anything to get Pima back, but he's just a kid."

Porter nodded as he listened. "Mind if I take a shot at it?"

"At what, speaking to my son? I don't even know you. The only reason I let you in is because you say Joe sent you. That name carries weight with Mike. But until he finds out exactly who you are..."

"I don't blame you." Porter adjusted on the supple leather and sank a bit deeper into the cushion. "Mind telling me about Pima?"

"Tell you what?"

"You said she's not a bad kid, that she wouldn't run away," Porter said.

"Never."

"Tell me what kind of kid she is."

Terri looked at Porter for a moment, then closed her eyes. "Pima is... different. She's just different. She is the sweetest girl you'll ever meet. So kind, has the biggest heart I've ever seen. Smart, too, but more book smart, you know?"

Porter nodded.

"She not very mature yet. I mean, she's only thirteen, for God's sake. People expect a kid her age to know how the world works and Pima's not there yet. She's quiet and shy, she'd probably go a week without talking if nobody asked her to. She's a watcher, you know?"

"I think so," Porter said.

There was the sound of a door opening and Porter looked to see Mike Newton shuffling out of his room, on steadier feet than when he'd gone in.

"Joe said you were okay. Said you were here to help and I could trust you. That's high praise coming from him."

"I'll take the vote of confidence," Porter said.

. . .

"SORRY I WAS..." He made a circular motion near his head. "...out of it earlier. I just... it's been hard." Mike's demeanor had shifted, and while he still looked like death, he was coherent and lucid.

"No apology necessary," Porter said.

A silence passed over the three for a few moments. Terri spoke first.

"Can I see you in the kitchen for a minute?" she said to Mike.

Her husband looked at her, then toward Porter. "Excuse us."

The pair walked into the kitchen and around the corner.

Porter stood and waited, looking at the artwork on the walls. It was nice, but he was sure Mike didn't make enough money to have a real Vermeer on the wall.

As he moved toward a sculpture of a moose, the man and woman of the house came back in.

"You want to talk to Bryce? Why? What good do you think that will do?" Mike said.

"Sometimes adults are shit at listening to kids," Porter said. "Or maybe he knows something and is just scared to talk. It can't hurt."

Terri eyed him warily.

"I'm great with kids," Porter said with a grin.

"I... okay. Sure. But we get to listen in," Porter said.

"I'd expect no less."

Terri stood and walked past the kitchen to the bottom of a staircase with wooden steps and a red runner leading up it. "Bry? Can you come here for a minute?"

There was a slight delay, then the clamoring of footsteps across the upper level.

A small boy appeared, his eyes nearly hidden under a shock

of curly hair. He was thin and slight, and Porter figured when he grew up, he'd be on the small side like his father.

"Who are you?" the boy said from the middle of the staircase.

"Porter. Who are you?"

"I'm Bryce," the boy said proudly.

"Bryce, Porter is a friend of Daddy's. He wants to ask you some questions. Is that okay with you?"

The boy shrugged and leaped the last four stairs to the bottom landing.

"Your mom and I will be in the kitchen, okay champ?" Mike said.

Bryce nodded absentmindedly.

Terri led her husband around the corner, but not before she pointed at Porter and tugged at her ear.

Porter nodded. "That your bike outside?"

Bryce shook his head. "No, that's Derrick's."

"Who's Derrick?"

"My friend. We played tag and he lost so he had to let me use his bike for a whole week. Can you believe it?"

"You must be good," Porter said, kneeling to look the boy in the eye.

"Nah. He fell down," Bryce said with a laugh.

"That's his own fault. He should be more careful if he's trying to beat Bryce Newton at tag."

The boy wiped his nose on the back of his sleeve and fixed Porter with a solid stare. He had his father's brown eyes. "You looking for Pima?"

"What makes you say that?" Porter said.

"Ever since she got lost, that's the only reason anybody wants to talk to me."

"I want to talk about whatever you do. Unless there's something you want to tell me about Pima?"

"No. I'm not stupid, you know."

"Who said you were stupid?" Porter said.

Bryce fidgeted in place. "I think everybody thinks it. They keep asking me if I forgot something when I talked to the last grown-up. I keep telling them no, but they won't listen."

"Fair enough. How about I just ask you a question about Pima? She's your sister, right?"

The boy nodded his head and his curls flopped around his face.

"Then you know her pretty well?"

"She's my sister, duh."

"Does Pima have a boyfriend?" Porter said.

"Eww, gross."

"What—you mean to tell me a handsome fella like yourself doesn't have a bunch of girlfriends?"

"No, that's silly. I only have one or two." He motioned Porter closer and lowered his voice. "Sometimes they fight over me at recess."

"See? I knew you were a ladies' man."

Bryce blushed.

"So, even though you have a few girlfriends, you never heard Pima talk about a boyfriend?"

"Nope," the boy said, shaking his head.

"Okay. One more question?"

"Mmmm, I guess so. *OK KO* is going to be on soon."

"I don't want you to miss anything," Porter said. "Who is Pima's best friend?"

"That's easy. Me."

Porter laughed.

Bryce's face grew dark. "I am."

"Of course you are, big man. I meant, who is Pima's best friend that's a girl? You know, does she have sleepovers or anything like that?"

Bryce brightened up. "Oh. That's different."

Out of the corner of his eye, he saw Terri Newton peeking her head around the corner, far enough away that her son didn't notice, but close enough to listen in.

"That's Scarlett," Bryce said. "She always spends the night and they won't let me in their room when they watch movies. It makes me mad."

"I'll bet it does," Porter said. He held out an enormous hand toward Bryce. "You answered all my questions perfectly. I guess your mom was right about you being the smartest kid in the world."

Bryce laughed and shook Porter's hand, then darted off, back upstairs two at a time. Porter watched the boy with a smile, trying to remember what it was like to be that young.

# NINE

"CUTE KID," Porter said as Mike and Terri exited the kitchen and walked toward him.

"Yeah, but he's a handful," Mike said. "Always have to worry about what he's doing and where he's at. If it's ever too quiet, you can be sure he's up to no good. Not like Pima, she always so quiet and she just..." The man trailed off and sniffed hard, like his sinuses were bothering him.

Terri looked from her husband to Porter. "Mike tells me you used to work for Joe?"

"A long time ago," Porter said, "I was his task-force officer."

"You still in?" she asked, having slipped herself supportively underneath Mike's arm again.

"Nope. Been out a few years," Porter said, taking slow steps toward the front door.

"Good for you," Mike said. "This job just takes from you. Chews you up day after day until it spits you out."

"Mike," Terri said.

"It's true," Porter said. "I figured I'd get out before I got chewed too bad."

"Smart man," Mike said.

Porter made it to the front door, the Newtons tailing along behind him.

"Joe said you were going to help. How?" Terri said. "You still haven't told me that part."

"I don't want to bore you," Porter said. "But you can help me with something."

Her eyebrows raised.

"Who's Scarlett?"

Mike squinted. "She's... she's from church, right?"

"School," Terri said. "They've been pretty tight the last couple years. We called her mom; she said she hasn't seen Pima."

"I'm sure she hasn't," Porter said. "Can I get her mom's number?"

Terri exchanged phone numbers with Porter, a text coming through his phone with a contact card for Scarlett's mother. Then she went into the kitchen and pulled a picture off the refrigerator. It was Pima and a girl with long red hair, in front of a wall with a falcon painted on it. "That's them."

"Go Falcons," Porter muttered. He put his hand on the doorknob and was stopped by Mike.

"I'll walk you out."

Porter nodded at Terri and stepped out onto the concrete walkway.

"Joe told me what you do," Mike said once the door was shut tightly behind them.

"What's that?"

"Please. You think I care what it takes to get my little girl back?"

Porter looked at the man.

"If there's something you can do, do it. If I can help, I will. Understand me?"

Porter didn't answer, instead looking at the small man, who was shaking with intensity.

"Do you understand me?"

"I'm tracking," Porter said.

"Good," Mike said. "Good." With that, he turned on his heel and went back into their home, slamming the door behind him.

Porter walked the rest of the way to the parking pad and back to his Yukon. He stopped for a moment, taking a deep breath of the crisp mountain air.

# TEN

WHEN PIMA HAD COME TO, she was tied to a chair with some kind of bag on her head. She could taste dirt and blood and snot in her mouth. She'd cried until she was out of tears.

She tried to remember where they'd taken her and how she'd gotten tied up. She tried to figure out where she was and why she had a bag on her head. All she knew was that her head was throbbing and she couldn't see.

When she concentrated enough to hear things, she could make out the sounds of people walking around and the faint din of voices. From time to time there was a slam, like a door somewhere.

And that was it.

Eventually, the footsteps drew closer to her and she heard a door creak open in front of her. There was a click, and light shone through her hood. Someone pulled it off her face.

Pima blinked, her eyes trying to adjust to the brightness. Once they did, she was looking at a girl with dirty blonde hair, not much older than her, wearing jeans with holes and a white tank top with her bra strap visible.

"What the hell, Seth?"

The girl stood up and looked across the room. Pima followed her gaze and saw the rest of the group. She recognized Seth and Dusty from the forest, but not the two other men.

One stepped forward; he looked like Seth, with better skin and teeth. "You idiot. You stupid idiot."

Seth took off his hat and rubbed his head. "Damn it, Richie, what was I supposed to do, huh? She saw our spot."

The girl with the jeans stepped closer to Seth. "So what, moron? That's why we put it where we did. We can move it all if we need to. We can leave it and let it get taken. Why else would we have disposable stuff in the forest? Shit."

Pima stayed quiet, looking around at the walls of the room. They were old and dingy, the carpet below her feet full of rips and burns.

"I thought we should interrogate her, huh? Find out what she knows," Seth said.

"You didn't think. You didn't think at all, you gigantic piece of shit," Richie said. "Because if you had, you would have known she was just some dumb kid playin' in the woods."

Behind Richie, a man in a full camouflage outfit stood leaning against the wall. He had a smile on his face.

Richie looked at him, daggers in his eyes. "You think this shit's funny, Bart? Huh?"

"Nope. Just goes to show that you can't trust your brother and his big retard," the man said as he rolled up a camouflaged sleeve.

"Who the hell are you talking to, huh? I'll beat your ass, Bart," Seth said, taking a step toward the man.

"Oh yeah? Let's go, tweaker." The two men grabbed each other and started to struggle.

"Get out!" the girl screamed. "All you idiots just get out."

"But Laura Bell, I was think—" Seth said, his hands on Bart's collar.

"I said get out, now, you dumb bastard."

"I ain't no bastard," Seth muttered.

"You got all of Daddy's taste for the smoke and none of his brains," Laura Bell said. "Daddy would have never done this. It was stupid."

"I'm just saying, I was thinking about a way—"

"Seth, shut your mouth right now or I swear to God, Bart will be the least of your problems," Laura Bell said.

"Okay, Sis, damn," Seth said.

"What are we gonna do?" Richie said.

"You let me figure out what to do about the kid. You idiots worry about making enough crystal, got it?"

There was a murmur of assent around the room.

"When's the last time she ate?" Laura Bell said.

"We ain't fed her yet," Seth said.

Laura Bell sighed. "What are you gonna do, starve her to death?" She reached into her pocket and pulled out a thick, folded wad of money bound with a fat rainbow-colored rubber band. She pulled off two twenty-dollar bills and handed them to Dusty.

"Please go get this girl some food."

"Okay, Laura Bell." Pima saw the man give the girl an ugly look. Dusty shuffled out of the room, his footsteps heavy on the hollow floor.

"Richie, go call Big Man. Tell him what happened and that it's not going to hold up production. Tell him we're still on target for the deadline."

Richie nodded and pulled his phone from his pocket.

"The rest of y'all, go. Get out of here and do something useful."

Bart and Seth went into the hallway first, pushing and slapping each other. Richie followed them out, cursing them the entire way.

Pima watched as Laura Bell shut the door behind the men, then turned around and looked at her.

"They got you all tied up." Laura Bell reached into her pocket and pulled out a small folding buck knife.

Pima felt her heart speed up and she started breathing fast.

"I ain't gonna hurt you." Carefully, Laura Bell cut Pima free, then returned the knife to her pocket. "Look, I need to make sure you don't have anything on you, got it?"

Pima shook her head, confused.

"Any kind of phone or tracking device or something. We can't have anybody who's looking for you find us. Stand up."

Pima stood on shaky legs, the blood barely returning to them. Laura Bell ran her hands all over her, patting her pockets and arms and even pulling the front of her bra a couple of times.

"That's to make sure you don't have anything in your cups there," Laura Bell said. She reached down and pulled Pima's shoes off and checked them as well. "Sit. You're good."

Pima did.

"My daddy taught me how to do that when I was younger. About your age, I guess," Laura Bell said. "He liked to make sure nobody had anything on them when they were doing deals. Most people didn't mind letting a girl search them. Bunch of perverts thought I was copping a feel or something."

Pima nodded, not sure what to say. She focused on Laura Bell's nose, which had a small stud in it.

Laura Bell looked at Pima's neck. "Did that big idiot try to choke you?"

Pima nodded.

"Hell, I'm sorry. Those two aren't the brightest, but they're family, ya know?"

Pima nodded like she did.

"Look, I don't want you to be scared, okay? Which I know is some dumb shit to tell somebody after they just had their ass beat and tied up to a chair. But Richie's smart; he's not gonna bother you. And I'll make sure my brother, Seth, and his trained gorilla leave you alone. They won't hurt you as long as I'm around."

Pima winced as Laura Bell's cool hand touched her swollen face.

"The thing is, I can't let you go right now. It's too risky. We have a lot going on right now; we're really going through it. The last thing we need is some trooper to pull us over with a missing kid in the car. You get me?"

Pima could barely understand the words Laura Bell was saying, but she nodded.

"Good. Don't worry your pretty eyes about it. We'll get you some food, and then I'll figure out what to do. Got it?"

Pima nodded again.

"You got a voice?" Laura Bell said.

Pima swallowed, her throat dry and scratchy. "Yes."

"Good." Laura Bell got up and left, closing the door behind her and leaving Pima alone again.

* * *

PIMA WASN'T sure how long things were like that. They left her untied and alone in the room. In a moment or two of sheer bravery, she'd tried to pull the plywood off the window, but it was no use. The wood was screwed in tight.

Laura Bell was in and out, checking on her and making sure she had what she needed, but Pima mostly saw Dusty. She'd hear his slow, heavy footsteps trudge toward her, then the door would swing open and he'd drop a sack of fast food on the bed for her. He always said the exact same thing.

"Here's your food. I hope it's good. Sorry I hurt your neck."

Then he would turn around and walk out of the room, leaving Pima alone again.

# ELEVEN

PORTER CHECKED his GPS for the third time, sure he was being led in circles. The small roads through the town all had multiple names and numbers, some seemingly changing mid-road to something else. He'd passed the same butcher shop three times.

Technology being no help, he turned the program off, and instead rolled down his windows and looked up at the city's meager skyline.

Having spent years in small towns looking for criminals, he'd learned one valuable trick: everyone was proud of their town hall. It was always the tallest building, or the nicest, or maybe it just had the highest spire awkwardly jutting into the sky. Regardless, when he saw the circular dome with a fifty-foot radio antenna, he guessed he was in the right place.

Porter drove toward it, through the downtown. Half its shops were vacant, the other half businesses that appeared to be on life support.

Eventually, the road dead-ended into an open green space, with several monuments erected in it. Porter nosed into the on-street parking and hopped out of his truck. After a brief stop at his lockbox to lock up his pistol, he slammed the door and started across the lawn toward the large building in the distance.

As he drew closer, he realized the monuments were a collection of granite pillars dedicated to the town's fallen veterans, with names inscribed as far back as World War One.

Porter stopped for a moment.

He always did when he came across these monuments. Every town, large or small, had its variation of this place. They were different, ranging from a small plaque in the sidewalk to sections of a park with walls and benches and statues. Porter lingered for a moment in these spots.

War was a political football. Every night, tone-deaf politicians would argue back and forth with each other, none of them really caring about their constituents. It made Porter sick to listen to them, and he wondered when the American people would get wise to the charlatans.

His stop at the monuments had nothing to do with war or politics: it was his way of remembering his father.

A Vietnam veteran, he was one of the men who didn't have to be drafted. A stern man of principle, Porter's father had chosen to go and serve his country, and had paid dearly for it.

Injuries from the war, both physical and mental, had made him difficult to deal with. In his youth, as is the way of most young men, Porter hadn't understood or appreciated his father. Now, with time and hindsight, Porter realized his father was just a man who had done the best he could at all times. This was a lesson Porter counted as learned.

A massive set of stone stairs led up to the town hall's entrance. Porter took them two at a time, then pulled the handle on the big double door, encountering a checkpoint.

There was no x-ray or standing metal detector as was

common in many federal or city buildings. No, there was just a man, even older than the man from the guardhouse at the Newtons'. He had a small, handheld metal detector in his lap as he tilted back in his rolling chair.

Porter paused for a moment as the elderly man heaved himself from his plush office chair.

"Good afternoon, sir." The man wore the uniform of a police officer, but on closer inspection, it was lacking a gun and a badge. A volunteer or auxiliary member of the force.

"How's it going?"

The man stood straight and kept looking up at Porter. "Hot damn, you're a big guy. You ever play ball?"

"It's been a while."

"You play around here? I watch all the games, maybe I'd know you."

"Nope. A long way from here."

"Well, I feel bad for those guys," the man said with a laugh. His shiny nametag read "Jerry."

"Jerry, I'm looking for the sheriff's office. Is it around here?"

"A few years ago, you would have been right. But they moved it, down the sidewalk and around to the back of the building."

"Great. And what's his name?"

"I'm Jerry."

"Not you, the sheriff. What's his name?"

Jerry cocked his head to the side and pointed his ear toward Porter. "Huh?"

Porter leaned toward the man. "What's the sheriff's name?"

"Ah. Sheriff Spaulding." He tugged on his earlobe. "I don't hear so good."

Porter gave him a thumbs up and turned to leave.

"Wait—you aren't coming in?"

Porter shook his head no.

"Good thing."

"Why?" Porter said.

"I don't think I could have gotten my little hand wand here all the way to the top of your head to check you. I'd have had to stand on a stool."

Porter laughed. "I'll bet you could do it, too."

The old-timer nodded vigorously as Porter turned around again and pushed out the door. He followed a sidewalk—colored with dark mildew and cracked in places—down the side of the town hall and around to the back where a smaller, free-standing brick building stood, with several marked sedans out front. Carefully painted on the glass window up front was a sheriff's badge with the name of the town and the words "Dennis Spaulding, Sheriff" underneath.

Porter pulled the handle and was met by a rush of warm air. The lobby smelled like someone was running a space heater. It was dark, and he could barely see the chubby woman sitting at the front desk.

"Help you?" a twang-accented voice spoke out.

"Hopefully. I need to see Spaulding."

"This is in regards to...?"

"Something I'd like to ask him," Porter said.

The woman stood and leaned over her small desk. "Regarding what?"

Porter eyed her for a moment. "Can I ask you a question?"

The woman shrugged noncommittally.

"Are you Sheriff Spaulding?"

"Obviously not," she said.

"Then it's none of your business."

The receptionist looked affronted and sat heavily back in her chair. "If you'll have a seat, I'll get on the horn."

"I'll stand, thanks," Porter said.

He wandered over to the front of the lobby, near the street window. The brightest place by far, the sunlight cast itself on a miniaturized model of the building and the small typed note that proudly displayed the architect's name.

Moments later, a door behind the receptionist swung open, the loud click of the one-way push bar echoing throughout the space.

"Sir?"

Porter turned, looking at two men, one in uniform and one in plainclothes. The uniform's nameplate read "Adams." "You aren't Spaulding."

"Can we help you?"

"I need to talk to Spaulding. What's so difficult about that? In a town this size, I know he can't be too busy. Either he's here or he's off somewhere having a coffee. If it's coffee, I'll come back later."

"Sir, I need you to calm down," Plainclothes said.

Porter laughed. "I am calm. Believe me, you'd notice a difference."

"Maybe we can help you?" Adams said.

"Why does everyone keep saying that? It's obvious you can't. Look, I'll try again later," Porter said, turning to leave.

Plainclothes had worked his way to Porter's side. "Actually, we need you to stay here for a minute while we get this sorted out."

Porter looked at the man, then back at Adams. "What's there to sort out? You guys aren't Spaulding, so I'll come back."

Adams reached for a pouch on his shiny black duty belt and unsnapped it. It was oleoresin capsicum spray. OC was like pepper spray on steroids. He pulled the canister and started shaking it.

"Really? You're gonna OC spray me? We're in an enclosed space, you idiot. You'll choke yourself."

Adams looked at Plainclothes, who shook his head, then put the can back in the pouch.

"It's like Mayberry," Porter said. "What's your issue? I haven't done anything. Move and let me out."

"Sir, you aren't leaving."

Porter couldn't understand the posturing of the deputies. Their reaction was way overblown. Still, he was no one's whipping boy. "Watch me."

When he turned around, Plainclothes had blocked the door and Adams was circling him.

"Okay. Okay," Porter said with a nod. "You take a minute to call the rest of your buddies. You try to stop me when I walk out of here and I'm going to throw you a beating, and the two of you won't be enough to stop me. You might as well call some friends."

Adams looked at Plainclothes, who nodded.

"If I'm going to jail, I might as well earn the trip," Porter said, stepping away from the two men. "Go on, call your backup."

Adams reached for the square microphone receiver clipped to his epaulet. As he keyed the receiver, a voice spoke up. "Belay that, Adams. It's all right."

Porter turned to the left and the metal door that the two deputies had come out of. A thin man in uniform was standing there. The stripes on his collar and sleeve told Porter he outranked the two idiots standing in front of him.

"What'd you say your name was?" the man said, blowing into his paper cup of coffee.

"I didn't."

"Fair enough. Mister, I can't have you kick my guys' asses in our own station. Imagine what a bad precedent that would set."

"Not my problem, Spaulding," Porter guessed. "You should really teach your guys how to interact with the public better."

"You might be onto something. Ruby said you wanted to see me?"

Porter looked to the receptionist, who was leaning over the desk with her eyes wide. "Yeah, I do."

"Fine. Let's talk."

"You bringing the goon squad?"

Spaulding shook his head. "That's not fair. They're just doing their jobs."

"If you say so. Which way?"

Sheriff Spaulding waved his guys off and motioned for Porter to follow him through the doorway.

Porter glared at the two deputies, then turned after their boss.

There were cubicles and office space, the linoleum floor dull for such a new building.

"You know, there's a better way to do that," Spaulding said over his shoulder, leading Porter to the office at the end of the hallway.

"Do what? Ask to speak with the sheriff? Because that's all I did. Your guys are a little jumpy."

Spaulding shut the door behind him and motioned to a folding metal chair across from his desk.

"No thanks," Porter said.

"Suit yourself," Spaulding said, dropping into a tattered office chair. "About my boys... I'm sorry. I realize they didn't do a great job, but I'm trying to make them better. Still, a little professional courtesy on your end would have gone a long way."

"What's that supposed to mean?"

"I mean, they didn't realize it, but you're a cop, right?"

Porter didn't say anything.

"Yeah, I mean, you look like a big monster, but you called it

OC spray. Civilians always say pepper spray; they don't know any better. And you moved yourself so those guys couldn't box you in. You're in the game, I can tell. Working?"

"No," Porter said.

"Want a job?" Spaulding said with a smile.

# TWELVE

"NOT A CHANCE," Porter said.

"Eh, I figured not. I could use someone on my team with some skill and know-how. My guys… they're just new, that's all."

"You seem a little more seasoned," Porter said.

"If you mean old, that's not hard to tell."

"Where'd you retire from?" Porter said.

Spaulding scrunched up his face. "How did you—"

"Your accent isn't from around here. Northeast?"

"Boston PD. Made captain and called it quits."

"Sounds about right. What, you give them a career and move down to run this shithole?"

"Hey, shithole's a little strong."

Porter didn't say anything.

Spaulding rocked back and forth in his chair. "Yeah. We used to come here for vacation. When I retired, we moved. I was home for about six weeks, then my wife said I was driving her crazy and I needed to get my ass out of the house. So I ran for election as sheriff, and managed to win."

"Now you're the man?"

"It appears that way. As much as I like this conversation, was there something you needed?"

"Pima Newton."

"What about her?"

"Where are you with the investigation?" Porter said.

Spaulding rocked a couple times in his chair. He pointed to his desk drawer. "Want a drink? I have some whiskey in there the DA brought me from someplace or another. It's supposed to be good."

"Pass."

Spaulding leaned forward. "Suit yourself. It is the policy of the sheriff's office not to disclose any information about an ongoing investigation."

"Is there an ongoing investigation? It doesn't seem like you guys are doing anything."

"What business is it of yours?"

"I'm a friend of the Newtons. Just want to make sure you guys are dotting your i's and crossing your t's. I was willing to accept that you just hadn't found anything, but after meeting your two local yokels out front, now I wonder if you don't have anyone qualified to run the investigation."

"I'll have you know I'm running it myself. Despite what you may think about the 'local yokels,' I've done this a few times."

Porter didn't doubt it.

Cops in big cities were usually a little better at the job. They had more resources and could learn more. They also had larger populations; there would always be a rape or a kidnapping or a murder. If Spaulding had come from the Boston PD and made it to captain in a big department like that, he had some experience.

"And you don't have anything?"

Spaulding exhaled. "No. The girl's just gone. No one's seen her. Nobody has any clue. She just disappeared."

"Fine," Porter said, reaching for the doorknob. "That's all I wanted to know. Is that so hard?"

"We don't always get what we want, Mr...?" Spaulding stood and met Porter at the door, reaching out his hand.

"Porter."

"Porter? One name, like Madonna?"

"It's just easier for people to remember. Your knuckle-draggers out front couldn't handle two names."

"I doubt my guys will forget you anytime soon."

"That a good thing?" Porter said.

Spaulding reached past the big man in front of him and opened the door, gesturing for Porter to exit first. "Actually, yes. These boys need a good scare now and then. You were the scariest thing they've seen in a while."

"You need new guys."

"I tried to hire you, didn't I?"

Porter didn't answer, looking at the empty cubicles to his left and right, pushing through the exit door and holding it for Spaulding.

Save for Ruby the receptionist, the lobby was empty. Porter ignored her as he walked by, and Spaulding moved in front of him to pull the door out and hold it for him.

"I was hoping you had something else," Porter said. "You haven't gotten much."

"Well, hope in one hand and shit in the other, see which fills up first."

Porter just looked at the man. "What your next move?"

"Me? I think I'm going to be digging the Newton girl out of a shallow grave sometime soon."

# THIRTEEN

THE TWO MEN parted ways and Porter stopped for a moment to take a breath. Despite it being a new building, the sheriff's office had felt old to him, and there was a smell he couldn't place.

The wind bit at him as he walked up the hill, past the veterans' monument and back toward his truck. He thought of the Newtons and Joe. He thought of Sheriff Spaulding and his idiot deputies. The reality was plain as day: there would be no easy way to find Pima Newton.

He realized that he'd hoped there would be some big puzzle piece everyone had overlooked. Something that, when he saw it, would make sense. Now he knew how foolish he'd been.

Although the deputies were marginally competent, Spaulding didn't seem too far off the mark. Sure, he wasn't in any hurry to set the world on fire with his cop skills, but Porter believed he'd at least looked into the matter.

As he crested the top of the small hill, the wind hit him again. Usually he didn't mind the cool weather, but something about the mountain air chilled him. When he reached his truck, he dug through the folded laundry, looking for a sweater or hoodie. After a minute or so, he gave up and pulled his Glock from the lockbox, and slammed the tailgate.

He let the truck idle as he collected his thoughts. With strikeouts at the family's house and with the locals, he was down to Pima's friends. Scarlett, the girl Bryce Newton had mentioned, went to a school not far away, but it was a little too early for them to be getting out. A hunger pang rumbled his stomach and Porter decided to fix that problem first.

He drove in slow circles around the town until he found a place that piqued his interest. The Burger Hut was a small place with a gravel parking lot and no drive-through. It must have been between the lunch and dinner crowds, because there were a scant few cars in the lot.

Porter walked up to the front door, cursing the gravel that dug through the thin sole of his shoes. The front door swung open on smooth hinges and a cowbell clanged above it to alert the staff to a new customer.

Leaning on the front counter was a tall brunette with a soft, pretty face.

"I absolutely think you're wrong," she said, speaking to someone in the kitchen. "There's no way the Saints beat the Panthers this weekend."

"Ahh, what do you know?" a man's voice said from the kitchen.

"You're sure? Want to bet your paycheck on it?"

Porter listened to the man grumble off the question and looked around at the booths and tables. He looked back to the front counter, where the woman—Claudette, according to her nametag—had fixed a crooked smile on her face.

"Hi."

"Hello," Porter said. "Can I ask you a question, Claudette?"

The woman looked surprised for a second, then looked

down at her nametag and laughed. "I'm not even sure why I wear this thing. Everybody in town already knows my name."

"It helps when strange men like me show up," Porter said.

"I guess it does. You had a question? Shoot."

"What's good?" Porter said, ignoring the menu on the counter in front of him.

"Hell, how much time do you have? I can say, humbly, that everything's good here, because I make most of it." She looked toward the kitchen, then back at Porter, and motioned for him to lean closer. "Except the pot-pie. Herschel makes that, and it's..." The woman made a back-and-forth motion with her hand.

"I heard that," Herschel's gravelly voice said from the back. "Don't you shit talk my pot-pie." Porter watched the older man lean through the passthrough and point his spatula for emphasis.

Claudette raised her eyebrows, her enormous grin flashing again. "Now I'm in trouble."

Porter couldn't help but smile. "As great as the pot-pie sounds, I should probably go with the burger. I mean, this is Burger Hut." He pointed to the back. "No offense on the pot-pie, Herschel."

The old man grumbled and went back to his griddle.

"Good choice. What do you want on it?" Claudette said, typing away on an ancient computer.

"No onions."

"I hate those too," she said. Moments later, Claudette gave Porter a very reasonable total, and it was only then that he saw the sign that said "No Debit Cards."

"No plastic?"

"You'd be amazed at what those companies want to charge for the privilege. We take checks..." she said helpfully.

Porter patted his pockets, looking for a checkbook he hadn't seen in years. He was ashamed to admit he never had cash anymore, the convenience of debit having won him over long ago. "I know this seems like a scam, but I don't have anything. Mind canceling my order?"

Claudette laughed. "What would I look like, turning a hungry soul away? Besides, Herschel's already got the meat going, and he gets pissy when he has to stop an order. He doesn't handle change very well. I'll tell you what, you go ahead and eat. If you can pay later, pay later. Deal?" She stuck her hand out.

Porter shook it, his massive hand enveloping her small, soft one. "Deal."

"Good. Go ahead and find a place to sit. I'll bring it out to you when it's done."

Porter walked past the cramped booths that he knew would be instant knee pain and found a small table near the rear of the store. As he looked around, he noticed that everything in the restaurant had the same feel as the computer on the counter: it was old.

Not dirty or in disrepair; in fact, the opposite. The floors were shiny and the windows clear and streak-free, and somewhere, beneath the scent of cooking meat, Porter could smell cleaning product. No, the place was just older, and in need of updating that probably cost too much for a small business.

As he listened to the sounds of the meat sizzling, he looked out the window, trying to piece together everything he knew. It didn't take long for him to realize he still had nothing, that the answer to Pima Newton's disappearance hadn't magically popped into his head.

Soon after, Claudette came to his table, tray of food piled high.

"Damn. Is that the normal portion?"

"Well, I figured a big guy like you might need a little extra."

"I'm supposed to be watching my figure."

"Honey, there's nothing wrong with your figure," Claudette said, before snapping her mouth shut. Her cheeks and neck turned red. "I mean... is there anything else I can get you?"

"Ketchup and mayo would be great."

"You one of those weirdos?" Claudette said as the blush drained from her face.

"Afraid so."

Claudette reached over to a booth and grabbed a bottle of ketchup, then went back to the counter.

Porter watched her walk away, impressed with the fit of her jeans. He looked back at his plate before she turned around and saw him.

She handed him the mayo. "Holler if you need anything."

"Will do," Porter said, before watching her walk away again. His mind firmly on her ass, Porter ate through the tray, stopping halfway to take a breather.

Porter wasn't overdramatic, but he could safely say it was the best burger he'd ever eaten. He gave up trying to figure out what made it so good and finished up. He bussed his table, sat the tray on the counter, and walked out, cowbell clanking above him. He was aware that Claudette had just gone into the back and didn't see him leave.

He drove around until he found an ATM, pulled out enough cash for a month of Burger Hut burgers, and drove right back to the restaurant. He opened the door and Claudette turned from the counter, facing him with her trademark smile.

"I thought you left."

"I had to get some cash," Porter said, handing her a bill. "I was feeling so guilty, it might have affected my digestion."

"Well, you should feel guilty, leaving without saying good-bye." She unfolded the bill. "This is too much."

"Stuff it in the tip jar," Porter said. "It's the best burger I've ever had."

"Glad to hear it. You in town long..." she said, the lilt in her voice asking for his name.

"Porter. How do you know I'm not from around here?"

Claudette laughed. "I told you, Porter, I know everyone in this town. Been here too long. Besides, if you'd moved in somewhere, it would be all over the place. The hens would be talking it up."

"The sewing circle is still alive, huh?"

"Out here it is."

"I'm in town for a little while. You work every day?" Porter said.

"I better. I own the place."

"So you're an entrepreneur?"

"More like too dumb to give up," Claudette said with a half-smile. She stuffed the change from Porter's order into the plastic tip jar by the register.

"Well, as long as I'm in town, you got my business. Deal?"

"I'm going to hold you to that," she said, the big smile returning.

"Please do."

# FOURTEEN

THE COWBELL CLANKED AGAIN as he left, and Porter looked down at his smartphone. He'd burned enough time at the Burger Hut that Pima's school was nearly out. He figured now was a good time to try to chat with Pima's best friend, Scarlett.

He was, however, acutely aware of the visual of a guy like him loitering around the school, asking after a thirteen-year-old girl. With his luck, Spaulding's two doofus deputies would show up and try to arrest him.

Porter wasn't a fan of going to jail.

No, he figured it would be best if he was a little more creative. He had the picture that Terri Newton had given him of the two girls, and he knew from researching Joe's file that the girl rode her bike home from school every day. It was easy enough to look at a map and figure which way she'd have to go.

He briefly considered going to her home and waiting for her there, but decided against it. Kids didn't always like to be honest in front of their parents, and if there was something Scarlett knew, he'd have a better chance if he talked to her alone.

Provided she didn't run away when he walked up to her.

He found an abandoned grocery store midway along the

most likely route she'd take home and pulled into the empty lot. Porter rolled the windows down and continued trying to stitch together Pima's disappearance.

Moments later the phone rang.

"Hello, Mother," Porter said with an affected British accent.

"How's South Carolina?"

"North."

"Whatever. You working?"

"Yeah. I couldn't tell Joe no," Porter said.

"That the only reason?"

"Pretty big reward," he said.

"Right. You're getting soft in your old age," his mom said. "Got any leads?"

Porter gave his mother the rundown, leaving nothing out. He imagined most sixty-year-old women wouldn't want to hear about a missing child, but most sixty-year-old women weren't retired federal agents.

"Sounds like a mess," she said.

"It is."

"Well, you be careful. You know I worry."

"Come on," Porter said.

"What? I do. Every time you start digging around in these things, there are always problems. Remember that time you stabbed a guy with a fork? Let's not have a repeat."

"I'll do my best," Porter said.

"Good. When you get back into town, I need help with my DVR."

"That's the whole reason you called, isn't it?"

"No," she said, the tone of her voice betraying her.

"Hey, I have to go," Porter said, looking at a kid on a bicycle at the street crossing, then back at the picture Terri had given him.

"Okay, Son, but no forks," his mother said as he hung up the phone.

Scarlett was stopped a block down. The girl wore a helmet, and dutifully got off her bike and walked it across the street when the light turned green for her to cross.

Porter slid out of the driver's seat and leaned against the hood of the car, waiting for her to get closer.

The girl made it through the crosswalk and started to pedal again. When she got close to the Yukon, Porter spoke up. "Scarlett?"

The girl kept pedaling by, neither slowing down or speeding up. She looked toward Porter. "Maybe. Who are you?"

"A friend of Pima's."

"No, you're not," the girl said, still rolling by.

He held up the picture of the two of them together. Scarlett put her feet down and stopped the bike. "Where'd you get that?"

"Pima's parents gave it to me. I'm a friend of theirs."

"You just said you were a friend of Pima's," Scarlett said.

"Same thing."

"No, it's not. I'm not friends with everyone my mom's friends with."

"Damn," Porter said. "You got me there. I'm just trying to help find her, how about that?"

Scarlett walked her bike toward Porter and put the kickstand down. She stayed on the far side, the purple ten-speed in between the two of them. Porter didn't want to spook the girl, so he stayed against the truck.

She looked at the picture he held up, then at him, then at his Yukon. "You a cop?"

"No."

"You sure?"

"Pretty sure. Why, you don't like cops?"

"I don't mind them, but they don't do a great job listening."

"I agree with you there," Porter said.

"Are you a private investigator?"

"Not really."

"What does that mean?" The girl took her helmet off and her thick red curls flopped out, hanging messily around her face.

"It means I'm not a private investigator."

"So if you aren't a cop or an investigator, and you don't even know Pima, how can you help?"

"You think wearing a shiny little badge makes you good at finding people?"

"Sometimes."

"If that's true, why haven't you told the cops where Pima is?" Porter said, slipping the picture back in his pocket.

"I don't know where Pima is."

"I think you know something you haven't told anyone. Right? It's just the way we are. We don't always tell the whole truth."

"I don't know, I swear." The girl started to shift from foot to foot.

"Listen, I don't care."

"What do you mean? Why are you here if you don't care?"

"I care about finding Pima. I don't care what you know or don't know, what you told the cops or didn't."

"What makes you think I know something?"

"Because the best friend always knows something."

Scarlett didn't say anything, instead looking down at her feet.

Porter looked at the girl for a moment. "When I was in junior high, I went to a tiny school. I'm talking thirty kids in the place, kindergarten to senior year."

"Sounds tiny."

"Super tiny. In the courtyard of this tiny school was a payphone. I used to—"

"Payphone?" Scarlett said.

"Yeah, payphone? You know, phone with a cord hanging on it, you put coins in to use it?"

Scarlett shook her head slowly, red curls shimmering. "No, wait, I think I have seen one in front of the drugstore. Never used it."

"Look, it doesn't matter, the story isn't that funny anyway. I used to prank call people from the payphone. I'm talking every day, I would call people and just say dumb stuff to them."

"Like what?"

"You know what, forget it. The point is, my best friend knew I was doing it. He didn't make any calls, but he laughed when I did. Well, eventually the school found out and they asked everybody who was making the calls.

"Of course, I lied my ass off and said it wasn't me; I didn't want to get into trouble. You know who else lied?" Porter said.

"Your best friend?"

"That's right. Ross lied his ass off, too, so I didn't get into trouble. Because that's what best friends do. So I feel like there has to be something, no matter how small, that you haven't told anybody else."

Scarlett chewed her lip.

"Does Pima have a 'special friend' that nobody knows about?"

"You mean like a boyfriend? Eww. Have you seen the boys at our school?" Scarlett said.

"Be nice to them. One day, one of those boys may grow up to be a ruggedly handsome not-private-eye with a terrific beard."

Scarlett laughed. "I doubt it."

The pair had not moved. Scarlett stood several feet away

from Porter, her bicycle a barrier between them, Porter still leaning on the front of his truck.

Porter saw the girl was thinking; he didn't push her. Often, when people were on the edge of making a decision, it was best to let them fall on their own.

His eyes drifted from Scarlett to the passing traffic. Amidst the pickup trucks and modest sedans, a sheriff's sedan pulled by. Through the lightly tinted windows, Porter saw the two deputies from earlier in the day.

The town was small, and it could have been a coincidence. Maybe they were responding to a call. Maybe Spaulding had told them to hit the road and get some experience.

Or maybe they were following him.

He watched as the sedan drove off into the distance, his attention brought back by the girl's voice.

"Maybe I don't know where Pima is, but maybe I know somewhere that we go sometimes, just the two of us. You think that could help?"

"It can't hurt. Maybe I can go there and see if she's there. Maybe she's just run away for a couple days," Porter said.

Scarlett nodded. "It's in the woods. Sometimes, when we don't have anything else to do, we go out there and hang out. A secret spot."

Porter liked the sound of a secret spot in the woods. It gave him somewhere to go, and he just might find a teenager camping out. He didn't say anything, so Scarlett would fill the silence with more information.

"We climb up into the trees and lie around taking pictures and stuff."

"Is it hard to find?"

"Super. It's a secret, remember? It takes a long time to walk there, a little less if we bike."

"Thanks for telling me. Why didn't you tell anyone about this place? Pima could be there."

"She's not. I went and checked the first day she disappeared. Plus, you know, I was worried. I didn't want to tell because of the drug men."

This time, Porter's silence wasn't a ploy. He had no idea what to say.

# FIFTEEN

"SCARLETT, what do you mean, 'drug men'?"

"The guys that make the drugs," she said, like it explained everything.

Porter just looked across the bike at the girl.

"Pima was out hiking around one day and she found the place. She saw a bunch of... you know, stuff. Tube and containers and stuff. The stuff our resource officer showed us when he had the meeting to tell us to stay away from drugs."

"Meth?" Porter said.

"I don't know, I don't do that stuff."

Porter thought back to the waning months of his law-enforcement career. There had been some new trends in the cooking of methamphetamines, both in the ingredients the cooks were using and the setups of their stills. They were trending smaller and smaller. Where the first meth operation he'd ever busted had taken up most of the inside of a mobile home, he remembered once arresting a man who'd managed to make a passable batch in a single two-liter bottle.

The problem was, meth cooking was volatile; there had

been plenty of tweakers who'd blown themselves up in the pursuit of the next batch. There had been whispers around the agency, particularly from some of the Midwest sub-offices, that the smart cooks were moving the labs outside. Hiding them in the middle of nowhere.

If the drugs exploded, no one died in a trailer fire. If the cops stumbled across them, they were on land that didn't belong to anyone. It was supposed to be the next phase in meth cooking, but Porter had gotten out before he'd witnessed any of it firsthand.

"You girls found a meth lab," he muttered.

"I guess so. But that was part of the fun."

"Fun?" Porter said, louder than he should have.

Scarlett stopped for a second and looked at him. "Yeah, fun. We really liked the area. It's so pretty. Those guys never saw us there anyway. We'd hide our bikes and we would climb high in the trees. They never knew we were there."

"And that's all you did? Watch the guys?"

"Sometimes Pima would take pictures of them with her phone. She said she'd show her dad one day, when she knew he wouldn't be mad at her."

"Cause her dad's FBI?" Porter said.

"Yeah. Pima said the bad guys should go to jail. We were gonna tell eventually."

Porter exhaled and ran his hands over his head. He wondered if he'd ever done anything so stupid when he was young, quickly deciding that it wasn't possible. "You realize these types of people will kill you if they catch you, right?"

"We never got caught; why would we worry about it?" Scarlett said, a perfectly rational thirteen-year-old.

"Could you pick the guys out if I showed you pictures?"

"What?"

"If I had a picture, could you tell me who they are?"

"I'm not sure. Maybe? We usually don't get a good look. There's a big one, even bigger than you. A couple skinny ones. I don't know, Pima has pictures."

Porter nodded. The mountain air blew again and he wished he'd taken more time to find his hoodie. "Can you tell me where this place is?"

Scarlett chewed her lip again. "Then people will know we were out there. Maybe they will think the drugs are ours, you know?"

"No one will even know you told me," Porter said.

"You promise?"

"I swear. I'll lie if anyone asks me how I found the place."

"Do you think something happened to Pima?"

"No telling, but I want to check it out," Porter said.

"Okay, let's go," Scarlett said, wheeling her bike toward the trunk of the Yukon.

"Negative," Porter said. "You aren't going."

"Don't you want to go?"

"Yeah, but if it's like you said it is, you shouldn't be there. Hell, you should never go back. Get my point?"

The girl nodded. She pulled out her smartphone and walked closer to Porter. "When Pima first found the place, she saved it as a location on her GPS and then sent it to me so I could find it. Here." Scarlett held up the phone and Porter copied the coordinates into his GPS and saved it.

"Good. I'm going to look into it."

Scarlett straddled her bike, pulled her hair back and then stuffed it under her helmet. "You swear you won't tell anybody I told you? Pima's folks? My mom?"

"I can keep a secret," Porter said.

Scarlett looked at him and held out her hand, pinky up.

Porter held out his pinky, intertwined it with her tiny finger, and shook it.

"You can't break that, no matter what," Scarlett said.

"I never lie."

Apparently satisfied with the pinky promise, the girl rode off, leaving Porter alone with the myriad of new decisions he needed to make.

# SIXTEEN

BACK IN THE YUKON, windows rolled up, his first instinct was to drive straight to the location Scarlett had given him and check things out. He looked up at the sun, which was dropping rapidly lower in the sky, the late-fall days not yielding long hours of light.

It wasn't a great idea to go out into unfamiliar woods at night.

He believed Scarlett had gone to look for Pima. If she had simply been hurt or stuck, her friend would have gotten help. So, either Pima wasn't out there and it wouldn't matter when he went, or she was still in the woods hiding out.

While it was going to be a cool evening, it wasn't kill-you-overnight cold yet. Judging by the warm clothes Scarlett wore and the fact the Newtons seemed to provide well for their children, Porter imagined Pima had sufficiently warm clothes on. If she was out there, it was because she wanted to be. Better for him to check in the light of day.

It didn't hurt that he didn't want to run into any meth cookers in the dark.

He briefly considered calling Spaulding and having him go

check it out, but changed his mind quickly when he remembered the ineptitude of the sheriff's deputies. Better to keep them in the dark unless he actually came up with something.

Mind shifting back to himself, Porter dropped the truck into gear and slowly circled around the town, looking while he could in the fading light. Before long, he drove past a motel he remembered seeing on his drive in.

He should have asked Claudette where a good place to stay was. It was always best to rely on local info for things like that. Between the burger and her smile, he'd been a little too distracted to think about the hotel plans, however.

In the absence of a recommendation, he figured one place was as good as another. Porter pulled into the parking lot of the motel with its half-lit sign. It was a small establishment, with all outward-facing doors. The building wrapped around a courtyard like a horseshoe, with an empty pool in the middle. Porter pulled into the mostly empty parking lot, taking his choice of spaces.

In the middle of the horseshoe, just below the empty pool, was a small building with wooden siding. Porter pushed his way through the door, a cowbell announcing his entrance.

"You guys like your cowbells around here, huh?"

A young man pulled his face out of a magazine. "Cheaper than an alarm system." The kid was clean-cut, with short brown hair and freckles. The placard on the counter said his name was Sam and that he was the assistant manager.

"Assistant manager? You're doing okay for yourself."

"I'm the only employee, other than the maid," the young man laughed. "They figured they'd give me a nifty title instead of a raise."

"Nice. Got any rooms?"

"I think I can rustle you up one," he said, pointing to a pegboard full of keys.

"How much?"

Sam pointed to a laminated piece of paper on the counter in front of him. "This month it's thirty-nine ninety-nine. Weekends go up to eighty-nine ninety-nine."

"Why so much? Are the weekends that exciting?"

"The next few weekends, at least. The leaves are changing, and tourists are suckers for that kind of thing."

"Not you?" Porter said.

"Nah. Been here my whole life, seen the leaves dozens of times. Bunch of idiots stomping all over the woods; me and my friends stay out of the way."

"Spend a lot of time in the woods?"

"Sure," Sam said, leaning against the counter. "Me and my girl go out a lot, hiking and trail running. Mountain bike sometimes when we're feeling brave."

"You know your way around pretty well?" Porter said, pulling out his smartphone.

"As good as I can, I guess. There's a bunch of space out there. It's easy to get lost."

Porter looked around at the lobby and got one of the cheap area maps out of its plastic holster on the wall. He showed Sam the coordinates he'd gotten from Scarlett. "How easy is this to get to?"

The young man turned the map around and after a few moments, grabbed a pen and circled an area of the map. "That's the national forest. Not hard to get there, easy to find parking. The problem is," he said, tapping his finger on the map, "it's a long haul back here. Take you a couple hours."

"Fun. Okay, Sam, mark me down for a couple of nights."

"Yes, sir." The young man didn't bother with any paperwork or ID. He asked Porter which room he'd like, and Porter asked for one in the middle somewhere. The young man obliged.

"Room Fifty-Five. One of our best."

"Really?"

"Nah. They're all the same. Tell you what, if you're still here this weekend, I'll give you the weeknight rate. You aren't some tourist; you must be a real outdoorsman if you want to be hiking in there." Sam tapped Porter's map.

Porter folded the map up. "I guess we'll see."

He thanked the young man and left, walking past his truck and across the lot to room 55, testing the door handle.

When he turned, movement on the main road outside the motel drew his eye. A sheriff's office sedan rolled by. At this point, it was too dark to see through the tint, but Porter didn't have to guess who was inside. He resigned himself to going back in the morning and talking to Spaulding about his new stalkers.

Or maybe he'd throw them the beating he'd promised.

When they'd rolled off, he opened the door and stood a moment. It was no frills, but serviceable. Under the front window was a noisy A/C unit, and in the middle of the room was a rock-hard queen-size bed.

The bathroom had generic tile and a tiny window for ventilation. It wasn't the upgraded suite he'd slept in last night, but it would do.

Satisfied, Porter pulled back the sheets to check for bedbugs. An old habit, but one he couldn't shake. Then he took the comforter off the bed, wrapped the TV remote and the small phone from the end table in it, and stuffed the mass into the top drawer of the squat dresser.

He stepped back outside to his truck and pulled his duffle bag out. Porter left his truck parked in the spot away from his room, and walked back through the parking lot.

After he'd closed and locked the door, and pulled the dresser in front of it for good measure, Porter dug through his bag and pulled out a bottle of Lysol and doused the room with its spray, not stopping until he started to cough.

He'd seen a documentary about the types of germs found in hotel rooms, and it had scarred him. Now he took no chances.

The documentary had also said the dirtiest, most fecal- and sperm-covered items in a hotel room were the phone and the television remote.

He opened the drawer and sprayed some on the balled-up comforter inside to be sure.

Porter showered, thinking of the new information he'd received from Scarlett, as well as the topography lesson from Sam. He was no woodsman, but he figured he'd be okay.

He dried off and was asleep the second his head hit the pillow.

# SEVENTEEN

EVENTUALLY, the group let Pima out of her room. Laura Bell had told the men she was doing it and no one could stop her. Richie put up a fight, until it was decided that Pima would have one of her legs tied to a chair so she couldn't run away.

Pima was hesitant at first, figuring it was a trick and they were going to kill her, but she was thankful to be able to see the daylight from the living room and sat so quietly that she hoped people forgot she was even there.

Whether they actually forgot or not was debatable, but they did grow comfortable enough around the girl in their midst to speak openly about much of their business. That scared Pima the most.

She didn't know who they were, not really—just a couple of names—so the hopeful side of her thought they could let her go and she couldn't ever snitch on them.

The terrified side of her hoped they weren't just being open because they planned to kill her regardless.

Richie was pacing around the trailer, pointing his finger at Seth. "That's not enough, you idiot. Big Man says we need more."

"Well, I'm working on it, Rich. I can't make the shit cook any faster than it does."

"Working on it, my ass. When's the last time you went to the spot to even check it out?" Richie said. He walked back and forth in front of the seated Seth, who had his feet up on a ratty couch.

"Not since I grabbed that little bitch."

"See, that's your problem," Bart said from the kitchen. "You don't take this shit serious." As always, he was head-to-toe in camouflage.

"You better watch your mouth. This is family business, and you ain't. You keep pushing me and I'll—"

"You'll what, tweaker? Huh? You come over here and I'll push your shit in," Bart said with a smile.

Pima tried to think about what that meant, and decided she didn't want to know.

Seth shot to his feet and Richie pushed him back down. "Not now."

"But Rich, that piece of shi—"

"I said not now."

There was quiet in the trailer for a few minutes. Pima thought she could hear Seth grinding his teeth.

"Okay," Richie said, standing still for a minute. "Bart, tomorrow morning I want you to go check the spot. See how much we can harvest. I need a count."

"Come on, Rich, you know I'm going bow-hunting in the morning. Deer season ain't but so long."

"And? Hunt, then go check it out. I don't care what you do, but you better not come back tomorrow if you can't give me a number, got it?" Richie stepped toward the kitchen.

"You should send that fiend of a brother of yours," Bart said, pointing at Seth. "I gotta waste my time on this shit."

Seth shot to his feet again. Before he could speak, Richie pushed him back to the couch. "Bart, get the hell out of here."

Pima watched the man in the camo slam the front door open and disappear into the yard.

"Why do you let him talk to me like that?" Seth said.

"Because he's right," Richie said. "This is your mess, you should be handling it."

"I'm just saying, I don't know why you keep him around," Seth said, arms crossed in front of him. "We don't need him."

Richie reached down and grabbed his brother's face. "I keep him around for the same reason I let you keep Dusty around. Because when the shit jumps off, there needs to be more than two of us. You're family, baby brother, and I love you. You, me, and Laura Bell—keeping us safe is all that matters."

Richie paused for a moment and stared at his brother. Pima saw Seth avoiding eye contact.

"You know what kind of numbers the Big Man is talking, right?"

Seth nodded.

"If we don't come up with that, he'll hang us out to dry. It won't be any time until the Mexicans have this place crawling with hit men. We can't take that on alone. We need Bart and Dusty if we have to go to war. But what we really need is enough crystal to keep these guys off our backs. Got it?"

"I know, Richie, damn."

"Are you sure? Because if you want, we can get out of the big leagues. Go back to selling those asshole bikers a pound or two a month. You want to go back to that?"

"Hell, no," Seth said.

"All we need to do is prove we can handle this demand. This one load and we're set. We'll be flush with cash and always have somebody to sell our shit to. The Mexicans have an endless supply of money. Let's make sure we're the people they buy from.

"In the morning I have a couple things to look into. I want you and Dusty to get as much equipment together as you can. I'll meet you guys out at the spot and we'll spend the day setting up new stills. We'll hit our deadline no matter what. You with me, baby brother?"

Pima watched as Seth looked up at his brother and nodded his head.

"Good. I gotta go make a call." Richie stepped out of the trailer.

Pima watched Seth dig around in his pants and pull out a glass pipe, then scratch a lighter a couple of times until it caught fire.

The trailer was filled with the sickly-sweet smell of his drugs again.

Pima held her breath for as long as she could.

# EIGHTEEN

AN ERRANT BEAM of sunshine knifed its way through the worn blinds and hit Porter in the face. He wasn't asleep. He'd been awake before his alarm went off, thinking about his hike in the woods, his mind running through contingencies and worst-case scenarios.

No point in waiting any longer.

After trying to drain the hotel's entire supply of hot water, he dried, dressed, and was out the door, scooting the dresser just enough to let him leave. Porter cut across the parking lot to his truck, sunshine warm on his still-wet beard, then fired up his truck and pulled out.

The GPS took him the most direct route, through what passed for traffic in the small town. After a series of turns, one leading him through the national forest, he came to a small dirt parking lot. He stepped out into the cool morning air and lifted his tailgate.

He dug through his clothes, looking for something that would be warm, but not too warm, as his large frame was sure to start sweating when he moved around. He'd almost detoured to buy a pair of proper hiking boots, but decided against it. Trying to wear a brand-new pair of boots before they were broken in was a recipe for chewed-up feet. Porter stuck with his Chucks.

The hardest decision of the morning was what else to pull out of his lockbox. He was wearing his Glock in a comfortable holster on his waist and had an extra magazine. He looked down into the lockbox at an AR-15 that he'd brought with him from Florida.

The first rule of a gunfight, he'd learned long ago, was to bring all your friends with guns. The second was to bring more guns than the other guy. Since Porter had no friends with guns, he considered bringing the rifle, in case he ran into the types of problems a pistol wouldn't solve.

In the end, he slammed the lid, leaving the rifle in place. While the thought of a gunfight against meth traffickers sent his pulse racing, he decided it was probably better not to terrify any soccer mom in designer yoga pants that he might encounter on the hike in.

He pulled on his backpack, which had several bottles of water inside, and set off down a gravel path.

For the first thirty minutes, the path was wide and flat and circuitous. He was instantly glad he hadn't slung his rifle across his chest. Somewhere there must have been another parking lot full of Volvos and minivans, because he saw more women pushing strollers than he would have thought lived in the entire town.

Porter's map took him past several of the trailheads, and all the soccer moms, until he came to a poorly marked path. Consulting the map again, he pushed through the wall of thickets until it opened up into a small but serviceable trail. Porter knelt and looked at several sets of tracks—multiple shoe prints and an errant bicycle track or two.

He kept moving, head on a swivel, possessed of a deep desire to see any meth traffickers before they saw him.

He was concentrating so hard that he noticed smells he never had before. With the faint dew still lingering and the musk of decay from the first volley of fallen leaves, Porter took deep breaths as he went—partly because he enjoyed the smell of the outdoors, and partly because he was sucking wind, moving around at that elevation.

Eventually, Porter reached the spot where Scarlett said he'd need to climb. He took a swig from a water bottle, then spent the next ten minutes trudging up a near vertical hill. He slipped on the already-fallen leaves and used the small trees growing out of the hill to pull himself up.

He wondered how the hell kids on bikes made it.

Cresting the hill, he squatted to stay low and looked out over the valley underneath him. He could see why the kids would like the spot. The valley was the size of a misshapen football field, with dozens of tall trees and a small creek that bisected it before snaking out of sight around a bend. Opposite him was another series of tall hills, lending the valley privacy.

Great for meth cookers.

Porter knelt, silently listening to his surroundings, eyes straining for any bit of movement in the valley.

Deciding there was no one down there, he descended the hill, half walking, half sliding.

At the bottom, he again stood, leaning on a tree, looking for another person in the valley. He didn't see anyone, but saw a small walking path that paralleled the stream and turned around the bend as well.

"The hell with that hill," he muttered to himself, "that's how I'm leaving."

He walked slowly along the valley floor, moving from one thick tree to another, looking for things that were out of place.

It didn't take long.

Buried in the creek at regular intervals were the types of

large water jugs one would find in a cooler at an office. Moving closer to the creek, Porter could see the rest of the setup, with tubes snaking this way and that, connecting the jugs.

The water in the stream was low, and more tubing was dug into the embankment. Porter looked left and right, finding the stream full of the devices, all in various stages of the meth-cooking process.

It looked like a hillbilly mad scientist lived in the area.

Porter was trying to figure how much meth the cookers had going when he heard a robotic, echoing sound.

Porter dashed for the nearest tree trunk for protection, pulling his pistol as he went. He knelt and stayed perfectly still. He would hear whoever made the noise again, this time before they saw him. He waited, still as a statue.

Not the type to easily dismiss odd things, Porter believed that everything meant something. There were rarely coincidences. The sideways glance from a stranger at the mall. The television remote not being where you left it. Seeing a couple of sheriff's deputies twice in the same afternoon, in two different locations. Still, he waited so long that he was ready to change his usual assumption and chalk the robotic noise up to hearing things.

Then the noise happened again. Porter snapped his head around, looking for its source. The large trees that were giving him cover were also playing havoc with the sound, and Porter couldn't tell where it was coming from. He waited, still and quiet, trying to slow his breathing.

Again, the echoing sound. This time, Porter stood and looked around the entire valley. While he couldn't tell exactly where the sound was, he could tell it wasn't moving.

Pistol pointed ahead of him, Porter moved from tree to tree, pausing to look and listen. He was sure there was no one else in the valley—no person could be that quiet moving on fallen, brittle leaves.

He looked up to the ridges of the hills around him, wondering if he'd see movement or the glint of a rifle scope.

The ridgelines were clear as well. He stopped moving and sat as still as he could, eyes closed, listening for the sound. Minutes later, it went off again. This time, he had a good idea of the direction it came from.

Pistol down at his side, he moved past two more big trees, then past a small bundle of thickets and stopped.

The leaves here looked different. They were not smooth and uniform, like the rest of the forest floor. These leaves had been disturbed and moved around messily. He slid his feet through them, scraping up big piles as he did.

After several minutes, his foot hit something that wasn't a rock or acorns. A second later, he heard the robotic chime again. He dropped to his knee, brushing away the rest of the leaves with his hand until he grabbed something thin and hard.

Porter pulled it up and wiped the smartphone off. He pushed the circular thumb button and the screen blinked to life.

The home screen was a picture of Pima and Scarlett, laughing at something happening off-screen. Their picture was obscured by a screen full of missed calls and texts.

"Shit," he said, wiping the screen off again.

# NINETEEN

PORTER STOOD, flipped the phone to silent, then slipped it into his pocket. He exhaled as he halfheartedly kicked through the leaves to see if he'd missed anything.

Pima had been here. And judging by the fact that a teenage girl had left her cell phone behind, it was obvious she hadn't left in a safe manner.

Porter felt a pang in his stomach. He tried not to get tied to the outcome of the cases he worked; it was too easy to hope a kid was still alive and smiling, and instead find them dead. He'd done it too many times.

He'd hoped she'd been with her boyfriend. He'd hoped she was high or drunk somewhere, angry about how her teachers or parents treated her. He'd lost a bit of that hope when Scarlett told him about their secret spot.

That hope was destroyed now, and things would get worse before they got better.

He followed along the path by the stream, away from the hill he'd slid down and off toward the bend he hadn't been able to see around. As he neared the sharp curve of the path, he saw a bicycle wheel sticking up, seemingly levitating above the fallen leaves.

Porter reached down and unearthed it, wiping off errant leaves stuck to the seat, and heeled the kickstand down, leaving the bike upright on the path.

"Damn."

As if the phone weren't enough evidence, Pima's only mode of transportation was still there as well. Porter looked around, trying to see if he'd missed anything else, when he heard the telltale sound of crunching leaves.

He stopped moving and trained his ears toward the sound. He didn't see anything, but a moment later, a searing pain tore through his forearm. When he leaned back against the closest tree, he was surprised to see an arrow sticking out of its trunk—the arrow that, moments earlier, had nearly buried itself in Porter's arm.

He knelt behind the tree, facing the bend in the path. He glanced down at his arm, blood already soaking his sleeve. "Son of a bitch."

Porter pulled his pistol and leaned around the tree, looking for the source of the arrow. He was driven back by another impact near him, a new arrow nearly taking his face off, slamming in the tree he was kneeling behind.

"What you doing here, big man?" a muffled voice called out. "You Mexicans here to sabotage our shit?"

Sound traveling within the woods like it did, Porter couldn't pinpoint the location of the voice. He needed another chance. "I look Mexican to you, asshole?"

The voice laughed. "Hell, I can't tell the difference."

Porter peeked around his tree. He felt sure the voice was elevated, from a position of advantage. He stood and backed away from the tree, then dashed to the next one. Another arrow impacted right as he ducked behind it. "You shoot an arrow about as good as you know a map."

The voice laughed again. "I'm just a little rusty. I got plenty of arrows; I'll get ya."

Porter leaned around the tree, looking at the hillside and the dozen or so trees in between him and it. He lingered for a moment too long, and an arrow ripped across the top of his thigh, sticking firmly into the ground.

Porter was at once furious and glad. The angle of the arrow meant it was coming from higher than he'd expected, and now he knew where. "Still missed," he lied.

"Give me time, friend," the muffled voice said.

"You can kill me," Porter said, peeking briefly around the tree, "or you can listen to what I have to offer. You like money, don't you?"

There was silence for several moments, and Porter heard the crunch of leaves in the distance. High on the hillside, he just caught the movement of a figure, camouflaged well. The figure stopped moving and was still again.

"Hey? You hear me? I asked if you liked money."

Porter leaned out of the other side of the trunk, and looked at the figure.

"I don't like your money," the muffled voice said. The figure sat completely still.

"Why?" Porter said. He raised his pistol and rested the front sight on the camouflaged figure. He took the slack out of the trigger, then stopped and let the trigger back out.

This guy might know where Pima was. If Porter shot him, he'd be back to square one. He took his finger off the trigger and slipped back behind the tree.

The camouflaged mass hadn't moved, apparently confident he couldn't be seen. Porter darted to the next tree, one closer to the hillside. He hid behind it for a moment, then peeked out to find the mass had moved and was coming down the hillside. In his hands was a black pistol.

"What happened to the arrows?" Porter yelled.

"You're right, I'm too damn rusty. This'll do." The man held the gun high, aiming it as he went.

"Screw this," Porter muttered. Still behind the tree, he fired his pistol into the ground several times. When he leaned out, the man in the camouflage had startled, and was running away from him toward the cover of a tree. Porter fired twice at the moving target, hitting the man and dropping him flat on his stomach.

The wounded man screamed and cursed. Porter didn't rush, instead moving from tree to tree as he closed in on the man. He made his way to a tree that was ten feet from the shot hunter and leaned against the trunk.

"Shit, shit, shit. Oh my God! My legs... why can't I move?"

"You didn't think I had a gun?" Porter said.

"Oh no," the man said. He screamed a blood-curdling cry.

"Roll over on your back," Porter said.

"I... I can't."

"If you say so. Where's your gun? Toss it."

A small black object came squirting out from underneath the man. "I didn't know, I didn't know, I didn't know..."

Porter closed the distance, his pistol aimed in on the man. "Where's the girl?"

"I didn't know, I didn't know, I didn't know..."

"Will you stop saying that? You did this. You shot at me first."

"I... I... smell yellow. Can you smell that?"

"Damn it," Porter said. He flipped the man over with his foot. "Hey! Pay attention. Where's the girl?"

"Amber... baby... do you have the..." The man trailed off.

"Hey. Hey," Porter said, nudging the man with his foot. "Hey!"

The man's eyes were glossy and fixed on something in the canopy.

Porter shook his head. "Asshole."

He stood for several minutes looking at the area. He wasn't in shock and he didn't have even a twinge of regret for what he'd done to the hunter. Porter had passed sympathy a long time ago on the highway of his life.

He didn't like being arrested. It happened to him often enough that he'd developed an aversion. He would get his lawyer to spring into action, and eventually the matter would be cleared up; however, Porter wasn't sure he trusted Sheriff Spaulding's clowns to handle the matter professionally.

Besides, he was in the middle of the national forest. This was federal land, and there was no telling what the park rangers would say, if he could even find one. They'd call the FBI in to help, and then it would be revealed that he was helping them out. Joe would never let him sit in jail—he would get involved. A black mark on Joe's reputation.

There was a dead body, guns, and copious amounts of methamphetamine. Porter wanted no part of it.

Porter checked the man's pockets and found nothing: no wallet, no money, and no phone. He stuck the hunter's gun into his back pocket, then grabbed the man by the camouflaged ghillie suit he was wearing, holding tight to the netting as he dragged him across the valley and toward the creek.

Porter rolled the hunter into the creekbed and, after wiping off the handle of the man's gun, tossed it into the creek with the hunter. He then looked left and right, walked fifty yards down the creek, and came to the first meth lab. He slid down the embankment, immediately angry at his soaked feet.

He pulled the first batch of tubing until it came free of the muddy earth. Then he pulled the big water jug, careful to keep from spilling any of the yellowish liquid inside on himself.

Porter trudged down, following the tubing until he found the spot where it connected to the next water cooler jug. The makeshift meth lab excavated, he took a couple of steps up the embankment, back to the forest floor.

He dragged the drug-manufacturing paraphernalia down the creekside until he got to the place where he'd dumped the man. He tossed the caustic brew of chemicals on the man's body. Then, he did it all again.

Nearly a dozen times he unearthed the cooking gear, and dumped it all on the hunter. When he was done, there were chemicals everywhere, and a big pile of water jugs stacked up in the creekside as well. He stopped for moment to catch his breath, the cool air burning his lungs. He pulled up the sleeve of his hoodie and examined the first arrow wound.

The arrowhead had sliced the top of his forearm open, but hadn't penetrated. Porter felt lucky about that. This was nothing he couldn't handle.

He pulled his pants down. The leg wound was a bit worse, but more of the same. No entry wound, just a glancing strike. He supposed he should feel good that he hadn't gotten stuck with one of the hunter's arrows, but he was too tired and pissed to look at the glass half-full.

Sliding his backpack off, Porter dug through a small, waterproof box and brought out the bundle of strike-when-wet matches and a small squirt tin of lighter fluid. He'd wanted to be prepared in case he got stuck in the woods overnight. Now, the fire-starting implements were going to serve a different function.

Porter liberally applied the lighter fluid to the entire area—water jugs, drugs, and dead body alike. Unsure he even needed to with the toxic soup of chemicals, he nonetheless used it all.

Then he struck a match.

# TWENTY

THE SHINY TAPE holding down the fresh bandage on his arm caught the sunlight just right, and reflected a small orb of light onto the Yukon's headliner.

The trip to the pharmacy had been quick, and there was nothing he'd needed that wasn't easy to buy and readily available. The pharmacist had looked at him sideways, no doubt due to the muddy footprints he'd left all over the store.

A quick stop to change, shower, and apply some first aid to himself at his hotel, and Porter was headed back to the Newtons'. He figured there was no reason to risk gangrene just to see them sooner. The bad news he had wasn't going to get better if they heard it immediately.

Porter drove up to the gatehouse. The guard opened the security gate without a second look. Porter was beginning to wonder if the old man was even alive.

A few turns and some gains in elevation, and Porter was at the Newtons' again. This time, he pulled into the driveway and parked. He looked past their house to the view and took a deep breath. Delivering bad news never got much easier, and it wasn't the first time he'd have to tell someone the worst. He hoped Mike could handle it, in his condition.

He popped the trunk to the Yukon and lifted out the bike that he'd struggled to carry out of the woods, then walked it to the front door. No sooner had his finger released the doorbell than Mike Newton slung the door open.

The man looked better, like he'd used some of his wife's Valium and gotten some sleep therapy.

"You're back. Did you find—" Mike looked from Porter's face down to the bicycle. He shut the door behind him and grabbed the bike, walking it away from the front door. "Come on. Bryce doesn't need to see this."

Porter followed him across the clean pavement to the side of the house. Mike leaned the bike against the garage door. "Where the hell did you find this?"

Porter told him, hedging a bit about the exact location in the woods. The last thing he needed was Mike trying to lead some posse out there.

"Wait, wait." Mike walked back around the front and came back in a few moments with Terri. His wife's face dropped when she saw Porter, and broke when she saw Pima's bike with no Pima. "Tell her exactly what you told me. She needs to hear it."

"I got a tip that Pima may have witnessed some meth traffickers at work."

"Tip from who?" Terri said.

"Some homeless guy. I didn't believe him, but I figured I'd check it out. Turns out she was out there, at least at some point. I didn't see her around, but I did find this." Porter pulled Pima's phone from his pocket.

"Where in the woods?" Mike said.

"I told you, I have no clue. I'm a city guy; I probably couldn't find the spot again. I barely found it the first time."

"And a homeless guy told you all this?" Mike said, eyes narrowing at Porter.

"Some transient. Said he sleeps in the woods a lot and thought he saw Pima roll by one day. Said he saw her going toward a place where he had seen some bad guys cooking drugs." Porter held a bit more back. It didn't seem like a great thing to tell an FBI agent he barely knew that he'd killed a man and burned his body.

"That doesn't even make sense," Mike said, rubbing his face.

"So that's it? You found her phone but we can't find her?"

"That's why I'm here. Can you open Pima's phone? Check through her pictures and see if she has anything we can use."

Mike thumbed the dark phone and it lit up, the picture of Pima and Scarlett on the lock screen. "I... uh... wow. I hoped this wasn't hers, you know?"

"Open it," Terri said.

Mike used his thumbprint to unlock the phone and it opened up. "That was our deal with Pima. She had to leave us access to her phone—me and Terri's prints can open it. There are too many weirdos, and kids can be victims so easy. I thought maybe we could keep an eye on her, you know? Keep her out of trouble."

Porter didn't say anything.

"Great job we did," Mike said, fumbling with the phone. "How do I get to the pictures?"

"Give me that," Terri snapped. She deftly maneuvered through the phone and opened the photo application. "Mike's a Luddite."

Terri swiped through the pictures, muttering to herself. "Who the hell are these guys?" She looked up at her husband, voice shaking. "Mike? Look."

Mike took the phone and swiped through the last pictures. Porter leaned over the man's shoulder as he did, recognizing the general landscape of the valley he'd just come from. "I've never seen these guys before."

The last few pictures were of a scrawny man with a baseball hat and a scraggly beard. Next to the scrawny man, and towering over him, was a much larger man. Pima had taken several pictures of them, including one in which the scrawny man appeared to be looking up at her.

"Who are they?" Mike said. "Who the hell are they?"

"I think they may have taken Pima," Porter said. "That's the only reason her phone and her bike would still be there."

Mike was silent. Porter could see the tendons in his jaw tensing.

"You think these are the guys? But you don't know, right? You don't know. It could be anything, it could be something else. She could be somewhere, maybe she's hurt or maybe she got lost," Terri said. "You don't know—how could you?"

"All I know is Pima was hanging out in a bad place where dangerous men were doing dangerous things. If they think she saw them, there's no telling what they would do."

"Yeah, but you may be wrong," Terri said. "You don't know. She could be... I mean, she could have..."

Mike reached his arm around his wife to comfort her. Porter could tell that they'd reversed roles, and now he was the strength when she couldn't be. He wondered when it would be her turn, in the upcoming days, to prop him up again.

"He's right. I know you don't want to hear it, but he's right." Mike turned and looked at Porter. "I don't care what you say, damn it, you're going to find your way back to that valley and you are going to take me with you. I'm going to bring a hundred agents. We'll find Pima."

Porter waited for a moment, then shook his head. "I already told you, I can't find it again. Besides, we should be concentrating on who these guys are. They're the key."

"But, but—but we could bring in a dog, right? He could track them down and find out where they live. Let's get a dog," Terri said, pulling at Mike's shirt.

"No good," Porter said. "I'm not sure how many streams I crossed to get there. Dogs will lose the scent. Not to mention that even if they did track them out, there's no doubt the guys threw her in a car and drove off. Dogs will never find her."

"So that's it?" Terri said.

"Hell no, it isn't," Mike said. He asked Terri to email the pictures of the guys to his personal and work email addresses. "We have their pictures."

Porter nodded, glad Newton was thinking like a cop again, but warned him, "Be careful how you look them up."

"What the hell does that mean?"

"You start using official databases for this and your ass will be in a sling."

"You think I give a shit about my job? My daughter's missing, you asshole. That's more important than anything. I couldn't care less about procedures." Mike was stepping closer to Porter, his voice growing louder.

"Think for a minute. I don't want you to do *nothing*, I just want you to be smart. You still have a family to provide for, no matter what happens to Pima."

"Happens?" Mike said.

Porter crossed his arms. "You know what I mean. Use your head. You're not supposed to be working the case, so send the photos to Joe. He can look everything up for you and then you won't get jammed up. Not to mention he already knows I'm out here helping."

Mike exhaled loudly, then stepped away from Porter.

"But that's it? Send them to Joe?"

"Believe me, if anyone can figure out who these guys are, it's him. In the meantime, I need a couple copies of the pictures, can you do that for me?"

"What? Why?" Terri said.

"I told you I was going to help find Pima, and I'm damn sure going to try. I need to run down a couple of leads," Porter said. "Having some pictures of these assholes would help. Could you print me off a couple?"

Terri looked at Mike, then Porter, and nodded her head. She stumbled away toward the front door.

When she was out of earshot, Porter put his hand on Mike's shoulder. "You have to keep your shit together."

"What did you just say to me?"

"You heard me. You losing your shit isn't going to help Terri, Bryce, or Pima."

While many would have considered Porter's words insensitive, he was gambling that Mike shared the same sensibilities as most of the law-enforcement officers he'd worked with. There was a reason why cops hung out together. It was a job where nihilism sometimes ran rampant, and jokes about death abounded.

This was because of the challenges the men and women faced. Porter remembered walking out of his office and scanning the surrounding areas for a sniper after one of their fellow agents was shot at through a window.

No one in corporate America worried about having an escape route on the drive home. An accountant never wondered if the knock at the door was the Mexican Mafia enforcer coming to make good on the threat he made in open court. The one about killing your entire family. Then setting them on fire. After raping them.

Cops treated each other differently, and Porter hoped Mike was no exception.

"I'm not—losing my shit. I just feel helpless. Pima needs me and I don't know what to do."

"Yes, you do. Pretend she isn't yours. Use what resources you can and point them in the right direction."

"Joe?" Mike said.

"You know it. That bastard will move heaven and earth if there's something he can do."

Mike uncrossed his arms and looked up at Porter. "You're serious about staying? Helping me find my girl?"

"I said I would, didn't I? I don't lie."

"Why?"

"I need a reason? Maybe it's the right thing to do."

"Please. Don't give me that shit. I can't even get guys whose job it is to do the right thing. Why would you?"

Porter looked out toward the mountains. "I owe Joe."

"He said you two were close. I'd hate for him to owe you something, be in hock a favor on my account."

"I'm the one who owes that ugly bastard," Porter said. "If it makes you feel any better, let's agree that I'm here for the reward money. Seventy-five grand is a lot of pocket cash."

"Well, whatever, I'm glad you're on my side. Hell, the bike and phone is more than anyone else found."

The front door slammed shut and Terri came back, a bottle of water in her left hand, several photos in her right.

"Couldn't get the damn things to print out in landscape mode," she muttered as she handed the pictures to Porter.

"Thanks. I'll let you guys know if I come up with anything."

Porter hopped into his Yukon, started it, and paused a moment.

He watched Mike put his arm around his wife, and the two of them stood there holding each other as he backed out of the driveway.

As he drove past the guard shack and the elderly sentinel,

he was hit with two thoughts. The first was that it wouldn't be a waste to see Sheriff Spaulding again. If these two losers in the pictures were local trouble, he might recognize them.

The second was that he hadn't eaten yet and it was late afternoon. His eventful morning had left him spent. Fortunately, he knew a great burger place near the sheriff's office.

# TWENTY-ONE

DESPITE FEELING like his stomach was going to eat itself, Porter figured he'd see Spaulding first. If there was anything he could learn from the sheriff, it would be best to know immediately. Maybe he would have an address on the two meth makers from the photos.

That might change Porter's dinner plans.

Without using the GPS, Porter navigated the streets easily enough and was soon parked in front of the sheriff's office again. He decided not to bother taking his pistol off. There was no metal detector, so what was the point? He grabbed a few of the photos from the stack Terri had given him and stepped out of the truck.

There were no other sheriff's department sedans out front, and Porter wasn't upset at the thought of missing out on a chance to see Deputy Adams and his plainclothes partner.

Not that he would have minded giving them the beating he'd promised, but his arm hurt, and his leg even worse. He didn't trust himself to play nice if pushed.

While he was never going to shed a tear for the man who'd shot arrows at him, he'd feel bad if he hurt a decent cop. The two deputies were idiots, but they didn't deserve to be hurt too badly.

Porter clicked the key fob and walked up to the front door, gritting his teeth against the stabbing pain in his leg. Inside, Ruby the receptionist sat alone, watching a soap opera on a small television on the corner of her desk. She looked up and saw him, then immediately picked up the phone.

"Better service this time, huh?"

Ruby whispered into the phone and furtively hung it up.

"You having a better day today?" Porter said. He gently smacked the rolled-up pictures against his palm.

She smirked and turned back to her soap. Moments later the door clicked open and Spaulding stood in the frame. "Mr. Porter? Back for a visit so soon?"

"It's just Porter. Have a couple minutes for me?"

"Sure, anything for a constituent. You would vote for me if you lived here, wouldn't you?"

"I don't do politics," Porter said. "Even local. I feel like everyone is lying."

"Ouch," Spaulding said, and motioned Porter to step back and follow him. "That's pretty honest."

"It is the best policy," Porter said.

The two men went back into Spaulding's office. "Interested in some Scotch this time?"

Porter looked at the sheriff and squinted. "No. No, I don't want any Scotch."

"You sure? I just got this new bottle in from the mayor. It's fifty years old, they tell me. It's supposed to taste like oakwood."

Porter ignored the man's offer. "Listen, I have somewhere to be. I just wanted to see if you knew these two losers."

The sheriff took the photos and slid through them. "You got a better one of the big guy's face? Bubbas are a dime a dozen around here."

Porter shuffled back toward the end of the stack and fished one out.

Spaulding rubbed his chin. "No, can't say I've ever seen them before."

Porter was searching the sheriff's face as he spoke, and thought he noticed a faint glimmer of recognition, but then it was gone.

"Why should I know them—who are they?"

"If I knew who they were, I wouldn't be asking you," Porter said.

"Maybe if you give me some kind of clue as to how you encountered them, I can help you out."

"I have some money to give them," Porter said. "One of those big checks, you know? I want to make sure they get it."

Sheriff Spaulding laughed, but the smile soon faded off his face. "That's pretty funny, Porter. I feel like I need to make it a point to let you know that you can't be hunting people down in my county. If these guys did something, or you need to find them for any reason, tell me. Leave it to the professionals, is that clear?"

"*Claro.*"

Spaulding scrunched his face up. "You speak Spanish? I tried to learn a little, but it all sounds like gibberish to me."

Porter ignored him and stood, boxing the photos into a neat stack.

"Mind if I hang onto these?" Spaulding said, reaching out for the pile. "Maybe I can show my guys when they get back. They're local boys, they might know these two."

Porter handed the stack over. "About your boys..."

Spaulding looked up from a photo. "Yeah?"

"Why are they following me?"

"What do you mean?"

"You know what I mean. I'm tired of seeing them everywhere I go," Porter said. "You should say something to them."

Spaulding leaned back in his chair. "Porter, this county isn't too big. There's a pretty good chance of running into anyone at any time here. When I can get my guys to un-ass their desks and go out into the world, there's a pretty good chance you could run into them somewhere."

Porter nodded. "Okay. Well, you tell them I'm tired of the coincidences and they should knock it off." Porter reached for the door handle and stopped, looking back toward Spaulding.

"On second thought, never mind. I'll tell them myself."

# TWENTY-TWO

THE CLANK of the cowbell announced his entrance into Burger Hut. Claudette was behind the counter, filling the individual salt shakers from a large bag. She looked up, her brilliant grin instantly plastered across her face. "My best customer."

"I said I was coming back," Porter said. "The food's too good to miss."

"Just the food?"

"The service isn't bad either," Porter said.

"Uh-huh. I'm sure you say that to all the girls."

"I meant Herschel," Porter said, pointing to the kitchen. The old cook leaned out the passthrough and saluted with his spatula.

Claudette's eyes were wide. "You better be careful, before he comes out here and hugs you, Porter."

"You remembered."

"Tough to forget. What can I get ya?"

"Same as yesterday?" Porter said.

"I can do that. You planning on mixing that unholy abomination and putting it on my masterpiece again?"

Porter smirked. "What's wrong with the mix? It's good."

"Sure it is," Claudette said. She tapped a few keys on her computer and gave Porter the total. "Unless you forgot your wallet today?"

"I figured you wouldn't fall for the same scam twice, so I brought cash," Porter said.

"Good thing. It would be just my luck to have a new favorite customer who was broke," she said with a smile. "Go sit, I'll bring it out to you."

Porter worked his way back to the same table he'd sat at before, with a nice view of the foothills in the distance. There were only a couple of other patrons in the restaurant, and they were quiet. Porter's mind drifted to Spaulding and Pima and the hunter in the forest. He wondered how the girl had gotten herself into such a mess, and felt a pit in his stomach when he thought about her chances of having survived an encounter with meth traffickers.

He felt sure that at this point, he was on a mission solely to recover her body.

Still, no family should have to bury an empty coffin. He wanted better for the Newtons. They deserved that.

Minutes later, Claudette appeared with a piled tray of food. This time, she had a glob of ketchup and mayo on separate plates. "I just can't bring myself to mix it, or even put them together. I'll leave that to you."

"You were serious about this much food every time, weren't you? I need to skip the bun or something."

"I told you yesterday you don't need to worry about it. Women like a big man."

"Yeah, but I eat a few more of these and I'll be Stay-Puft marshmallow big," he said with a smirk.

She laughed and walked away. Porter was impressed that she had another pair of jeans that hugged her curves so well.

Lost in thought, Porter tore through his food. He tried

piecing together everything he knew. All the info from Joe's file, everything he'd heard from the Newtons and Spaulding. He wondered who the two guys in the photos were, and what they had done to Pima.

In the back of his mind, something was rattling around. A loose thought, something he wanted to tell himself. He tried to figure it out, but it wasn't there. Thoughts like that were like butterflies—run after them and they float and fly and disappear. Sit back and watch them, and there was a chance they would hang around for a while.

Porter pushed the errant thought from his mind.

Claudette was back a few minutes later. "I see you didn't like it today."

"Terrible," Porter said. "The worst."

She started cleaning up the plates, and Porter stopped her. "Got a minute?" He pointed to the chair opposite him.

"Sure," she said, sitting down. "What can I get you?"

"Nothing. I'm just tired of eating by myself. Figured I could use some company."

"But you're already done eating," she said with a smile.

"Yeah, but I'm still sitting. That counts."

"Give me a minute," Claudette said, standing up and clearing the table. Porter watched her walk away until she disappeared in the back. Moments later, she came out with an enormous brownie, cut into two pieces. "There, now you're still eating."

The brownie was nearly as good as the burger, and Porter ate it quickly.

"Slow down. That's how you get agita."

"Agita?"

"Yeah, agita."

"No fair making up words to try to trick the tourist," Porter said. "Next thing I know, you'll try to convince me to hunt snipe."

"It's not made up," she said, "it's real."

"Let's say I believe you, which I definitely don't. What the hell is an 'agita'?"

"It's like heartburn."

"See? You're messing with me," Porter said.

"No, I'm not. My grandfather was from Italy and he used to say it all the time. It was even in an episode of *The Sopranos*."

"Really? Fine, I'll check it out when I go home," Porter said. "If I see Tony say it, then I'll concede."

"Where is home?" Claudette said, picking at her brownie.

"Tampa."

"How's Florida? I've never been," she said.

Porter shook his head. "It sucks."

"No way. The commercials make it look so great."

"Too hot. Too humid. It rains all the time."

"Yeah, but you have the beach," she said with a smile.

"Then sand gets everywhere. Trust me, you guys have it better up here," Porter said.

"What? This cold weather? You're crazy."

"I guess I am a little better insulated than you are," Porter said, patting his abdomen.

"Believe me, when winter hits, that ain't enough," she said with a laugh.

"Maybe so," Porter said. "But beyond that, this seems like a nice enough place."

"It used to be. Now... I don't know. It just feels like it's stuck in time. Stale. Jobs leave and they don't come back. Hell, what do I know? I was an English major in school; economics wasn't my strong suit."

"So was I," Porter said.

"What? An English major?"

"Sure," Porter said.

"Really? Who's your favorite poet?" she asked flippantly.

"Flannery O'Connor," Porter said without missing a beat.

Claudette eyed him suspiciously. "You're serious? I thought you were busting my balls."

"Nah. I'm lousy at math, so I figured I should go a different route."

"Hmm. Can't say I expected that," Claudette said. "You know, since I completely judged a book by its cover."

"I don't blame you. I probably look like I can't even spell the word 'book,'" Porter said.

Claudette blushed. "I didn't mean it like that. It's just, you don't seem like the type, that's all. You probably spent your time stuffing people in lockers."

"You'd be surprised."

Claudette stood and picked up their shared plate. "Honestly, at this point, I'm not sure I would be." She walked back to the kitchen.

Porter watched her go.

He collected his things and moved toward the front door.

Claudette leaned out from the kitchen. "So, am I going to see my best customer again tomorrow?"

"The burger's too good to miss," Porter said. "Service ain't bad either. And I don't mean Herschel."

"Good. It's a date," Claudette said with a big smile.

Porter pushed out the door, cowbell clanking as he went.

# TWENTY-THREE

THE BIG BOX store in town was easy enough to find, with its oversized building and enormous parking lot. Porter ran in to grab a couple of things. He figured it would take him a few days to find out what happened to Pima, and he'd need some provisions to make the motel feel like home.

The inside of the store felt sterile, with its artificial lights and squeaky clean high-traffic linoleum floors. Porter squinted as his eyes adjusted to the brightness. He filled his cart with a couple of cases of spring water, and more supplies from the pharmacy to keep his injured arm and leg clean.

With any luck, he'd be able to keep them from getting gangrene.

As he pushed his cart toward the checkout line, he saw the very unstealthy Deputy Adams loitering near the produce department. The deputy turned his back as Porter walked down the aisle, as if he'd miss a tan-and-green uniform and a big shiny gun belt.

Spaulding had been right about them needing training, but Porter hadn't realized how badly. Still, at this point, he was tired of being followed, and if it weren't for the perfect lighting and hundreds of security cameras, he'd have taught the deputy a lesson on the spot.

Instead, he paid for his items and pushed his way to the parking lot and loaded up his truck. He waited for a few moments to see whether Adams or any other member of the sheriff's office followed him out of the store.

Seeing no one, he threw the Yukon into drive and peeled out to the main road, heading back toward the motel. He couldn't be sure he was going to be followed, but he was going to take it as a given until he was proven wrong.

Porter ran three lights to get back to the motel, sliding on the loose gravel of the parking lot into a spot that wasn't near his room. He hustled to his front door, opening it and flipping the exterior light on, before stepping outside again and making a phone call.

"Hey man. What up? How's the case?"

"It's going," Porter said, watching the road by the front of the motel. "Right now I just need to pretend to be on the phone for a couple minutes."

"Well, while you're pretending, tell me how it's going."

Porter filled Ross in—the one person who always got the unabridged details.

"You just left the hunter there?"

"Yeah," Porter said, leaning against the window of his room.

"You have to hide the body or something, right?" Ross said.

"I set it on fire."

"Set it on fire? That's not smart. There's still evidence," Ross said.

"It'll be fine. Besides, I'm not trying to get into it with you right now. I just need to kill a few minutes."

"What's that supposed to mean?" Ross said.

Porter explained that he was sick and tired of being followed.

"What are you gonna do about it? You can't mess with them—they're cops."

"I'm gonna mess with them."

"I just said you can't do that," Ross said. "Don't you listen to anything I say?"

"Uh-huh," Porter said.

As if on cue, a familiar pair of headlights pulled in to the front of the motel and into a spot, then blinked off.

"Hey man, I gotta go."

"Porter, no. Listen, maybe you should—"

Porter hung up the phone and stuffed it in his pants. He lingered for a few moments, waiting to make sure he was seen.

The car the deputies had pulled up in wasn't a marked unit, but it was still the same make and model as the rest of the sheriff's office sedans. Besides that, even in the failing light, anyone with eyes could see the light bar stuck to the inner windshield.

And they wondered why criminals always made them when they were trying to be sneaky.

Making sure he'd been seen going back into his room, Porter reopened the door, stepped inside, and flipped all the lights on. Then he shut the door behind him. He made sure the blinds were cracked just a little bit and that his room was lit up like a Christmas tree. A very inviting Christmas tree.

Porter sat on the bed and waited for a few minutes. He needed the cops to relax and settle in. He needed them to let their guard down. Then he planned on having a talk with them about boundaries.

He peeked out the partially open blinds and saw the car still sitting next to his Yukon. Porter was impressed that the cops at least had the shrewdness to not park in front of his room. That was the most impressive thing he could say about them.

Porter shut the blinds fully, then drew the shade and flipped his light off. Anyone who'd been watching would assume he'd settled in to doze off to a peaceful night's sleep.

Instead, he went to the bathroom and pried open the small window. Porter looked at the window, then looked down at himself, then looked at the window again.

He was used to being the biggest guy around. His physical attributes had served him well many times in his life, from his youth playing football and wrestling to his stint as a bouncer to his career as a federal agent. He was deceptively fast for his build and his strength could not be ignored.

The bathroom window didn't care about any of that. Its narrow frame taunted Porter. He made sure the window was all the way open, then fed his head and arms out of the opening.

Porter continued pushing himself along, inch by inch, until his hips caught on the windowsill. Halfway through and upside down, he pushed along the wooden siding of the motel until he was past the sill and the rest of him slid freely out.

He tucked his head and rolled, ending up on his ass in the dirt.

Porter stood and dusted himself off, then hugged the back of the motel, following the curve until he was at the edge of the building. He peeked his head around the corner until he could just see the front of the hood of the car the men sat in. Most of their sedan was obscured by his own Yukon.

Porter waited a few minutes to catch his breath, hoping that the deputies would leave their vehicle. That would make things a lot easier. But neither of the men moved a muscle.

Porter looked around in the dirt at his feet, toeing up a softball-sized rock and gripping it tightly in his hand. He wasn't sure what he'd done to make these good old boys so upset, but he was going to make sure they had a reason to be angry with him.

Convinced the deputies' attention was on his room, Porter

took a few big steps over to his Yukon and leaned close to his truck. The deputies' sedan was in the adjacent spot.

Porter stole a look around, finding the coast clear. Even the light in the check-in hut was turned off.

He moved around to the back of his truck, leaning on the tailgate. He looked at the back of the sedan and took a step toward the car, raising the rock as he went.

Then the driver's door opened up. Porter thought for a second and stepped back behind his car. He wondered what the men were going to do. The passenger joined the first man at the trunk of the sedan. There was whispering and rustling, and Porter couldn't make out what they were saying from the other side of his truck.

What he could hear, as clear as Claudette's laugh, was the sound of a shotgun shell being chambered.

# TWENTY-FOUR

THE SOUND of a shotgun racking had a tendency to change things. In this instance, it changed Porter's mind.

He no longer assumed the cops were guileless idiots trying to prove a point. There was something bigger going on, something that involved a loaded shotgun.

Porter felt his Glock resting in his waistband and knew he was outgunned. A long gun beat a pistol most times. He wished he could get into his truck and grab the rifle inside, but that wasn't possible. He'd have to handle this another way.

Timing the click of the deputies' boot heels as they moved away from the sedan, Porter stepped in between the two vehicles and kept his head down as he moved to the front of the cars. Up and to the right, one man was moving to the front door of his room. The one with the shotgun was headed around the back. Both were wearing balaclavas to hide their faces.

Porter knew the man with the long gun was the bigger threat. He waited until he turned the corner to the rear of the U-shaped motel, then sprinted from his hiding spot to the edge of the building. When he peeked his head around the corner, the man with the shotgun was moving slowly away from him, toward the bathroom window.

Porter stepped to the rear of the building and took several large steps until he fell in a couple of feet behind the deputy. His Chuck Taylors helped him to move as quietly as a size thirteen foot could move, which was silent compared to the noise the man in front of him was making, stomping through the dirt and rock and grass.

Every so often, the deputy would slow down and sweep the barrel of the shotgun left and right, looking for anything suspicious. He never looked behind him, where his biggest threat was slowly advancing on him.

At this point, Porter was within arm's reach of the man, just waiting for the right moment to wreck his night. Up ahead, his bathroom window glowed into the darkness. Porter had waited long enough.

He took two quick steps, then slammed a right hand into the man's neck. It was like someone had flipped off a light switch. The man fell into a heap, his arms stiffly stretched out in front of him. Porter pulled off the man's balaclava, revealing the plainclothes deputy from the day before.

A few moments later, he'd moved to the wall next to his bathroom window, his body pressed flat. There was a loud bang, the sound of the other man kicking his door in. Porter waited. He wasn't a mind reader, but he knew the man was confused, expecting to see Porter sound asleep in his bed.

Porter waited, still as a stone as he heard the intruder pull open the bathroom door, the overhead light projecting his silhouette out into the forest behind the motel. The man's boots clicked across the flooring, closer and closer, until Porter was sure he was in the window next to him.

He stepped away from the wall and reached up into the window, grabbing the man by the side of his head. The man with the mask tried to squirm away, but Porter squeezed and held his head in a vise grip.

Then he yanked the man's head, pulling him clear through the open window. Since he was smaller than Porter, he didn't get stuck on the sill; he was yanked all the way out and landed on the ground beneath Porter.

The masked man struggled beneath him. Porter let go of his head and grabbed the man's arm, locking it up and tearing the man's elbow out of place. There was a muffled scream from beneath the balaclava, which Porter put an end to with several powerful elbows to the face.

His assailant limp beneath him, Porter pulled off his mask, confirming it was Deputy Adams.

"Son of a bitch," he muttered.

He was up in an instant, leaving Adams unconscious and bleeding from a large gash that his elbow had gouged out. Porter winced as the wound in his own leg stung, presently unhappy with his squatting up and down.

The other deputy was beginning to stir, snorting as he was coming back to consciousness. Porter kicked him in the side of the head, rendering the man inert again. He pulled out his pocket knife and cut the straps on the man's shotgun, pulling it away from him.

"This is mine now," Porter said as he stepped away from the fallen man.

He jogged to the corner of the building and looked around it. The parking lot was empty enough to show no new cars. No one was out for a late-night stroll or cigarette break. Porter jogged over to his truck, threw the shotgun in the back seat, and peeled away, rear tires sliding in the loose gravel.

# TWENTY-FIVE

"AND IT WAS like that when you got there?"

"Yep," Porter said. He sat in his idling Yukon in the parking lot of the big box store that seemed to never close.

"Well, Porter, I'm sorry this happened," Spaulding said, looking up at Porter from his heavily marked cruiser. "I'd hate for anyone to feel unsafe in my town."

"I don't feel unsafe, I'm just not happy my door was kicked in. I have underwear in there. What if they stole them?"

Spaulding smirked. "I'm not sure anybody wants your drawers."

"Did you say 'drawers?'"

"Isn't that what people call them?"

"Not saying it like that, it's not," Porter said.

"Eh, I tried. When I went to the scene, both guys were gone. Any clue who did it?"

"No," Porter lied. "No clue. I told you—"

"It was like that when you got there. Then you drove here and called us. I know, I know." Spaulding yawned. "You've told me."

"It's kind of late for you to be out. Don't you have underlings for this type of shit?"

"I do, but I can't get any of them on the phone. Probably drunk or sleeping it off someplace. I'll deal with them when I can. Just know that no matter what, someone will respond if you have any issues. I give you my word."

"That makes me feel better," Porter said, a dry bite to his voice.

"No need to be sarcastic. I'm here, aren't I? Besides, you can't say I didn't warn you."

"What the hell's that supposed to mean?"

"I asked you to leave the police work to the police. A day after you show up in town asking questions about the Newton girl, this happens. You think that's a coincidence?"

"I don't believe in coincidence," Porter said. "If me asking questions stirred up some shit, good. Something's got to give."

Spaulding nodded. "Something did give: it's called your door frame. Just... try to let us handle this. If you find anything out, tell me. I'm committed to finding this kid."

"Uh-huh," Porter said. "I'll be sure to come down and file a report if I find anything."

"Why do I think you're bullshitting me?"

"Because you're not an idiot?"

Spaulding frowned. "I think I'll take that as a compliment. I'll write this up in the morning; I can't do anything until I get a little coffee. If the hotel needs to know what happened before that, have Ron call me. I'll make sure they don't charge you for the door."

"Mighty nice of you," Porter said, dropping the Yukon's shifter into drive.

"Porter?"

He looked out the window, down at the sheriff.

"Don't... do anything. Call us. I'm serious."

Porter gave the man a halfhearted salute. "Yes, sir."

He stomped the gas and drove out of the parking lot, leaving the sheriff and his sedan behind.

Porter drove back to the motel. He had no reason to believe the deputies would be back that night. They were probably somewhere trying to figure out how to put Adam's elbow back together. He parked and went into the check-in building. Sam was there again, nose in a magazine.

"Hey, man, Sheriff Spaulding was here a little while ago. You know somebody broke into your room?"

"I'm aware," Porter said.

"That kind of thing never happens around here."

"Never is a long time," Porter said.

Sam nodded, like he'd heard sage advice. "I like that."

Porter squinted at the man. "Think you can give me one with a door that still works?"

Sam fished Porter another key from the pegboard and handed it to him. "Look, I called the owner and he said to comp your room for as long as you want to stay with us. Like, compensation for the break-in."

"That works," Porter said.

"Just come back sometime tomorrow and I'll switch your paperwork out."

Porter nodded and left Sam to his magazine.

"Never is a long time," he heard the young man mutter.

He'd lied to Spaulding about several things, one being that his underwear were in the room. They weren't; he'd packed everything in his duffle bag when he'd left that morning. With no reason to visit his former room, he went straight into the new one.

It was exactly the same as the last. Porter went through his ritual of quarantining the remote and phone, then dumped Lysol disinfectant everywhere. Satisfied he wasn't going to get some exotic strain of leprosy, Porter went out to his truck, bringing in his bag and dropping it on the bed. Then he went back out again.

Porter pulled the confiscated shotgun from the floorboard in the second row and put it into his lockbox. He pulled out his own AR-15 and an extra mag, and locked everything up behind him.

He pushed the dresser in front of the door and lay down fully dressed, rifle on the bed next to him, and let sleep take him.

Mercifully, it wasted no time.

# TWENTY-SIX

PIMA SAT AS QUIETLY as she could, her mouth closed, trying to make herself as small as possible.

"What the hell are you talking about?" Laura Bell said.

"Did I stutter? I mean all of it. It's all gone. Nothing's left. Not a thing. And I think... Bart..."

"Slow down, man, you're talking way too fast," Seth said.

Pima watched Richie pace back and forth, sweat pouring from his head despite the chill in the trailer. "Where was I going today?"

"The spot," Seth said. "Dusty's out getting some supplies. We were going to head over there and meet you in a little bit."

"Don't bother," Richie said. "It's all gone."

"You keep saying that." Laura Bell was sitting on the kitchen counter. "What does that mean?"

"What did I say, woman? It's. All. Gone."

"You're talking about our shit?" Laura Bell said.

"Yes, I am talking about our shit!" Richie screamed. "What don't you people get? It's all gone. All of it. We don't have shit anymore. Nothing."

Laura Bell hopped off the counter, landing lightly on her feet. "What happened?"

"I ran some errands and I thought I'd get to the spot early. I hiked my ass all the way out there and I found all of our stuff, burned up."

"Was it an explosion?" Seth said.

"Not an accidental one. Our stuff was piled up into one place and it was all melted down in the creek. And there was a body in there with it. I swear it's Bart. They killed him, then they burned his ass up."

"Must have been the cops," Seth said.

"It wasn't the cops, moron. They collect evidence," Laura Bell said.

"Then who? Who could destroy our site and kill Bart?"

"The Mexicans," Seth said sagely.

Pima watched Laura Bell's face drop. "Why wouldn't they just take our shit, Seth? They wouldn't waste it by melting it down. It wasn't them."

"Then who?" Richie said, pausing his relentless pacing for a moment.

"I don't know, but right now it don't matter. We don't have enough to give the cartel."

For the first time, Pima saw Laura Bell look worried. Or maybe scared. She couldn't tell, so she kept her mouth shut.

"We don't have enough," she muttered.

"I know those bikers have some," Seth said.

"So?" Richie said. "Whatever they have isn't enough."

"I've been talking to Colton. He was telling me his brother's in the Peaks and they've been stepping up the production," Seth said.

"Even if they have, we don't have enough money to buy it off them."

"Buy it? Let's just rip them," Seth said.

"Are you crazy? We can't rob the bikers. There's too many of them," Richie said.

"They're pussies and you know it. I've done more work than any of those guys. We just march our asses in there, lay some bodies down and take what we need. I'll kill the whole fucking club if I have to," Seth said.

"I know you'll try, baby brother. But maybe it doesn't have to come to that. I can get Big Man to arrange a meeting with the Mexicans, tell them we had an explosion and we need more time. Sometimes operations explode. Shit happens."

"Don't be stupid, those boys don't care. Besides, you scared to rob the bikers? There's only a dozen of those guys. How many cartel boys will be up here in a flash if we start jerking them around?" Laura Bell said.

"I don't know what else we can do," Richie said, sitting down on the couch. "I ain't running from nobody. No, I'm going to have a meeting and explain it to those bean-eating assholes. I'll tell them they can have a better cut when we do deliver; they'll like that."

Laura Bell stood behind Pima, playing with her hair. "That's not a good plan, Rich. You know they won't agree to that. No chance. I hate to say it, but I think Seth has a better idea for once. We're better off going after the bikers."

"Damn, Sis, you're supposed to be the smart one," Richie said. "You know what? I'll handle this myself. You guys just make sure you get enough equipment to start some new stills. We need to get back up and running yesterday." Richie moved to the front to leave.

"Don't do this. Stay and let's figure it out," Laura Bell said. "We can make something happen."

Richie stepped over to her and gave her a kiss on the cheek. "You just worry about figuring out our next spot, Sis. I got this." Then Richie was gone.

"Damn it," Laura Bell said, rubbing her face. "You guys just don't listen."

"What's there to listen to? We got no other chances. I don't care what Richie thinks, I'm going after the bikers."

"Seth, please, just listen—"

"You know that clubhouse of theirs has a back door?"

"So what if it does?" Laura Bell said.

Pima watched Seth get up and pull his pistol from his waistband. She hadn't seen the gun since he'd tried to point it at her when she was in the tree.

"You know what that means. I'll sneak in the back, then bang-bang. Their shit is my shit. And we're good."

"Just because I thought that plan was better than Richie's doesn't mean it's a good plan. You're both idiots. What if the bikers don't have enough?"

"Who cares? At least I'll get something. I'll bet they got cash laying around. I'll take that too. Then I can buy crystal anywhere. I've heard the Thompsons over in Morganton been making moves. They'll sell to me."

Laura Bell crossed her arms. "Okay, genius, let's say this goes off. Who's going with you? Richie's out and I ain't no good with a gun."

"I'll take Dusty."

"Dusty?"

"Hell yeah. All I have to do is set him loose."

Laura Bell sighed. "He's the biggest guy in Western North Carolina. Everybody will know it was you guys."

"So? I told you I ain't scared of their asses."

"Come on, think," Laura Bell said.

"Damn it, I am thinking. We gotta do something."

"We will, Seth. We will. Let's just wait till Richie gets back. Then we'll sit down and figure this out together," Laura Bell said.

There was silence in the room for a few moments. Pima watched Seth's face scrunch up.

"Fine. I'll wait. But if his ass doesn't have a plan when he gets back, I'm doing what I think is best." Seth reached into his pocket and pulled out his glass pipe.

"Do you have to do that right now?" Laura Bell said.

"Hell yeah. It helps me think."

Once more, the sweet smell of meth filled the trailer.

And again, Pima held her breath for as long as she could.

# TWENTY-SEVEN

FRESH FROM THE SHOWER, Porter took a few minutes to dress his wounds. They didn't look bad, by his standards. Given the events of the previous day, the deep gashes could have easily been gunshot wounds, which would have taken a bit more to take care of.

Like a trauma surgeon.

Instead, he felt confident that he'd be able to manage things, as long as he was careful. Fully dressed, Porter stepped out into the bright light of the day, rifle in tow.

There was a family loading up a vintage station wagon in the parking lot, the mother pulling the young daughter close as Porter walked by, rifle dangling from his hands. Moments later, he was driving through what passed for morning traffic, following the directions on his GPS. In the distance, he saw the technicolor trees, rendering the hills and peaks in inimitable shades of fall colors.

He pulled up in front of the brick building and turned the truck off. He reached into the back, pulling out his laptop bag and dragging it out of the truck with him. He paused for a second to reach back to the passenger seat and grab a couple of pictures of the meth cookers, then slammed the door behind him.

The library was smaller than the ones he'd used when he was a kid. Or maybe he was bigger. Either way, the space had tan floors and tan walls and a tan desk, and didn't seem large enough to hold more than two dozen people at once.

Standing at the front counter was living proof that Porter wasn't the darkest person in town. The man looked to be in his mid-fifties and very fit, busy doing whatever it was that librarians did.

"Hello, young man." The librarian's name tag read "Lonnie."

"Mr. Lonnie," Porter said. "Any chance you guys have a wi-fi I could hook up to?"

"We sure do. Got it installed just a couple years ago. It runs pretty damn fast if you ask me."

"Good. My motel didn't have it. I'd usually go to one of the big bookstores and use theirs, but I didn't see any around."

"I think that's a good thing. Keeps a place like us busy," Lonnie said.

Porter looked around at the half-empty space.

"We pick up after school," the librarian said with a smile. "You just need the number from your library card as the login. Password is the same for everyone."

"I'm fresh out of library cards," Porter said.

"How on earth can you live on this world with no library card?"

"I'm not from around here," Porter said, "hence why I said my motel didn't have wi-fi."

"So? You don't have a library card for wherever you're from?"

"Nope," Porter said. "I'm guilty."

"Well, I'll have to fix you up," Lonnie said, leaning over to a keyboard. "Name?"

"Smith."

"First name?"

"John," Porter said.

"You have been gifted with a common name, haven't you?" Lonnie said with a smile. "How about your address?"

"Don't got one of those either," Porter said.

"No problem, I'll just use town hall. I do it for our indigent population. They like to come in and read a little bit. Well, they mostly nap on the couches, but better here than out there," Lonnie said, pointing to the street.

"You have a lot of homeless folks in town?" Porter said.

Lonnie stopped typing, his smile dimming. "You know, we didn't use to. Last few years, though, it seems like we get more and more. Drugs, you know? People give them a try and get hooked, it's a short trip to the streets, you know?"

Porter nodded. "Drugs a big problem here?"

"More than it used to be. Seems like it's everywhere nowadays."

"Sheriff do much to stop it?"

"Spaulding? He tries, but what can you do? People gonna do what they want, no stopping it, you know?" Lonnie said, shaking his head. He punched a button and the printer behind him whirred to life. Moments later, he handed Porter a plastic library card, still warm from the printer. He scribbled something on a Post-It note and stuck it to the card. "That's the password. You go on and get comfortable."

That was easier said than done at the desks in the library. Porter smacked his knees into one of the small spaces, then sat on the chair, only for the hydraulic mechanism to hiss and slowly lower him to the bottom. It was a blessing in disguise, since he was now a bit more comfortable.

Porter fired up his laptop and started his search. His first plan was simple: check the jail. Google pulled up the link to search the jail's roster. Most jails, even tiny ones, had an online database of who was in jail for what. The often-basic web pages would generally also show the amount of the bond, if any, required for the defendant to be let out of jail.

While every sheriff touted this as a way to interact with the community better, Porter knew better: it was just a place to pawn off family members asking questions about their incarcerated loved ones.

He started with the list of currently incarcerated people. Porter's search of the page brought up twenty-three currently incarcerated inmates at the local jail. With nothing else to go on, Porter clicked each link that popped up, trying to see if he'd get lucky. Maybe one of his guys had managed to get put in jail in the last couple of days.

That didn't happen. After fifteen minutes of watching the slow page open and shut, he'd struck out.

"Figures," he muttered. He opened up his search parameters, asking the website to show him anyone who'd been in custody in the last year, but had been released for whatever reason. There were options to filter things by race or gender, but Porter didn't use them. He'd seen too much sloppy data entry in his life. Leslie or Stacy being marked the wrong gender, a black person marked as white and the like. It would be better to check them all so he didn't miss anything.

Two hours later, he was still crawling through the web page.

Lonnie the librarian appeared across the desk from him. "You're working hard, Mr. Smith."

"Please, call me John," Porter said with a smile.

"Right, right. Can I get you some coffee?"

Porter shook his head. "It doesn't agree with me."

"Doesn't agree with you? You mean the caffeine or...?"

Porter raised his eyebrows. "Trust me, you don't want details."

"Definitely not," Lonnie said, walking off between a set of bookshelves.

Porter kept looking, digging through the jail's roster of formerly locked-up people. An hour later, he felt like his eyes were starting to cross. As he clicked the close window tab on the face of Harold Sumter, a black man arrested for DUI, Lonnie appeared again.

"John, I feel like you need to take a break," Lonnie said, holding out a bottle of water. "I figure this won't send you running to the toilet."

"I hope not," Porter said, accepting the water. He looked at the man for a minute. "You lived here long?"

"My whole life," Lonnie said. "I mean, you take out the few years I was in the service. Then my Uncle Sam moved me around to a few different places, but when I got out, I came right back home."

"You know most of the people?"

"Sure. There may be a few I missed out on meeting, but I'd say you're the first new person I've met in six months, John."

Porter picked up one of the photos from the small stack he'd brought in. "You ever see this guy?"

Lonnie took the picture and slipped the reading glasses that hung around his neck onto the end of his nose. He moved the picture closer to his face, then back again. "No, can't say I have. I mean, he looks familiar, but that might be me tricking myself into being helpful."

Porter took the picture back and slid it to the bottom of the stack.

The librarian looked down at the table and pointed to the other picture Porter had laid there. "Hell, I know this one, though."

"Who, the big guy?"

"Yeah, I know him. That's Dusty Walker."

Porter scribbled the name on a piece of scratch paper. "You sure?"

"Oh, I'm sure. Everyone knows Dusty."

"Why's that?" Porter said, picking up the photo and looking it over.

"He was a pretty big deal. Best damn lineman in the state. That guy had scholarships to go anywhere he wanted. Boy must have been in the Saturday paper every week during the season. Lots of people were real proud of him."

"How'd he do in college?"

"Well, that's the problem. Ol' Dusty wasn't the brightest. Most of those offers got pulled off the table when he barely graduated. Still, State took him. I'm sure they were glad for any talent to show up at that school."

Porter looked at the photo of the big man again, putting a story to the face he'd stared at. "How'd he do?"

"Not so good. Blew out his knee his second year and couldn't pass the classes so he came home. He's been causing trouble ever since. Damn shame." The librarian tsked.

"Lonnie, you just made my life much easier," Porter said.

"That's what librarians do," Lonnie said, chin slightly tilted up. He walked away, back off into the bookshelves.

Armed with a name, Porter had a new set of tricks. He plugged Dusty Walker's name into the jail search screen and a list of the times the man had been in jail populated the screen. Porter clicked the blue link at the bottom of the screen.

A mugshot of Dusty came up, much more clear than the grainy photo he'd been looking at. He had a big face that matched his body and an eyebrow ridge that looked Cro-Magnon. He'd been arrested for speeding and DUI.

The next link was more of the same. Porter clicked through

them until he came to a property crime page: burglary, theft, and breaking and entering.

Then came the first of many arrests for assault. It was as if the giant had learned that he could just hurt people and get what he wanted. There were multiple convictions for assault, both regular and domestic, and the cherry on top was a manslaughter conviction, for which Dusty had been a guest of the North Carolina Department of Corrections for forty-seven months.

"Nice guy," Porter muttered.

He'd been taking notes as he looked at Dusty's rap sheet. Addresses—where crimes were committed and of his home—particulars about each case, and co-defendants.

One of Dusty's cases had a co-defendant's name listed. Porter plugged it into the jail search and came face-to-face with a mugshot of the scrawny man from Pima's photo.

"Seth Rollins."

Only two links came up when Porter searched, so he clicked the first one—a forcible entry charge with Dusty. The other was for possession with intent to manufacture or distribute meth-amphetamine. He only served eighteen months for that one.

Now that Porter knew who the two men from the photos were, he needed to figure out where they'd be. Fortunately he had a pad full of addresses from his search. He went through them all on Google. The street view showed him most were apartments and random houses in run-down neighborhoods. Except one.

One was a trailer surrounded by woods. It was a couple of acres away from anything, and the directions app told Porter it was only twenty minutes away.

Porter clicked on his phone, looking at the time. It was only one o'clock. Plenty of time to go see if these two were dumb enough to be home. He briefly considered telling Spaulding what he'd found, but quickly decided against it.

Aside from the fact that he had no confidence in Spaulding or his men, there wasn't any point. Even if they were on board with going to the trailer, all they could do was knock on the door. They had no warrant, and everything Porter knew was circumstantial.

Porter didn't imagine Dusty or Seth being in a good enough mood to talk to the sheriff. They'd clam up.

"Nah," Porter said under his breath as he stood. He gathered his things and stuffed them into his bag. "But I bet they'll talk to me."

# TWENTY-EIGHT

PIMA RARELY SLEPT. Even in the dark of the trailer, she could barely manage to keep her eyes closed long enough to nap. It wasn't just the discomfort from the tape strapping her leg to the chair. It was different, a feeling she couldn't shake.

Any time she'd get close to sleep, her eyes would involuntarily shoot open, darting from person to person around her, making sure no one was coming to get her.

No one ever was.

Since Laura Bell had told them to leave her alone, everyone had—even Seth, although he'd shoot her a look from time to time. Like he'd be glad to kill her and not think another thought about it. Like he'd eat her, or worse.

Unsure how long she'd been awake, Pima's eyes were drawn to the coffee table, to the phone whose shrill ring shattered the silence.

Asleep on the couch, Laura Bell groped blindly for the ringing nuisance. "Yeah?"

The woman was quiet for several moments, and Pima heard a voice through the other end of the phone.

"No, that's fine. What's the matter?"

Phone to her ear, Laura Bell got off the couch and stood motionless in the gloom. "What the hell do you mean he's dead?" Her breath came faster and faster, and Pima thought Laura Bell was going to hyperventilate.

"Are you sure it's him? Don't play games with me right now. You say this shit, you better be sure."

Laura Bell's voice was getting louder and there was a garbled quality, like the back of her throat was closing up. Pima looked at the two men, asleep on their couches. Seth and Dusty had been up late, the pipe passed back and forth between them for hours.

"Okay. I got it. No, you did right, thanks for calling." Laura Bell hung up the phone. She stood motionless for a long time, looking neither at Pima nor the other occupants of the trailer.

Pima was silent as the grave, not sure if Laura Bell knew she was awake in the darkness of the trailer.

Then Laura Bell let out a deluge of sobs. Fast and shallow, her crying was as soft as it could be, but stretched for minutes.

Pima closed her eyes and tried to give her privacy.

Then, just as suddenly as the tears had started, they stopped. Laura Bell gave one big sniff, then clicked on the light to the trailer. "Get up, idiots. Hey, get up."

Seth rolled away, turning his back to his sister. "Come on, girl, why you being so loud?"

"Get your high ass up. I just heard from Donna at the salon. Richie's dead."

Seth sat up, leaning to one side with his hand on his head. "The hell you say."

"I'm not playing. They found his head in a sack at the sheriff's office. Somebody just left our brother's head, right there for everybody to find."

"Hold the fuck on, Sis. What are you telling me?"

Laura Bell sat on the couch next to Seth. "Listen to me.

Richie is dead. We haven't heard from him since yesterday, right? That stupid meeting with the Mexicans didn't work and they killed him."

The change in Seth was sudden. "Hell no they didn't. Not my big brother. They don't know what they starting." He was up on his feet, dancing back and forth, the way Bryce did when he had to pee and couldn't find a bathroom.

Pima closed her eyes again, but peeked out of one, still able to see the room.

"Look, we gotta go," Laura Bell said, walking into the small kitchen. "Wake your boy up and get him going. We need to leave now."

"Why the hell would we move house? We need to be out there looking for those cartel boys right now."

Laura Bell stopped and stared at Seth. "They got Richie, Seth. If they did that, then they might know where we are. If the cartel would leave his head on the sheriff's steps, what do you think they'll do to us?"

"How will they know where we are, huh, genius?"

"They cut his head off, Seth. Don't you think they could have convinced him to give us up?"

"Not Richie. He'd neve—"

"Cut. His. Head. Off. That changes the game."

Seth rubbed the last vestiges of sleep from his face. "You're right like always, little sister. We need to get the hell out of here." He reached over and smacked the still-sleeping Dusty. "Get up, big 'uns, we gotta go."

Dusty lumbered to his feet, his barely awake look no different than the look plastered to his face all day, every day.

Laura Bell opened a bag and started stuffing stacks of money, bundled with rainbow-colored rubber bands, into it. "I'll get the money we have here; you grab whatever crystal you two morons haven't smoked up."

"On it. Dusty, do the kid," Seth said, as an afterthought.

Pima's heart started racing as Dusty stepped toward her, the same look on his face as always.

From the kitchen, Laura Bell screamed out, "What the hell are you doing?"

Dusty stopped, looked at Laura Bell, and then back at Seth. "No?"

"Think, you bag of dicks. Why the hell would we kill her now? And take a dead body with us? Huh?"

"We just do her and leave her," Seth said.

"In the trailer that has our names on it? Are you serious? This is why nobody ever lets you think."

Seth stopped for a minute and looked at Laura Bell. "Hell, you're right. So what do we do with her?"

"Nothing. We bring her with us, set up in a new trailer, and worry about her and what to do about Richie when we get there. Nobody hurts the girl, got it?"

Seth nodded. "Fine. Dusty, go put her in the trunk."

Pima watched the big man come close to her, but instead of grabbing her throat, he reached down and tore the duct tape from her leg, then effortlessly slung her over his shoulder. He ducked as he walked out of the trailer, ambling down the stair and unlocking the trunk of the silver car that sat waiting.

Dusty set her in the trunk gently. "I'm glad I didn't have to hurt you. Sorry about your throat."

Pima nodded quickly, looking through the open front door, watching Seth and Laura Bell gather all the things from inside.

Dusty rummaged through the trunk next to her and pulled out a silver roll of duct tape. "I have to tape you up again."

Pima glanced at the trailer, then up at Dusty. "No you don't. No you don't. You're a nice guy, I know you are. Just let me hop out and I'll run off into the woods and you'll never see me again. Everybody's busy; no one will ever know. Please."

Dusty looked at Pima, then back at the trailer. Then he ripped a length of the duct tape off and stuck it firmly to Pima's mouth.

"I don't think so. Seth would be mad at me."

Dusty taped her wrists and her ankles as well.

Pima sat still for the entire process, watching Seth and Laura Bell as they exited the trailer, each of them with a pistol stuck in the front of their pants.

Laura Bell stepped over to the trunk and pulled her loose hair into one of the rainbow-colored rubber bands that had been around the money. "You didn't make it too tight, did you?"

"No," Dusty answered truthfully.

"Good." She leaned down and looked at Pima. "Look here, pretty eyes, we have to go right now. I promise that as soon as we get where we're going, I'll get you out of there. Just chill out."

Seth stepped next to his sister, looking down at Pima. "I'm just saying, Sis. One match and this entire place goes up, her in it."

Laura Bell glared at her brother. "What did I tell you? Huh? Stop trying to think."

Seth laughed and pulled out his pipe as Dusty slammed the trunk, leaving Pima alone in the darkness once more.

# TWENTY-NINE

THE GPS, spotty at other times during his stay in the mountains, had a perfect bead on the trailer in the woods. The drive was quicker than the twenty minutes he'd expected, and Porter's mind had been firing the entire time.

The hunter in the woods had been part of the crew he was now hunting. It stood to reason that if the man had been so unhappy to see him in the valley the day prior, any of his friends would be equally as enthused if Porter showed up at their trailer. Porter doubted they would throw him a welcome party.

Driving up to the front door seemed like a poor idea. The map he'd looked at earlier seemed to indicate the drive up to the front of the trailer was almost three-quarters of a mile long. The road was gravel, and Porter could imagine the racket he'd make just driving up there.

Plenty of time for a murderous giant and his drug trafficker friend to pick up a hunting rifle and shoot at him.

The GPS told him to turn right onto a gravel road that was nearly hidden by trees. Porter debated, then turned the app off and continued up the main road for about half a mile. He'd looked at the trailer and the surrounding areas on his laptop, and had a better idea.

On the right, an unfinished strip mall appeared. Porter slowed and turned into it, pulling all the way to the rear of the structure.

The walls of the building were up, a nice brick on the sides. The parking lot was paved and the roof was on, but there were no tenants in the spaces yet. Porter didn't see a construction crew and figured they were on a lunch break somewhere. Even if they weren't, it looked like all their work would be on the inside of the building.

He should have some privacy in the back. Porter took a moment and collected his things, then slid out of the Yukon.

With a drive or walk up to the front door already ruled out, Porter made a new plan. He'd use the woods as concealment and move until he was close enough to see the trailer and anyone in it. With any luck, he'd see the two he was looking for before they saw him. Maybe he'd even find Pima.

Porter shook his head, pushing that thought from his mind. He'd learned long ago about getting his hopes up.

Instead he focused on what he could handle. He popped his tailgate and took a few extra minutes to search for the hoodie that had previously eluded him. He found that, as well as a pair of the Mechanix gloves he favored. After slipping both articles on, he opened his lockbox and took stock.

His rifle was there, waiting and ready like it always was. He'd been outgunned the night before with Sheriff Spaulding's men and he didn't want it to happen again. Still, it probably wasn't a good idea to bring it out. If something happened and he had to use it, he'd probably never get it back. He liked his rifle too much to let it rot in Spaulding's evidence room.

Instead, he picked up the shotgun he'd taken from the deputy at his hotel. He made sure it was in working order and found it to be loaded, with a shell in the chamber. Five rounds. He took a minute to wipe it off with his gloved hand, anywhere he may have inadvertently touched it the night before. Then he closed his trunk.

"Thanks, idiots," he said to himself, glad the deputies had actually managed to do something worthwhile. He slammed the trunk, then stepped off the pavement and into the woods.

He moved as quickly and quietly as he could, listening to the birds chirping above him, his feet making a rhythmic crunch on the leaves as he went. After a few dozen feet, the woods tightened, the large trees with their bare branches giving way to smaller, thicker bushes and shrubs.

Porter picked his way through these thick spots, using the barrel of the shotgun to move some of the thorny vines out of the way. Even so, the thorns caught against the sleeves of his hoodie and tore at his face like so many papercuts when he didn't move just right.

His mind ablaze with a stream of profanity, Porter was nevertheless as quiet as he could be, until the thickets opened up a bit and he could make out the trailer in the distance. The trees grew less dense, and Porter paused by each trunk long enough to take a hard look at the trailer.

Soon he was fifty feet from it, pausing at a cluster of three trees that could sufficiently hide him. Shotgun by his side, he waited, watching the trailer and listening, looking for movement.

He saw nothing. No one moving around, no one coming or going. No one pissing off the front porch.

He heard nothing. No yelling or laughing. No music. No television blaring.

After a time, Porter looked at his phone. An hour had elapsed since he'd left his truck. Estimating that he'd been in this stand of trees for half that, Porter decided he'd waited long enough.

Shouldering his shotgun, he stepped out of the tree line and sprinted to the trailer, keeping tightly to the side of it, where the windows were boarded up. It was small, as far as trailers went, a basic rectangle with a roof. The siding had probably been blue once, but it was weathered and faded by the sun.

There was a blue tarp on the roof, held down by a dozen tires.

He listened hard, trying to hear anything inside, but there was still nothing. Either everyone inside was asleep, passed out, or the place was empty.

Porter decided it was time to find out.

# THIRTY

PORTER EASED off the side of the trailer and worked around clockwise, to the back of the place. He paused for a moment at the corner, giving a quick peek to the back side. There was no one, so he moved smoothly along the back wall of the trailer, stopping at the sliding door that granted entry.

It was slightly ajar, and Porter gave it a tug.

The track was not smooth. There was a dry screech as the windowed slider slid out of the way.

"Damn," Porter muttered. He pushed the door the rest of the way open, the noise getting louder, then abruptly stopping.

No need to be quiet now.

He stepped through the threshold and into the living room, which held a trio of filthy couches. Porter shouldered the shotgun and swept it across the space. He crossed the living room and turned left down a hallway that dead-ended into a bathroom.

He turned around and walked past the kitchen before moving into another hallway. This one had two doors, one open and one closed. After a brief debate with himself, he passed the closed door and looked into the open room.

The windows were boarded up and, other than one small chair and a mattress and box spring on the floor, it was empty. He left the room and walked back to the closed door, floorboards creaking as he did.

Porter twisted the handle and found it unlocked, so he pushed the door open, letting it slam into the wall behind it. A laundry room, with no washer or dryer. There were bags of trash tied up on the floor. Porter closed the door to get away from the smell.

Shotgun by his side, Porter went back to the room with the boarded-up windows. He saw remnants of duct tape on the arms of the chair, and a couple of empty fast food bags in the corner next to the bed.

It seemed like a room where someone was being held. Porter ground his teeth. Pima might have been here, but if so, he was too late.

Walking back into the kitchen, he opened cabinets and drawers, finding them to be mostly empty. On the coffee table in the living room was an ashtray overflowing with cigarette butts and ashes, and several rainbow-colored rubber bands. He picked one up, turned it over in his hands and dropped it on the floor.

Porter was in the process of ripping the cushions off the couch when he heard the familiar sound of tires coming up the loosely packed gravel road. He peeked through the dingy curtain, eyes trained on the road that snaked away from the trailer. Just barely, through the trees, he could see a vehicle approaching.

He considered leaving out the back, to get out of there before the occupants of the vehicle showed up. He scratched that idea almost as soon as it entered his head.

He'd probably be seen if he left, as the area around the trailer was devoid of trees. Porter didn't want anyone else shooting at him, with an arrow or otherwise. Not to mention that whoever was approaching could very well know where Pima was.

And if they knew that, they were just the person Porter wanted to talk to. He strained his eyes until the noise of the tires on loose rock was accompanied by a vehicle: a silver four-door Civic.

This was exactly the reason Porter hadn't driven up to the trailer. Someone could have watched his entire approach. Instead, he was the one watching the Civic, bumping along as it went over the road, tires slipping as it turned the corner to the clearing where the trailer sat.

Hoping to see Seth Rollins or Dusty Walker get out of the car, Porter instead saw three Hispanic men swing the doors open and step out of the Honda. It didn't shock him—people of all ethnicities had to buy their meth from somewhere, and from everything Porter had read, it seemed selling meth was the only thing Seth Rollins had going for him.

What did surprise him was the fact that the three men were carrying AK-47s.

Whatever they were at the trailer for, it wasn't a peaceful transaction.

All three were short and powerfully built. Two wore jeans, one a pair of khaki pants. All three had bandanas wrapped around the lower half of their faces.

Porter thought for a moment, his mind running through all the options he had. The two with the jeans walked up to the front and Porter watched the third go around the back of the trailer. Porter heard them creak their way up the dilapidated wooden stairs out front.

He stepped back from the window and raised the shotgun to his shoulder and pushed the safety off. There were no good options, but as much as he liked the state, Porter didn't plan on dying in North Carolina.

He stood in the hallway by the kitchen, muzzle of his shotgun pointed at the front door. There was a muffled conversation out front, but Porter was ten feet away and couldn't hear what the men were saying.

Briefly sneaking a look through the kitchen and to the back-slider, Porter hoped the guy out back stayed out there. Maybe a contingency plan to grab anyone the two guys up front flushed out.

He heard the front doorknob jiggle. The voices outside were louder now.

"*Uno, dos...*"

The attempt to kick in the door was laughable. It didn't move. There were three more kicks before the door finally flew open, slamming into the wall behind it, handle sticking into the drywall.

Porter kept his shotgun pointed at the now-open door.

The two men rushed into the trailer in an undisciplined manner, both going straight in and looking toward the hallway on the right. Porter stepped forward, aiming the front sight at one man's back and pulling the trigger.

At such a short distance, the buckshot didn't have time to fully open, and slammed into the man like a bomb. His feet were taken out from underneath him and he fell into the wall.

Pumping a fresh shell into the gun. Porter tracked his front sight to the next man, who was turning around, trying to find the person who'd shot his partner.

Porter had a worse shot on the second man, from the side, but he took it anyway. The man took the full brunt of the blast somewhere in his upper torso—Porter wasn't exactly sure and didn't care. Neither of them were moving, let alone using their rifles on him.

This left only the man behind the trailer. As Porter swung his shotgun to the rear slider, the trailer erupted with the sound of 7.62 rounds slicing through the flimsy walls. With the big rounds chewing up all the space around him, Porter knew he had to move.

Without aiming, he shot two shells through the back wall of the trailer. Porter understood ballistics: he didn't like his odds of hitting the shooter, but he didn't care. Hitting the man would have been a bonus, but it wasn't his objective.

He wanted to get the man's attention and suck his concentration into the trailer. Porter sprinted out of the open front door, nearly falling down the decrepit stairs in the front of the trailer. As soon as he touched ground, he darted clockwise around the trailer, back to the side with the boarded-up window.

He looked first, then ran around the corner, pausing underneath the plywood. He listened as a rifle fired over and over again, the shooter trying to kill him through the back wall.

But Porter wasn't there.

He stepped to the corner, then snuck a look at the back side of the trailer.

There was a brief flash of khaki pants turning the corner opposite him. The killer had clearly had the same idea as Porter, and was moving to flank him. He'd just waited a little too long to start moving. Now, Porter was behind him as they circled the trailer.

Porter sprinted again, this time the entire length of the rear of the trailer, passing the blown-out sliding glass door and bullet-pocked walls. He peeked around the next corner and saw the man in khakis, who was looking around his own corner at the front of the house.

Wasting no time, Porter stepped out and squeezed his trigger again, sending buckshot slamming into the man's lower back. Normally, he would have aimed higher, but he at least wanted a chance. A chance he could speak with the rifle-wielding man.

The force of the blast had knocked the man off his feet and turned him, so he landed on his back, AK out of reach and of no use to him now. Blood soaked the dirt around the man.

Porter stood where he was for thirty seconds, not advancing. If the man was going to make an effort to reach the AK, Porter didn't want to be too close.

The wait wasn't necessary. The man moaned the entire time, his intermittent and barely understandable words coming in Spanish.

Porter stepped over to him, looking down at him.

The man was calling out for someone named Rosa.

"Rosa can't help you," Porter said. "Only I can."

The man looked up at Porter, the fear in his eyes replaced by anger. Porter reached down and pulled his bandana off. "What's that?"

"And nobody can help you," he said through a mouthful of blood.

Porter smiled. "Do I look like I need help? I'm doing okay, asshole."

"*Tenemos muchos hombres.*"

"You have lots of friends? I'm sure you do, but that doesn't matter right now. Tell me about the girl."

"*Tenemos muchos hombres.*"

"Yeah, I got that part," Porter said. "The kid. Where is she?"

The man breathed faster and faster. He tried to sit up, but the combination of his injuries and Porter's foot on his chest kept him flat on the ground.

"They're gonna find you," the man said.

"Doubt it. You guys don't even know who I am. Where's Pima?"

"*Muchos hombres.*"

"*Entiendo*," Porter said. "I heard you. Can you tell me where the girl is or not?"

"*Cuál chica?*"

"You don't know any girl?" Porter said.

The man shook his head and spat at Porter, the glob of blood narrowly missing.

"Then what good are you?" His shotgun out of shells, Porter reached over, picked up the man's AK-47, and put him out of his misery.

# THIRTY-ONE

HE DROPPED both his borrowed shotgun and the AK on the dead man's chest.

Porter took a minute to look at the man's tattooed face, which was now completely exposed. His ink was a roadmap of where he'd been, where he'd done time, who he'd worked for and, if his tattoos followed the rules, the surprising number of people he'd killed.

Porter shook his head. The shooter was a hitman for a big-time cartel called Los Primos. It had fallen out of favor to call them cartels, but Porter didn't think "Drug-Trafficking Organization" rolled off the tongue quite the same.

He recognized their symbols and tattoos from his time chasing down gangbangers with Joe. The Los Primos cartel was one of the most vicious he'd ever come across, and he was more than a little surprised to find them in small-town North Carolina.

This was not good. If the Los Primos were in town, he wasn't just dealing with some hillbilly drug cookers.

If the Los Primos were in town, things were worse than he thought.

Porter rifled through the man's pockets. He found no ID and only a cursory amount of money. He moved around to the front of the house, up the rickety stairs, and searched the other men, both long since dead. They also had no identification.

Standard procedure for cartel hitmen. No names, no IDs, and if they were caught by the cops, they'd give them fake information. There was nothing for Porter to go on.

He glanced at their Honda, still running except now there were bullet holes spiderwebbing the front glass from some of the errant AK rounds the man had shot through the trailer. Porter checked the seats and found nothing. He popped the trunk and, in addition to several boxes of 7.62 rounds, found a couple of small bundles of money, banded together with rubber bands—the same rainbow-color design as the ones from inside the trailer.

Porter stuffed the money into his back pocket, then stepped away from the Honda.

His route back to his car was quicker and more direct than his approach to the trailer. As remote as the location was, there had still been enough shots fired that even Sheriff Spaulding's guys could have found their way.

After a few minutes he stepped out of the clearing and fished his keys out of his pocket, unlocking the Yukon and hopping in. He tossed his gloves onto the back seat and drove away from the construction site. Porter pointed the truck toward his motel.

He needed a shower.

# THIRTY-TWO

"SLOW DOWN, DUSTY, DAMN."

Laura Bell leaned forward from the back seat to look at the speedometer, then sat back and grabbed tightly to the handle anchored to the roof of the car. She'd heard them called "oh shit" handles, but this was the first time she'd really understood the phrasing.

The Lumina was hurtling down the highway, which, thankfully, was mostly empty. They'd passed joyriders on motorcycles and cars in the slow lane, taking pictures of the remnants of the leaves. She gripped the handle, pistol digging uncomfortably into her waist, as she watched her brother smoke more and more of their meth stash.

Seth hadn't stopped ranting since they'd gotten into the car.

"I don't give a shit, you hear me? I don't. Those motherfuckers killed my brother. I'll dust them all. I'll go to Mexico and kill their families. Their wives and kids. Hell, I'm going into nursing homes and snuffing out their grandmothers. They're all dead."

"Be quiet and put that pipe down," Laura Bell said, barely recognizing the vacant look in her brother's eyes.

It had been like this the entire ride. Laura Bell had told Dusty to head to one of their old cook spots, so they could lay low and regroup. As Dusty sped toward the trailer, Laura Bell had to brush off every one of Seth's dumb ideas about how to get rid of Pima.

In the end, Laura Bell stopped trying to correct him and just prayed for the Lumina to safely get where it was going.

"I'm thinking we need to hit those bikers," Seth said.

"Don't," Laura Bell said, her hand aching from her grip on the handle. "I'll think of something. I'll call the Big Man and see what he can—"

"The Big Man? Don't get me started on him. That son of a bitch set Rich up."

"You don't know that, maybe—"

"Hah. Who's the smart one now? Who else sets up the meetings and gets Rich in touch with the Mexicans? The Big Man did it, and he let Richie die. When I get back from Mexico, the Big Man's next. Once I find out who he is, I'm going to kill all the—"

"I got it, I got it," Laura Bell said with a sigh.

"No, listen to me, now. If he has kids, I'm killing them. I know the bastard has to have parents. He's going to get it, right when I get back from Mexico. You know what? He's local, right? I'll swing by and do him on my way out of town."

Laura Bell sighed and looked out the window, thinking of how she could fix this situation and stop her high-as-a-kite brother from making it worse.

There were several blissful seconds of quiet. Then Dusty shattered the silence.

"Uh-oh."

"Uh-oh, what? What uh-oh, Dusty?" Laura Bell said, leaning forward into the front seat.

"Look," Dusty said, eyes on the rearview mirror.

She turned around, rewarded by the flashing lights of a trooper from the North Carolina Highway Patrol. "Shit. Shit. I told you to slow your dumb ass down, Dusty."

"I'm sorry, Laura Bell."

"Doesn't matter, I'll do him first," Seth said, stuffing his pipe into the glove box.

"You shut your mouth. Don't do anything. The car isn't stolen, your idiot friend was just driving too fast. All they want to do is give us a speeding ticket." She reached up and touched Dusty on the forearm. "Dusty, just be cool okay? Do what the cop says."

"Yes, Laura Bell."

The lights drew closer, the shape of a car finally recognizable. Dusty pulled over to the shoulder and put the car in park.

The group waited for what seemed like an eternity until the lean, fit trooper arrived, circular hat clamped to the top of his head. He stooped just behind the driver's side window, forcing Dusty to turn to face him as they spoke.

"I'm Trooper Pirelli, North Carolina Highway Patrol." His accent made it seem like there was no R in "North" and an H somewhere in "Carolina."

"Sir," Dusty said.

"Do you know why I stopped you?"

"I think I was driving too fast," Dusty said.

"Bingo. I clocked you at eighty-nine in a fifty-five," Pirelli said.

"Wow," Dusty said.

"Most people don't notice that the speed drops when going over the little bridge back there."

"I didn't," Dusty said.

"Understandable. License, registration, and proof of insurance please."

Dusty got his information and driver's license out, and

handed it to Pirelli. The entire time, Seth was shaking his leg so violently that the car was rocking.

"Back in a minute," the trooper said as he walked back to his vehicle.

Laura Bell stole a glance behind her, then leaned up into the front seat again. "You're doing good, Dusty. Keep doing what you're doing. We'll deal with the ticket later."

"Okay."

She turned her head toward Seth. "Stop with your leg, you're gonna freak the cop out. Sit still."

"Sorry, Sis," Seth said, his forehead freely dripping sweat. He stopped shaking his leg and started grinding his teeth.

Laura Bell watched as the minutes on the dash clock crawled by, listening to Seth grind his teeth the entire time.

Ten minutes later, Trooper Pirelli came back, his walk a bit looser. He stepped all the way up to the driver's window. "Here's your information back, Mr. Walker." He leaned down into the window.

"Thank you."

"You know, I didn't recognize you, sitting in the car and all. We played against you guys back in oh-one."

"My memory is bad," Dusty said. "Sorry."

"It was the semi-finals of regionals that year. You guys beat us, but we put up a fight," Pirelli said.

Dusty thought for a moment. "The Bearcats?"

"That's us. I played receiver, so we never lined up against you, but I can tell from standing here, I'm lucky I didn't."

Dusty smiled. "You look tough."

Trooper Pirelli laughed and then the smile was gone from his face.

"Look here, my computer told me you're on probation. I'm supposed to let your PO know I pulled you over for speeding, since you were going so fast."

Laura Bell sat still as a rock, listening to the trooper. Seth's teeth were still as loud as walnuts cracking.

"I don't think I need to do that, do you?" Pirelli said with a smile.

"No, sir. I won't speed again ever," Dusty said.

Seth was back to rocking the car again with his leg shake.

"Let's not go too far. Just try to slow it down, got it?" Trooper Pirelli laughed.

"Yes, sir," Dusty said.

"Can't let the best player to ever come out of Western North Carolina wrap himself around a pole one day."

"I'll slow down." Dusty raised his fingers in a strange sort of half salute.

Trooper Pirelli patted the top of the Lumina. "Have a good day, folks."

Then he was gone.

"You did good, Dusty," Laura Bell said, resisting the urge to look behind her again.

Seth was back to grinding his teeth. "Yeah, yeah. Glad that pig is gone."

"Shut up, Seth. Pull back on the highway," Laura Bell said. "Go real slow."

"Yes, Laura Bell."

Dusty eased the Lumina back onto the highway, starting out exaggeratedly slow.

"A little faster than this, Dusty; this looks weird," Laura Bell said as the man accelerated a bit. "That's good right there."

"Tell you what, that pig's glad he liked you, or I was gonna have to do his ass. Ain't gonna let no cop stop me. A pig ain't shit, you know what I'm saying?"

"Just shut up and sit there, idiot," Laura Bell said, and leaned back against the seat, thinking of ways to get the money or drugs they needed.

"Uh-oh," Dusty said.

"What?" Laura Bell said, sitting up.

"The trooper again."

Laura Bell looked out the rear windshield at the familiar lights. "He probably has to go to another call. Just keep driving the same. You're okay, he'll just pass us by."

Except he didn't. The vehicle was behind them in moments and Dusty pulled over again.

"He probably wants your autograph, hero," Seth said.

"What do I do?"

"Just be cool. This guy likes you," Laura Bell said.

"Fucking pig," Seth muttered to no one.

Trooper Pirelli swung his door open and walked back to the Lumina, this time, lingering by the trunk for an extra moment.

He stood behind the glass, like the first time, forcing Dusty to turn and face him.

"Mr. Walker, I'm sorry to bother you again, but I wanted to check on something," Trooper Pirelli said.

"What?" Dusty said.

"When I was walking back to the car a few minutes ago, I could have sworn I heard a thumping noise coming from your trunk. I figured it was my ears playing a trick, but I just heard it again. Mind if I take a look?"

# THIRTY-THREE

"THUMPING?"

"Yeah, pretty distinct," Pirelli said.

"The car's old," Dusty said.

Pirelli laughed. "I can tell. Still, I know I'm hearing something. I once read about this case where a man didn't know his daughter had locked herself in the trunk. She was playing hide-and-seek or some such nonsense, and she was too young to know how to release the lock. Everyone drove around looking for her but she was trapped just a few feet from him. I wanna say it got too hot and she died."

"We ain't got no toddlers," Seth said.

Pirelli leaned down a bit more, and watched Seth for a few moments. "All the same, mind popping your trunk for me?"

"Okay," Dusty said.

Trooper Pirelli stepped around to the trunk, waiting for Dusty to get out and meet him.

Dusty slowly removed his seatbelt and began the arduous task of unfolding his bulk from the car.

"Tell him no," Seth hissed. "He needs a warrant to get in the trunk."

It was the first smart thing Seth's drug-addled mind had come up with, Laura Bell thought. Pirelli technically needed a warrant to search a locked trunk. Her mind raced to find a way to stop the train they were on and get off.

She knew that despite the law, if Pirelli wanted in, he was getting in. All he had to do was call for backup to come out with a warrant. Easy enough to obtain if he thought there was something dangerous in the trunk.

Dusty heaved himself from the car and shut the door behind him.

"Dusty. Dusty," she said quietly as he passed her window, but the big man didn't hear her and joined Pirelli at the trunk.

Seth muttered, "Fuck this," and opened his door.

Before she could stop her brother, she heard Pirelli speak up. "Sir, stay in your vehicle," he said to Seth.

Laura Bell spun and watched through the back window.

Seth held his hands up. "Dusty doesn't know how to open the trunk. It sticks sometimes and our boy is a little slow. If you'd let me—"

Trooper Pirelli backed up as he spoke and kept both men in front of him. Laura Bell saw him rest his hand on the butt of his pistol.

"But I just need to—"

"You know what? Go lay down on the shoulder. Right now, on your stomach."

Seth kept walking toward Trooper Pirelli.

"Stay still," Laura Bell said from the car.

Seth didn't.

Pirelli unholstered his pistol and leveled it at Seth.

"Shit," Laura Bell said.

"I said get on your stomach, now," Pirelli said.

Faced with the possibility of being shot, Seth took several

steps backward and lay down flat on the shoulder, half-in and half-out of the tall grass on the side of the road.

"Arms out to your sides. Do it now," Pirelli said.

Seth stuck his arms out like he was playing airplane. "Stupid ass pig. Dumb ass redneck piece of shit..."

Laura Bell saw Pirelli sneak a look at Dusty. He waved with his pistol. "You get over there, too. Lay down next to your buddy."

"But, sir—"

"I said do it, Dusty."

Dusty obliged, lying down a few feet from Seth.

Pirelli stepped over and cuffed Seth's arms behind his back. Seth grunted but didn't say anything.

"I hate that you made me do this, but you were disobeying orders. Not to mention you've been mad-dogging me this entire time. I can tell you're high off your ass. Any more drugs in the car?"

Seth mumbled a stream of expletives.

Pirelli did a quick pat-down of places that Seth could reach, even while cuffed. A thin, limber person could reach most of the way around their body while cuffed, so cops liked to check everywhere.

His eyes went wide when he felt the front of Seth's waistline. "Well, what the hell's this?"

He pulled out Seth's pistol and stood up with it. "You have a permit for this?"

"Sir," Laura Bell said from the car.

"You stay right there. Do not move, do you understand?"

"Yes sir, but—"

"Don't move," Pirelli said.

Laura Bell watched Pirelli stand up and set the gun on his own hood, then move back to the trunk of the Lumina. The keys were dangling from the lock.

"You two stay right there," he said, pointing at Seth and Dusty. "We'll sort all this out once I get a peek inside."

Laura Bell reached for the door handle and Pirelli popped the trunk.

"What the hell?" the trooper said as the lid opened.

Laura Bell imagined it was a shock to find a taped-up, kidnapped girl in their trunk.

Pirelli stood there unmoving for several moments. Then, as he lowered the trunk to speak, he came face-to-face with Laura Bell's revolver as it barked out a round.

Laura Bell saw the bullet rip through the trooper's shoulder, his shirt instantly awash in blood.

"What the fu—"

She pulled the trigger two more times, missing him.

Pirelli was moving, bailing from behind the Lumina and racing to the safety of his own hood. He knelt behind it, pulling out his weapon with his one good arm and trying to aim it at Laura Bell.

The trooper's back was to Seth and Dusty. This was his mistake.

During the chaos, and the ringing of gunshots, Seth was screaming, "Get him, Dusty, get him!"

Dusty pushed his hands against the earth and heaved his bulk up, showing some of the prowess that had made him such a highly regarded college recruit.

Pirelli zeroed in on Laura Bell, but she kept her eyes fixed over his shoulder as Dusty slammed his shoulder into the trooper's back, denting in the hood of the car. Pirelli's gun went skittering across the blacktop of the lonely road.

"Kill him, Dusty, kill him," Seth screamed, hands still cuffed behind his back.

As Pirelli leaned half-dazed against the hood of his car,

Dusty grabbed him by the shoulders, lifted him into the air, and slammed him to the ground.

Then Dusty's hands were around the trooper's throat.

"Dusty, stop," Laura Bell said. "Stop, let's go."

As Trooper Pirelli clawed at Dusty's hands and face, Dusty slammed the man's head onto the hard earth, over and over again.

"Dusty, stop!" Laura Bell was pushing and pulling at Dusty, trying to get him to stop. His eyes were blank as he continued slamming the trooper's head until it was cracked and broken.

"Kill him," Seth screamed, barely able to raise his face off the ground.

Dusty continued until the trooper's lifeless body lay underneath him. Laura Bell had given up trying to stop him; it was no use. She just couldn't move the massive man.

The giant stood, covered in blood up to his forearms. He dug through Pirelli's pockets until he found a cuff key, then unhooked Seth from his bonds.

Once on his feet again, Seth ran over to the trooper's gun and stuffed it in his waistband, as well as grabbing his own from the hood of the running patrol vehicle. He spat at the trooper's lifeless body.

Laura Bell stood staring at the two men as they moved. She felt numb, like her hands didn't belong to her. The revolver she'd used to shoot the trooper hung limply by her side. Dusty slammed the trunk and started the car.

Seth grabbed Laura Bell and dragged her back to the car.

"Get in, Sis, we gotta go."

"I didn't—I mean, I wanted..."

"Let's go, baby sis." Seth shoved her into the back seat of the Lumina, then slammed the door after her.

Dusty stomped the gas and the Lumina tore away from the scene, leaving the body of Trooper Pirelli behind.

# THIRTY-FOUR

BEARD STILL DAMP from the shower, Porter stepped into his new favorite restaurant. He'd been busy all day, and all the thinking and shooting had left him famished. The familiar clank of the cowbell signaled his arrival.

"So, Flannery O'Connor, huh?" Claudette held up a small, paperback copy of a book.

"You looked into her?" Porter said.

"I'd heard of her—I mean, you don't study literature in the South without hearing about her. Just never really my thing. If she's *your* favorite, I figured I'd see what I was missing."

Porter leaned on the front counter, all thoughts of cartel hitmen temporarily driven from his mind. "What do you think?"

Claudette's hand waffled back and forth. "Ehh. I'm more of a Tolkien girl. Not bad, though."

"I can't say I blame you," Porter said. "Can I get the usual?"

"You think you've been here enough to have a usual?" she said.

"Three days in a row entitles me to have a sandwich named after me," Porter said with a laugh.

"Not quite, cowboy; that's for a whole week of eats," she said. "Go sit."

Porter obeyed, the slight limp from his injury more pronounced since his sprinting session at the trailer earlier. He sat at his regular table, but pulled an extra chair over and propped his leg up.

"What happened?"

Claudette was standing near the table, cup in her hand.

"I'm clumsy," Porter said.

"Hell, you aren't the only one. I fall on flat ground sometimes. The craziest thing. I think I'm going okay, then bang, down I go."

"Maybe we need to wrap you in bubble wrap," Porter said.

"Sure, if that's your thing. Sounds a little kinky to me," she said with a smile as she turned back to the kitchen.

For several minutes, everything was quiet. Porter's mind jumped through all the things he'd uncovered. It wasn't a conscious thing, more like his computer was always running in the background.

The cartel thugs who had showed up at the trailer were a wrinkle in the usual order. He was trying to figure out how they were involved, and all he could come up with was one thing: it was his fault.

It could be no coincidence that the men showed up at the trailer of Seth Rollins ready to kill him after Porter had destroyed a metric ton of Seth's drugs. No, this was purposeful.

Porter wasn't sure if Seth owed the Mexicans drugs or money or both, but it was evident he was past due.

This was a problem for Pima.

If the girl was even still alive, he couldn't even wrap his mind around how she might survive the Rollins crew and the cartel gun thugs running around. He felt his heart pick up a bit, growing frustrated with his lack of progress in finding the girl.

"I said I'm not letting you ruin another burger," Claudette said as she approached, another absurd tray of food in her hands.

"I thought the customer was always right," Porter said with a smile.

"That's true, unless they're wrong. Why not try it without the crazy mixture this time? You might like it better."

"You're the boss," Porter said. She walked away again, this time looking back just as Porter leaned out into the aisle to watch her go.

"Eyes on your own work," she said with a laugh.

Porter grinned and went to work on the tray, but it was a halfhearted effort. He mostly picked at everything.

Minutes later, she was back, this time taking a seat across from him. "Not good today?" she said, genuine concern on her face.

"It's not that; it's great. I mean, it's probably the best thing this town has to offer. I wouldn't eat anywhere else."

"The Burger Hut is the best," she said with a mock British accent.

"How long you owned it? I figured it was a mom-and-pop place when I drove by the first time."

"Well, it was, kinda. A young mom-and-pop couple, at least. Till pop stepped out and mom won the restaurant in the divorce."

"That was good, I guess," Porter said.

She shrugged. "It pays the bills... most of the time." She fixed Porter with her dark eyes. "So if it's not the food, what's the matter?"

"I got a lot on my mind," Porter said.

"Pima, right?"

Porter stared at her for a few moments. "Is the town that small?"

"Well... yeah," she said. "Word travels fast. You're pretty memorable, so people talk."

"I guess so," Porter said, picking at his fries.

"So do you think you will?"

"What? Eat all this? No, I need a take-home bo—"

"No, find Pima."

Porter chose his words carefully. He didn't want any other information about him or the Newtons traveling the grapevine if he could help it. "Tough to say."

"I imagine. It scares the hell out of me."

"You got kids?"

"Two. They're still way too young to get lost riding home on their bikes, but still. What if they were gone, you know?"

"It would be shit. I feel bad for the Newtons," Porter said.

"Do you and your wife have any kids?"

Porter looked at the woman for a couple of seconds, impressed with how smoothly she'd asked him if he was married. "We never had any."

"That was past tense," Claudette said, taking a fry from Porter's plate.

"Yep. She didn't step out on me, but it just didn't work, you know?"

"Believe me, I know." She leaned forward, elbows on the table. "Speaking of the grapevine, did you hear about the shooting?"

"Shooting?" Porter said, feigning ignorance. "What shooting?"

"At the trailer? Three guys got killed. The news is saying it's a drug deal that went bad. This town didn't use to have trouble like that," she said.

"What can you do?" Porter said.

"Worry about what I can control, I guess."

"I agree with that," Porter said.

There was a comfortable silence between the two. Claudette was looking out the window at the pinkish sky, the sun just beginning to lower behind the mountains. Porter was looking at her, wondering why he hadn't noticed she had dimples before.

"So, it's my early night," she said, turning from the window. "I let Herschel close up so I don't drive myself crazy being here all day, every day."

"I'll bet Herschel loves the solitude."

"Yeah, he likes to get into his flask without me giving him a hard time, that's what he likes," she said with a laugh.

Porter smiled.

"If you... need any information about the area, I could come by your place and help you."

Porter raised his eyebrows. He hadn't been prepared for the statement.

"That sounded pretty desperate, didn't it? Oh God, that was bad."

"No, it sounded okay," Porter said.

She covered her face with her hands. Porter could just see the red creeping down her chest, disappearing below her cleavage. "I mean, when you're younger it's easy to meet people. There's high school and college and friends and friends of friends. But when you get older, those chances aren't really there anymore."

"Smaller playing field," he said.

"Right? And then kids and work and an asshole ex. I... I..." she stammered, then slid out of her chair and began to pick up Porter's tray.

"I'm very flattered you would include me anywhere on your playing field," Porter said.

"I'm just saying, why isn't it appropriate to walk up to

another adult and say, 'I have no venereal diseases and I think you're attractive and I'd like to sleep with you'?"

"You kind of just did," Porter said.

"Like an idiot," she said.

"Claudette?"

"Yeah?"

"I have no venereal diseases and I think you're attractive and I'd like to sleep with you."

"You're serious?"

"Why not? I don't have a curfew," Porter said.

She smiled. "Yeah. Yeah, I'd like that."

"Great. How long until you're out of here?"

"Half an hour?"

"That works," Porter said.

"You're not kidding, right?"

Porter told her what motel he was in and the room number. "Find out."

# THIRTY-FIVE

CLAUDETTE WAS RIGHT; they weren't in high school any longer. He didn't have the old, unused condom leaving a ring in his wallet that he did twenty years ago. Still, he was no fool.

He walked through the big box store, the artificial light beaming down on him, looking at a plethora of contraceptive options. In his pocket, his phone vibrated, and he answered without looking. "Yeah."

"Are you okay?"

He pulled the phone away from his face to check the caller's name, then answered. "Yeah, Joe, why?"

"First thing this morning, Mike Newton sent me a bunch of pictures he says you found, but won't tell him where."

"And now you're worried about me?" Porter waved at the pharmacist and pointed at a pack of prophylactics behind the locked glass case. "Pictures aren't dangerous, Joe."

Joe ignored the jab. "I called that idiot sheriff out there, what's his name?"

"Spaulding."

"Yeah, that's him. I sent him the pictures; he didn't recognize any of them."

"I tried the same thing. Nice guy, but worthless."

"But I'm not worthless. I figure, why not dig around myself? I get paid way too much and do way too little cop work anymore. I can dig up an ID on two morons from a photo, right? Turns out I still got it. I come up with the names of the jabronis. Then I run a search on the real property and county records, and find a place the Rollins boy was on the deed for. But I'm not telling you anything you don't already know, am I?"

"Joe, I—"

"No, you listen. When I look into the address a little more, I find out there's been a multiple homicide, not three hours before I call about the place. Now, does this seem like a coincidence to you? If I found the place, I know you could, too."

"Joe, I'm fine."

"Was that you at the trailer?"

Porter didn't answer, instead signing the card machine on the counter with his finger.

"Porter?"

He nodded at the pharmacist and took his bag. "What?"

"I asked if that was you at the trailer."

"What do you want me to say?" Porter said.

"I just want you to tell me the truth."

"Who do you work for?"

"What kind of question is that?" Joe said.

"Come on, who pays for the beer in your fridge?"

"You know," Joe said.

"Yeah, I do. Until you don't work for those guys anymore, you can't expect I'll tell you everything about what's going on. You asked me to come out here and take a look, and that's what I'm doing. Don't ask me questions you don't want the answer for. Plausible deniability, remember? Your words, Joe."

There was silence on the phone. "When did you start listening to me?"

"I pay attention sometimes," Porter said.

"Fine."

There was silence for a few more seconds. Porter exited the store and fired up his Yukon, bag from the pharmacist firmly in hand.

"At least let me know you're okay," Joe said. "From the report I got, it seemed like the Wild West at the trailer."

"I already told you, I'm fine. You worry like an old woman."

"I'm not that old yet, asshole. If you're fine, what are you doing right now?"

"I'm meeting someone," Porter said.

"Anything good? You got a snitch or informant?"

"I'm trying to get laid, Joe. Is that all right with you? Do I have to be on the job twenty-four-seven?"

"Oh." Joe was quiet for a few moments. "I mean... after the trailer, though? You still... you know...?"

"I'll compartmentalize," Porter said.

"Hmm. Well, that makes one thing clear," Joe said.

"Yeah?"

"I'm definitely never hooking you up with my daughter," Joe said, and hung up the phone.

Porter pulled into the hotel, selecting a parking place far from his room. Despite a slight rush of anticipation, he wasn't in enough of a hurry to be stupid. The last thing he needed was to be interrupted by someone recognizing his truck from somewhere and looking for him.

He locked the door behind him and hopped into the shower, for the second time in two hours, then dried and put clean clothes on. He sat the bag of condoms on the table, then moved them to the dresser, before putting them into his duffel bag.

Porter sat on the bed and took a deep breath, feeling like he'd been on the move for two days straight. He wanted a minute to relax.

He didn't get it. His mind kept working on solving the puzzle with the pieces he'd fed it. Porter couldn't help but feel like there was something he was missing. Something that was obvious and right in front of his face. He took a deep breath and closed his eyes, trying to remember what he hadn't even forgotten yet.

Moments later, there was a small knock on the door. Porter checked the peephole and, seeing Claudette, slipped his pistol from his waistband into the dresser drawer. The last thing he needed to do was terrify the poor woman.

Claudette must have showered as well. Her hair was damp and she had a bit of makeup on. She had likewise changed, into jeans and flip-flops.

She beamed a big smile at him. "I guess you were serious."

"Just wait," he said.

Porter let her into his room and told himself he'd do his dead level best to figure out what he was missing—first thing in the morning.

# THIRTY-SIX

THE ROOM FELT SMALLER than it was. Laura Bell sat on the folding chair and struggled to breathe, feeling as if all the oxygen had been sucked out of the space.

Their old trailer was really no better or worse than the other one they'd camped out in; it was just different. A bit more out of the way, a bit more run-down. Still, it was the best option right now.

Laura Bell shook her head, trying to clear the vision of Dusty and the trooper from her head. Mostly, she was trying to forget her part.

She'd been part of the family her whole life and it was far from the first time she'd seen someone killed. It was, however, the first time she'd helped.

Seth paced back and forth, the ember in his pipe bright red. He passed it to Dusty, who was seated on a big stump that he'd dragged in from the yard. "You smoked that pig, Dusty. Damn, it was beautiful."

Dusty slowly nodded, drawing the smoke into his lungs.

"You that happy, huh?" Laura Bell said, blinking away the

memory in her head. "You didn't have to kill him. The whole world is gonna be looking for us now."

"Hell, Sis, you shot the son of a bitch. What you think we was gonna do?"

Laura Bell shook her head, but didn't answer.

"It was him or us and it's us left. That's all I care about," Seth said.

"Well, you should care about more than that. I've checked online—they already have our faces all over the news. Everybody knows it was us, Seth. Where can we go? We're stuck."

"I was thinking about that," Seth said, accepting the pipe from Dusty.

"You think you can lay off the smoke for a little while? You ain't thinking clearly."

"Don't tell me what to do, woman," Seth said, his voice echoing throughout the small room.

Laura Bell knew she'd get nowhere, so she walked over to the tattered, corduroy chair in the corner and let her brother rant.

"We need to get out of town—like all the way out. Somewhere else than here."

Laura Bell just stared at Seth while he paced around. Dusty leaned his head back, seemingly asleep on the dirty drywall.

"Problem is, we need some damn money. We can't get far without it, right?"

Laura Bell nodded.

"See? I know what the hell to do. I got me an idea that will kill three, maybe four birds with one stone."

"I can't wait," Laura Bell said.

"See, these cartel clowns need to pay for Richie. Don't think I forgot. I'm high but I ain't that high."

"How do you—"

"Don't interrupt me," Seth said.

Laura Bell looked at him and started to speak, but closed her mouth.

"Yeah, we need a little payback. What we need to do is set a meeting and act like we have the product. Then when they show, take the money, and off the fuckers. Payback."

Laura Bell said nothing.

"But first we need the product, to trick the Mexicans. That's why me and Dusty-boy over there are gonna go to the Peaks bar and take what we can from the bikers. We do that, then we meet the Mexicans, then we get out of town."

"If you're going to rip off the Mexicans, why even bother with the bikers' stash? You don't need to have product to lie to the cartel," Laura Bell said.

"Look, baby sister, for the smart one you sure act dumb sometimes. Of *course* we're going to rob the cartel. But why not get more money from the bikers while we're at it? Think about it, we can use every bit we can get," Seth said. "If I'm going on the run, I want to stay in nice places like the Hyatt and shit like that. None of these fleabag spots for us."

"Seth, please. This is a bad idea. Let's just go, right now. We can run, we'll be okay, I'll figure something out. Let's leave the girl here and she can find her way home. You don't want to screw with the bikers and you damn sure don't want any part of the cartel. They cut our brother's head off, remember?"

"That's exactly why I gotta do it," Seth said.

Laura Bell rocked back and forth in her chair. She'd given up; there was no changing Seth's mind, and Dusty was dumb enough to go wherever her brother told him to.

"You ready, big man?" Seth said.

Dusty opened his eyes and stood up. Laura Bell swore the trailer shifted when he moved to the front door.

"Good. When we come back, we gonna be coming in hot.

We won't have time to tie up loose ends," Seth said. "Let me do this before I leave."

With that, Seth threw the door open and was out into the front yard. Laura Bell jumped off her chair, knowing full well where he was going.

She'd been unable to convince her brother to bring Pima in when they'd arrived. He wouldn't listen to a word she'd said. "Seth. Seth, no!"

By the time she'd gotten outside, Seth had the trunk open and had dragged Pima out by her elbow, throwing her roughly on the patchy brown grass.

The girl was still bound with the tape, and she wiggled to sit up, her eyes wide with fear.

Seth paused for a moment, looking straight up into the nighttime sky. "Damn, look at that moon."

Laura Bell watched him stand there, swaying back and forth for several moments, until he snapped out of it. Seth grabbed Pima again and pulled her further from the Lumina. "Can't get blood all over our ride."

"Seth, no," Laura Bell said, stepping between her brother and their captive.

"The trooper was this damn girl's fault. If I'da killed her somewhere else, we wouldn't be wanted people right now. Your fault, little sugar," Seth said. He reached into his waistband.

"Leave her alone," Laura Bell said, grabbing and clawing at Seth to keep his hands from the revolver. "I said leave her alone."

Seth tried to push Laura Bell out of the way, but the woman fought back, slapping at his hands until she delivered a stinging blow to the side of her brother's face.

Seth stopped, still as a stone, and stared at his sister.

"This is your fault. You should have never taken her from the woods. This little girl didn't do anything," Laura Bell said.

Seth stood there, swaying back and forth. "You're wrong for this. I love you, Sis, but you're wrong." He took a step back and turned toward the car. "Dusty, let's roll."

The two men were in the car and fishtailing out of the front yard before Laura Bell could stop them.

She took a few breaths, then reached down and pulled the duct tape off Pima's mouth. The girl had tears streaming down her face and the tape was so wet that it slid off easily.

Laura Bell knelt down on the ground next to the young girl, hugging her. "Shhh, it's okay. Just hush."

"T-They're gonna k-kill me next time. I didn't do anything. I didn't do anything," Pima sobbed.

Laura Bell squeezed her tightly. "Nobody's gonna kill you while I'm around."

"B-But why do you help me?"

Laura Bell was quiet for a few minutes as she rocked Pima, then spoke up. "Because I used to be a scared little girl in a world she didn't belong in, either. Nobody tried to make me feel safe. You deserve better. You didn't ask to be dragged into this. And you know what?" She pulled back and looked Pima in the eye. "Neither did I. But here we are."

Laura Bell cut the tape off the younger girl's wrists and ankles, and walked her into the trailer and shut the door behind them. She sat on the brown chair and pulled the trembling girl in next to her. They were so small they both fit.

"You keep helping me, but one day you won't be able to stop him. He's gonna kill me."

"No, he won't. I won't let him."

Pima swallowed hard. "You could let me go..."

"Then he'd say I'm working against him. He probably *would* kill me." Laura Bell pulled away far enough to look into Pima's tear-soaked eyes. "You let me worry about him, okay? Just let me worry about him."

# THIRTY-SEVEN

AN HOUR as the crow flies from the small town where the Newtons lived was a solitary building, ten feet off the lightly used two-lane highway. On the opposite side of the highway, the mountains rose over the building, casting a wide shadow during the day. Behind the building, the view was into a valley. At night, the entire valley was lit up with the lights of the city far below.

In another place, the building would be called a roadhouse, a joint where people stopped in and left just as quickly, hoping to never return.

As it was, the place was a dive bar and headquarters, old and run-down, with nothing going for it except its regulars, which kept the place afloat. Any given night, there would be a mixture of pickup trucks, motorcycles, and weed roaches sitting in the parking lot.

The bikes were all Milwaukee-made, not the type you would see driven by actors on television shows. These were gritty bikes driven by hard men.

The bar was likewise the same. There were scant neon lights, and no advertising of shot specials or ladies' night.

There were shots every night, and ladies when the men wanted them.

Al Jackson was in his usual place behind the bar. One way of looking at it would paint Al as the owner of the bar. Another would reveal that he was the only one with sufficient credit history—and lack of criminal history—to get a loan for the building and to be put on the deed.

He had, however, been given a very large endowment to use as a down payment, courtesy of the Peaks Motorcycle Club, LLC.

Despite being a relative figurehead of an owner, Al took his job seriously. The bar was always stocked and the cigarette machine was always full.

He hobbled through the back room, looking for another case of Kentucky bourbon to put behind the bar, before the men inside got nasty about the lack of their favorite booze.

"One of them bastards could help me carry it," Al muttered to himself, his back locked up like it was on so many nights.

Before he could cuss his fellow brothers out for their laziness, he felt something cold and hard in the divot just behind his ear.

Al raised his hands.

"Where's the drugs, old man?"

"Son, do you know whose bar this is?" Al said, eyes fixed on the metallic door to a walk-in cooler that no longer worked. "You know who you're stealing from?"

"Of course I do; why else would I be here? Now tell me where the fucking meth is. I want all of it."

Al kept his hands high. His doctor said he had a small spot of cancer in his lung, but he wasn't ready to die yet. Not like this, not over drugs. "You got it."

"Let's go. Now," the voice said.

Al limped his way down an uneven tile floor, into a stark

office with four dingy walls and a large safe on the floor. He knelt down to see the dial, his back spasming when he did.

He fumbled the combination twice.

"You playing games with me? You wanna die, old man?"

"Just hold your damn horses. Hard for me to see these little numbers, let alone you got a gun at my head."

"That's right, don't forget the gun. Music's loud in there tonight. I pull this trigger, nobody will even know."

"Yeah, yeah, I got it," Al said, hitting the combination the fourth time he tried, pulling down the handle with a loud *thunk* and then struggling to his feet.

He felt a strong hand pull him out of the way and he lost his footing, falling onto the floor.

"Damn, now give me a minute, shit. I gave you what you want, no need to push me around."

Al got to his feet again, looking up at a man in a ski mask.

"Oh, hell. I'll ask again: you boys know what you're getting yourselves into? It ain't hard to tell who the two of you are. Not with big-ass Dusty standing right there. I know you gotta be Seth."

The masked Dusty looked at Seth, who turned around from the safe. "Shut him up, Dusty."

With that, Dusty sent a backhand into Al Jackson that knocked him clear into the corner, where he rolled once and was still.

"You have to hit him that hard?" Seth said.

"Sorry," Dusty said.

Seth went back to the safe, pulling out everything inside and stuffing it into a tan duffel bag he'd brought with him. There were several bundles of cash and two shoeboxes full of ugly yellow rocks, already prebagged for individual sale.

Satisfied he had it all, Seth pushed past Dusty and back into the hallway. "Let's bounce."

The men hurried toward the back door they'd snuck in through. When they turned a corner, there was a stout man in a leather vest with no shirt on underneath.

"Damn, Al, you distilling that shit yourself—"

The man locked eyes with Seth and his eyes opened wide, like he was surprised to see two ski-masked men standing in the back of his *sanctum sanctorum*.

"Who the fu—"

Seth pulled his pistol and raised it, firing at the man, sending six rounds of unaimed shots in his direction.

The man also had a pistol, but his reaction to the gunfight was too slow. He got his own pistol out after Seth was already firing, pulling the trigger, but badly behind the curve. Seth gunned the man down, flinching and moving as he did, in an attempt to avoid the man's return fire. At least one of Seth's rounds found their target. The biker staggered back against the wall and dropped his own gun, hand to his chest.

Seth yelled at Dusty to move and the two took the hard left in the hallway, away from the front with the rest of the Peaks MC members, and out the back door.

A driving rock beat followed them out into the cool night air.

# THIRTY-EIGHT

PORTER HAD LIED. He'd promised himself that he would devote his attention to the Pima Newton problem first thing in the morning. That wasn't true.

First thing in the morning, he took Claudette in the shower, which was small but managed to accommodate both of them. Then they lay on the bed, air-drying.

"I brought you something," she said, standing stark naked and walking to her purse. In the daylight, Porter realized the pants she wore while working were a valid advertisement of her figure.

"I didn't get you anything," he said with a sheepish grin.

"Please, it's not weird. I figured since I read one of your favorites, I'd give you one of mine," she said, tossing it onto the bed and lying back down.

"Whew. I thought this was a six-hour anniversary present."

"Looking for a window to jump out of?" she said with a laugh.

He flipped the book over in his hands. "*The Graveyard Book*?"

"It's like if *The Jungle Book* took place in a cemetery. Gaiman is one of my favorites. You ever read him?"

"Sure," Porter said, flipping through the book.

She frowned. "Really?"

"He wrote some comic books I liked when I was a kid. Never read a novel of his, though."

"Comic books? You?"

Porter shrugged. "Should I lie?"

"I think you'll like that, then."

"Can't wait to check it out."

"That's my personal copy, so you give it back when you're done with it, okay?"

"Scout's honor," Porter said.

"Were you a Boy Scout?"

"Not even close," Porter admitted.

"I was about to say... there are some things even I won't believe." She got up again, this time to dress and get her things together.

Porter slipped shorts on and walked her to the door. Claudette opened it and looked up at him.

"So about this," she said, pointing to him and the bed. "I had... I mean, it was... you know... the thing is..." She reached up and kissed him, then left the room, the door slamming behind her.

Porter smiled, then got dressed. Having felt the nip in the air when he'd walked Claudette out, he took the time to find a long-sleeved fleece shirt, then stuffed his pistol in his waistband and stepped out into the day.

Back to thinking about Pima, he felt his stomach chewing on itself and resolved to fix it.

The Burger Hut was open for lunch, but Porter was wary. He wasn't sure what the conventions of the day called for;

seeing Claudette this soon would probably make him look desperate. No one wanted to look desperate.

Instead he drove around until he found an open diner with plenty of cars out front. The lunch rush was real, and if this place was good enough for the locals, it was good enough for him.

He sat himself, ordering quickly and staring out the window while the waitress rang in his order. The older woman was pleasant, but no Claudette.

His phone vibrated and he checked the caller ID before answering. "Still worried about me?"

"Not anymore. I'm assuming I haven't caught you at a bad time?"

"Well, I'm buck naked, admiring myself in a mirror," Porter said, a little too loudly. Two old men seated at the counter turned and looked at him.

"That's a visual I don't need," Joe said.

"You asked."

"Look, I dug into things a little more. If you can pull yourself away from the mirror, I think you're gonna want to hear this."

"I'm all ears."

"So our guy, Seth Rollins, he comes from a pretty big family. Had an older brother named Richie who was in on the business as well."

"Define 'had,'" Porter said.

"Richie Rollins was recently disaffiliated with his head."

"Disaffiliated? Someone cut his head off? When?"

"Couple days ago. Apparently they dropped the head on the steps of the sheriff's department," Joe said.

"Sounds like some cartel-type business, don't you think?"

"Those bastards are sick enough to do it. And to drop it on

the cops' front door? They're daring anyone to catch them. That's bad, Porter."

"When you're right, you're right," Porter said, smiling at the waitress who brought his food.

"The Rollins family, they're into some shit."

"One's got no head. How many of them are there?"

"Still a couple. A few years ago, Papa Rollins went away for forty-five years for meth trafficking. It looks like that left Richie and Seth, and a daughter who hasn't been in much trouble."

"Fine family," Porter said.

"I'll keep beating the bushes," Joe said. "If I figure anything out I'll call you back. Porter?"

"Yeah?"

"Try to have some clothes on next time I call, will ya?"

Porter laughed as he hung up the phone. He shoveled the food in his mouth, left more than enough money on the table, and left.

Joe's intel had been helpful, but now he wanted to see if the sheriff had anything new to tell him.

The drive was quick, and Porter was walking through the door of the sheriff's office in no time. Ruby the receptionist was there, nose deep in her soap opera. To her credit, she was more attentive than on Porter's previous visits.

"Spaulding in?"

"He's in a meeting. If you'd have a seat, I'll let him know you're here, sir."

"No thanks, I'd rather stand," Porter said.

No sooner had he made it over to the big front window than the door to the back swung open. Deputy Adams was the first out of the door, followed by his formerly plain-clothed partner with the buzzcut. Both men were in their uniforms, and both looked like hell.

Spaulding looked angry and was following them out the door.

Deputy Buzzcut had a bruise going from the side of his neck around and up the front of his throat. It was one of those terrifically colorful ones, and was various shades of purple and green. He moved stiffly when he turned to look at Porter, as if it still hurt a couple of days later.

The entire side of Adams's face was a swollen mess. His eye was blacked and completely closed. He was also wearing a sling with some sort of orthopedic appliance stabilizing his right elbow. Porter assumed that at some point someone had put his elbow back into place. If they'd done it soon enough, Adams probably hadn't needed surgery.

Probably.

A small smile crept across Porter's face. "You guys look like shit. What happened?"

The deputies looked at Porter, neither of them speaking. Each not only knew that Porter had caused their current states, they also knew that *he* knew it had been them at the motel that night.

Coming to with their balaclavas pulled off must have been quite a shock. Still, they had to put on a show for their boss.

"Car crash," Adams said.

"Really? Must have been a bad one. What about you, Buzzcut?"

"Same."

"Damn. You were both hit by the same car? Must have been big, like a truck or something, huh? I'm glad you two are okay," Porter said.

Sheriff Spaulding stood next to his deputies. "Apparently, that's why they couldn't get their ass over to your motel when you called the other night. These two idiots were in a car crash together." He put his hands on his hips. "I suspect they'd been drinking, but I can't prove it."

"Hopefully you two learned your lesson," Porter said.

"You guys get out of here. Take another couple days and heal up. I swear to God, you're a waste of damn payroll..." Spaulding trailed off as the walking wounded shuffled away. He waved his hand for Porter to follow him to his office. Once the two men sat down, Spaulding looked at Porter and lowered his head. "I have a question for you, and I need you to be honest with me."

"I cannot tell a lie," Porter said.

"Did you bring all the crazy with you when you came to town?"

# THIRTY-NINE

"HOW'S THAT?" Porter said.

"Ever since you showed up, there's been nothing but trouble. I'm wondering if you brought it with you, like people bring the weather."

"Considering I only showed up because a kid went missing, I can't say I'm the root of the problem," Porter said.

Spaulding leaned back. "Maybe not, but I know for damn sure things have... escalated... since you've been in town."

"Sounds like a problem for the local law enforcement."

"Fair enough. I'm sure you've heard, this tiny ass town being what it is and all."

"Heard what?" Porter said. "All I've basically done is eaten burgers and slept since I've been out here."

"Many of those burgers over at the Hut?"

"Does it matter?"

"Not in the least. Just heard you've been over there every day," Spaulding said.

"Now you're following me around?"

"Me? Hell, no. The town has eyes, though. People talk; it is what it is. Personally, I don't blame you." He leaned forward over his desk and lowered his voice. "Claudette? The ass on that girl—"

"I hadn't noticed," Porter said. "Besides where I eat, what else have you managed to hear around town?"

"I don't have to try too hard; it's on my front door. Literally."

Porter fixed Spaulding with a blank stare.

"You heard about the severed head, right?"

"No," Porter lied. "Must have slept through that one."

"Hell, it was a mess. Local guy, named Richard Rollins. Somebody just dropped his head off in a burlap sack. Crazy thing is, he's the brother of..." Spaulding fished around in the papers on his desk. "This one you were looking for. Seth Rollins is his name, in case you never found out."

Porter leaned back in his chair, watching the sheriff as he spoke. "Last time I showed you that, you didn't have any clue who he was. Now you know the whole family?"

"It wasn't hard to show the picture to the boys and find out who he was. Apparently, him and the big guy used to get into a lot of trouble, but I haven't run across them since I've been sheriff."

"You could have told me who they were," Porter said. "You know I'm looking for them."

"Why the hell would I do that? You're a civilian; I don't owe you anything. I shouldn't even be telling you all this right now."

"Suit yourself," Porter said, pushing his chair out and standing to leave.

"Sit," Spaulding said, pointing at Porter's chair.

"You asking me or telling me?"

"Just sit down, all right? I haven't gotten through with the crazy. You might as well listen."

Porter sat down on the edge of his chair. "What else?"

"Me and the boys went to the Rollins place to notify the family about big brother's head in a sack."

"How'd that go?" Porter said, already knowing the answer.

"It was like a goddammed massacre. Three Mexican guys dead, all shot up. I hadn't seen anything like that down here before. Not since I was in the city, you know?"

"I didn't even know you guys had three Mexicans in this town," Porter said.

"We don't anymore. Then the trooper gets killed and—"

"What trooper?" Porter said.

"You really don't watch the news, do you? One county over, a trooper gets himself killed on the highway. Dashcam shows your two boys doing the killing."

"Damn it," Porter said. He hated that anyone lost their life in the performance of their duties. All for a public that couldn't care less. There would be a funeral and then it would be lost from the mind of the populace.

That Seth and Dusty had killed a trooper was unwelcome news. It showed a loss of control. And the fact that they were a county away meant they were running. It was already hard enough to find someone who didn't want to be found; it was even harder trying to find a moving target.

"Not too long ago, Sheriff Upton calls me and tells me about a shooting they had in one of their biker bars last night. The guys that run it are a tough bunch, and they won't say anything, but I have a theory."

"I like theories," Porter said. "Lay it on me."

"I'd be willing to bet my fat Northeast pension that it was your two boys again."

"My boys? Believe me, we're still unacquainted," Porter said.

"The thing is, I'd never even heard of these two assholes until you showed up. Now, I got dead Mexicans, a head in a bag, and a murdered trooper. So, I gotta ask: what part do you play in this?"

Porter smiled. "Me? Come on, Spaulding, I'm just looking into things, same as you."

"Well, this old law-dog gut of mine tells me that's not true. I can feel something isn't right."

"That's probably agita," Porter said. "Take an antacid."

Spaulding just looked at Porter.

"Hey, Spaulding, I've been wondering something. I hope you can help me, since you serve and protect and all that shit."

Spaulding nodded. "What's that?"

"Ever since I was a little kid, I've loved motorcycles. Didn't you say there was a biker bar somewhere?"

"I don't think they're really looking for tourists," Spaulding said.

"I'm sure they'd love me. Mind pointing me in the right direction?"

Spaulding eyed Porter for several moments. Porter noticed the man's blue eyes had flecks of green in them. He reached out and scratched an address on a piece of paper. "You'd just find it anyway."

"Very generous of you," Porter said, reaching out to accept the scrap of paper.

Spaulding didn't let it go. Each man pulled slightly on an end. "Listen, you didn't take my advice when I told you to let us worry about the Newton girl, so I'm probably wasting my breath right now, but here goes nothing—don't go to this bar. For your own good."

"But I love motorcycles so mu—"

"Joke all you want to. The cops don't go there if they can help it. Besides that, those boys are some real 'the South will rise again' types, if you get my drift."

"I don't," Porter said, deadpan.

"Yes, you do. You're... you know..."

"Tall?" Porter said.

"Black. They aren't too keen on that."

"Ahh. Well, I've always thought I'm more of a medium brown. But if it will help break walls down, I'm sure I have a copy of *Roots* somewhere I could give them. In the name of progress, of course."

Porter walked out of the office, slamming the door behind him while Spaulding shook his head.

# FORTY

THE DRIVE out to the biker bar was relatively straightforward, as far as directions went. Straight on I40, no turns until you found the bar. Actually driving the highway was a different beast. The road itself was winding, with sheer rock faces on the right and drop-offs on the left.

Porter had to blast the air conditioner to keep from getting nauseous.

Eventually, the color-soaked views changed and there was a small building on the left side of the divided highway. In this case, it wasn't just a double yellow line, but a several-hundred-foot stretch of tall concrete barricades that Porter could just barely see over.

He took the next right, up a steep grade and into the parking lot of a church. It was neither Sunday nor Wednesday, so the church and the parking lot were both empty.

Because of the hill the church sat on, Porter could see over the barricade and into the parking lot of the biker bar. He reached into his back seat and grabbed a pair of binoculars, looking through the windshield at his target.

The parking lot wasn't paved, just loose gravel spread in

front of a one-story building with brown shingles and brown siding. The cars out front were a motley assortment of pickup trucks with rust damage to the body panels and motorcycles that looked as though they had been put together the hard way—in someone's garage, not a factory.

The sign out front read *The Peaks MC*, with the familiar-to-Porter logo of a mountain ridge covered in blood.

"Son of a bitch," Porter said. "These guys are everywhere."

He guessed there were eight to ten people in the bar, and they didn't seem to be moving around much. With the sunlight directly overhead, he had a clear view of the entire place. No one was showing in the windows; nobody stepped out into the parking lot.

Papers taped to the front door fluttered in the breeze as Porter looked over the area one more time. He'd expected men outside, twirling revolvers and shooting them off into the air.

This looked more like a bunch of old guys had fallen asleep.

He saw a path that led to the rear of the building and briefly thought about sneaking in, but stopped himself. He needed to talk to someone, and sneaking wouldn't help him do that.

Porter tossed the binoculars onto the front seat of his car. Then he popped the trunk, slipping a couple of magazines for his Glock on his waistband, and slammed the tailgate. He reached back onto the front seat for a picture of Seth and Dusty.

He left the Yukon running.

Jogging down the hill, Porter looked both ways before he crossed the quiet highway. The concrete divider was taller than him, but he climbed up and over it, landing in a crouch on the other side before jogging across the parking lot to the front door.

There was a small squeak as he stepped on the rickety staircase and he stopped a moment to look at the papers plastered to the front door.

There were notifications of meetings, a list of brothers who were delinquent on their dues, and a flyer for an upcoming charity ride. There were also donations being taken to help two Charlotte brothers replace their bikes, which had somehow been melted to slag.

Porter took a deep breath and swung open the door, stepping into the bar. He waited a few moments for his eyes to adjust to the gloom inside.

"Dive bar" was a descriptor that wasn't thorough enough. The floor was a patchwork of ratty carpet and linoleum. The brown ceiling tiles were saggy, and the couches were ripped and torn, obviously used as the sole place to extinguish cigarettes in the entire establishment. Strewn across the furniture was a variety of men, all reeking of booze. Porter didn't have to get too close to recognize used condoms, tacked up on the wall behind the pool table. A man and woman were asleep on the frayed felt.

Behind the bar, a man was straightening vodka bottles.

"You own this place?" Porter said.

The man looked up into the cracked mirror that ran the length of the bar. "We're closed to the public." He looked back at his vodka bottles.

"Thank God for that," Porter said, looking around.

"I said beat it. You can't drink here."

"Don't worry about that, I'd prefer to pass on the hepatitis," Porter said.

The bartender turned around and looked at Porter. There was a large, freshly purple bruise across the entire side of the man's face.

"What are you, an idiot?"

"I've been called worse," Porter said.

"How are you gonna come into my place and insult it?"

"I didn't insult it, I just made an observation and a firm decision about my health."

"Okay, dickhead, time to go." The bartender hollered a

couple of names and two men rose from the mass of humanity on the couches. They staggered to their feet, looking at Porter, then at the bartender.

"Who the hell is he?" the smaller one said.

"Nobody," Porter said, turning back to the bartender. "I just want to ask you a couple questions, then I'll get out of your hair."

"You want him out, Al?"

Al the bartender looked at Porter for a couple seconds, then to his guys. "Yeah. Get him out."

"Come on, Al, I'm just here to talk. You don't have to get physical," Porter said.

"Physical?" the smaller of the two men said. "I'm feeling pretty Olivia Newton-John right now."

"What?" Al said.

"Come on, you seen her ass in that video?"

"We're just gonna pretend you never said any of that," Al said, then gestured to Porter. "Go on, get him out of here."

The two men made their way closer to Porter. He didn't like turning his back on Al, but he needed to deal with the two heroes first.

The larger man made the mistake of grabbing Porter. "Al told you to—"

Porter backhanded the biker in the throat and he went down in a coughing fit. Mr. Physical wasted no time jumping into the fray, slamming Porter's shoulder with a punch, not tall enough to hit much else.

Porter reached out and grabbed the man by the back of his head, clamping tightly on to his greasy hair, and slamming him face-first into the bar. Then, using the man's denim jacket as a handle, he picked him up and threw him over the bar at Al, who ducked out of the way.

Mr. Physical smashed into the wooden shelf that Al had

been arranging bottles on, taking them and a big stack of glasses with him. The ruckus echoed off the walls of the bar.

"Hey," Al yelled when he reappeared. "What the hell's your problem?"

"I just wanted to talk. You guys attacked me," Porter said.

"And we ain't done yet." Al whistled sharply, and anyone not woken by the crashing of the glass behind the bar staggered to their feet. "Get up. Get this son of a bitch."

Porter wasn't sure if Al thought it was a fluke his guys got worked over, or if he was hopeful more numbers would even the odds. Either way, the three men who stood and stumbled toward him were in much better shape than the other guys.

But three barely awake, hungover guys weren't a concern. Porter moved toward them, stepping over the biker that was still coughing and clutching at his neck, and grabbed the man closest to him. Before Porter could disconnect him from consciousness, the man in the middle reached into his waistband and produced a small revolver, pointing it at Porter's face.

Getting shot *was* a concern. He thought briefly about going for his own pistol, then discounted that, since he'd never be fast enough. He'd do it the hard way. As he tensed, ready to lash out and disarm the man, Al spoke up.

"Not in here, idiot. We had enough cops in here already today. Take him outside first."

"Yeah, not in here, idiot. Take me outside first," Porter said.

"You call me an idiot?" the man with the revolver said. "I'll show you idiot."

He stepped closer, touching the muzzle to Porter's forehead. "Move."

So Porter moved.

# FORTY-ONE

THERE WAS no doubt it wasn't the movement the man expected. Porter wasn't cowed by the revolver; instead, he snapped his head to the right as he pushed the pistol away from his face. He grabbed the gun in a vise grip, tearing it from its owner's hands.

The man had his finger sunk deep into the trigger guard, and as Porter torqued the revolver free, there was an audible crack and the man's finger snapped. He dropped to his knees, howling in pain and holding his bad hand with his good one. The revolver skittered free across the floor.

After one step to close the distance, Porter smashed several knees into the wailing man's face, leaving him sprawled out on the floor.

The man on the left wasted no time swinging a pool cue at Porter, who took it square on the back, leaving no damage. What was damaging, however, was the punch the other man leveled to the side of Porter's head, leaving his ears ringing. It was much harder than it should have been for a hungover older man.

He stole a quick glance to the right and saw the glint of brass knuckles in the man's hand.

"You asshole..." Porter growled, and took a big step toward Brass Knuckles. He tried to swing them again, but Porter was too close, and was much taller than the man.

He hooked him around the neck and brought an elbow crashing onto the top of the man's head. The man went slack in his arms, and Porter slammed him with another elbow for good measure and let him slump to the ground.

Pool Cue was still swinging away, some strikes missing Porter and some hitting him. Now that Porter was done with Brass Knuckles, the man with the stick had his full attention.

The cue had snapped at some point and the man stood there, awkwardly waving the shard at Porter. He tried a couple of fake swings, but Porter didn't fall for them. Instead, he walked toward the man, backing him up until the man was flat against the wall closest to the bar.

"Come on," Porter said, "swing it. Put me out of my misery."

As if on cue, Pool Cue swung the shard at Porter, who reached out and grabbed it as it hurtled toward his head. He ripped it free and swung it back at its owner, sinking it deep into the man's shoulder. Then he pushed the man's head down and wrapped him in a front headlock, lifting him off the ground.

He turned and faced Al while he choked the struggling, screaming man unconscious. "This is your fault," he said as he let the man collapse into a heap, pool cue sticking out of his shoulder.

Al's eyes were wide as he stammered, "But, but, but—"

Porter stepped over to the revolver on the floor and picked it up, pointing it at Al. "When I want you to talk, you won't, and now you won't shut up." He touched the side of his head where the knuckles had impacted, glad to find he wasn't bleeding.

Porter stuffed the revolver into his back pocket, then reached over the bar and grabbed Al by the shirt collar, dragging him across the bar. With the bartender fully in his grasp, Porter picked up the photos he'd brought with him and dragged Al outside into the cool, bright light of day.

"Hey man, I'm sorry, I had no idea—"

"What? That I would stomp a mudhole in you backwoods assholes?"

Porter pushed Al against one of the rusty pickup trucks, then smashed the photos of Dusty and Seth into his face. "You know these guys?" Porter rubbed the pictures along Al's face as he spoke. "Huh? Speak up."

Al's words were muffled as the paper crushed into his face. Eventually, Porter pulled the photos off. "Well, hell, at least let me have a look. Damn."

Porter let go of the man and handed him the pictures. Al took one brief look and nodded. "Of course I know them. They was the ones that did this to my face."

"When?"

"Last night. They was here last night," Al said.

"They the ones who killed your boy, too?"

Al didn't answer, instead looking down at the gravel of the parking lot.

"Why didn't you tell the cops?" Porter said.

"Please. Would you? Hell no you wouldn't, not seeing the way you are. It's up to us to take care of our own. We have our own rules. You ain't any different."

"Fair enough," Porter said. "What were they here for? What did they want?"

"Why the hell you think, man?"

"Al, I'm getting tired of the guessing games," Porter said, pulling the little revolver from his back pocket and pressing it to the bartender's chest. "Start making sense."

"It was drugs, what else would it be?"

"You sold them drugs? You bought drugs from them? Which was it?" Porter said.

"It was neither."

Porter pulled back the hammer on the revolver. "I told you I'm done guessing."

"Wait, wait, wait," Al said, hands raised in front of his face. "Now, just wait a damn minute."

"A minute? Okay, that's all you got. Talk."

Al looked around, as if there might be someone to hear him spill the beans. "Heard talk that those Rollins boys got some big-time hookup with the Mexicans. They supposed to be supplying a big amount and now they're short."

Porter thought about the trash he'd destroyed.

"Yeah, they real short, so they thought they'd sneak in here and get our stuff. That way, they don't all wind up with their head in a bag," Al said with a smile.

"These guys are idiots," Porter said. "How'd they get hooked up with a cartel?"

"Hell if I know; none of my business. I'd never sell to beaners anyway—not my business model."

"Better to poison your own people, right?"

Al scrunched his face up like he was confused.

"Never mind," Porter said. "Any clue where Rollins and his ogre are right now?"

"Hell no. If I did, we'd be there getting our shit back instead of hanging around here so you can put a boot in our ass."

"You sure?" Porter smashed the photos against Al's face again. "No clue where they are?"

Al mumbled faster until Porter took the photos off of his face again. "I don't know where they are, that's the God's honest truth. You see the news? Everybody's looking for them. Besides..."

"Even if you knew you wouldn't tell me?" Porter said.

"You blame me for wanting my own payback? They killed my boy. Their ass is toast."

"I guess we'll have to see who finds them first."

Al kept his hands raised, a gesture of compliance. "Look, you're pretty good at this stuff, but I have a whole club full of hard-nosed assholes who are going to want those two. I like my chances."

"Once they wake up."

Al shrugged.

Porter smiled. "Then I guess I'll need a head start." He looked down at the large Bowie knife hanging in a sheath at Al's side. It wasn't uncommon for bikers to carry them. The large blades drew less attention from people, and weren't the same headache with the cops. "Pull that knife out for me."

Hands raised, Al looked at his hip, then back at Porter. "You ain't trying to trick me, right? Like you won't kill an unarmed man, so I pull my knife and you smoke me?"

"Just get the knife."

Al pulled it out, holding it with two fingers like it was radioactive.

Porter motioned with his head. "Stick it in that tire."

Al looked at Porter and then down at the tire, then stuck the knife in the tire, leaving it in the sidewall as the air hissed out.

"Keep it; you're gonna need it." Porter pointed again.

Once Al understood what Porter wanted, it didn't take long. He made Al slash every tire in the parking lot. All the trucks, all the bikes, all the spares, everything.

"See, that wasn't so bad, was it? I should take your phones, so you guys can't call a ride, but I don't want to wait around this dump any longer than I need to."

"The boys won't be too happy when they wake up."

"Good point. I don't need a dozen angry rednecks following me around for the next few days." He pulled the borrowed revolver from his waistband. "I could go back in there and make sure none of them ever wake up again."

Al shook his head. "Nah, I think they'll get the point. I'll smooth things out."

"Good answer." Porter smacked Al with the revolver, right on top of the bruise he'd gotten during the previous night's robbery. The bartender collapsed in a heap, his leg awkwardly underneath him. Porter opened the cylinder of the revolver and ejected the rounds into his hand, and dropped them onto Al's chest. Then he wiped the gun with his shirt and tossed it down the hill behind the bar.

The highway was deserted, so Porter moved across the divider and back to his truck, which was still running. He hopped in and gunned it down the hill, followed the highway until there was a break that was supposed to be for police use only, flipped a U-turn, and punched the gas.

As he passed by the bar again, he saw Al outside, still asleep on the gravel parking lot. Porter liked to think the bartender was dreaming of large men punching him in the face.

# FORTY-TWO

"SIT STILL AND QUIT WHINING," Laura Bell said. "You did the thing to yourself, you don't have nobody to blame."

She looked down at her brother's arm—a bloody mess—and changed the dressing for the third time in as many hours.

"Why can't you get it to stop bleeding?" Seth said, writhing on the chair.

"Because there's a bullet in there. You need to get to a hospital, Seth, I don't think I can plug this up."

"Hell no. I'm staying right here until we rip the cartel. Then I'll go when we run. Maybe I'll go to a doctor in Mexico. How funny would that be, huh?"

Laura Bell frowned. She knew the arm was worse off than Seth was willing to accept, but as of late, he wouldn't listen to anything she said.

"This is why I told you not to go to the bar. Those bikers weren't going to let you take their shit without a fight. Now look at you."

"So? You should see the other guy," Seth said with a laugh, standing and letting his arm hang by his side.

Laura Bell glanced at Pima, quiet as ever, sitting on the

couch, making herself as small as possible. "Good for you, you killed a guy. That make you feel better? We already had enough heat on us, now you do this? My Facebook is all blown up with pictures of me. The bikers know it was us and everybody's talking. What are we supposed to do?"

"You know exactly what we do. We meet the Mexicans somewhere. We take all their stuff, then we run."

Laura Bell shook her head. "You just killed that Peaks guy for no good reason. All you did was bring more heat down on us, and you got a shot-to-shit arm on top of it all."

"That's pretty rich coming from a gal who just killed a cop," Seth said, squinting his eyes as he looked at his sister.

"That's not even the same and you know it," Laura Bell said. "Let's just go. You got a little money from the bar, we can run. Right now, no waiting."

"Fuck that," Seth said, stepping over to the kitchen counter and fumbling with his pipe.

"Will you leave that shit alone for a minute? Use your head. We aren't going to make it out of this."

Seth took a big hit and blew the smoke across the counter toward the seated Laura Bell. "Trust me, Sis."

"But Seth, I—"

"I said trust me." Seth set the pipe down and picked up his phone. "I'm going to set it up." With that, Seth pulled open the trailer door and was gone.

Laura Bell stood and walked in front of Dusty. "Are you with him on this? You gonna march in there and get killed?"

Dusty looked down, trying to avoid eye contact.

She put her bloody hands on the side of his face and raised it until the two were eye to eye, then stared at him. "You aren't as dumb as everybody says, Dusty. You went to college, you can think for yourself. Don't let Seth go and don't you go with him."

Dusty smiled awkwardly and forced his head down again.

"Dusty, are you ready to die? Because my brother seems like he is."

Dusty smiled again and then stood, Laura Bell's hands falling from his face. "I'm gonna find Seth."

The trailer door slammed behind him.

Laura Bell fell into the couch, holding her blood-soaked hands between her knees.

"This is how it happens," she said.

Pima didn't reply.

"When Daddy went away a few years ago, it was just like this. Things just kept going wrong until everything was bad. Daddy's way smarter than Seth and even he couldn't see the writing on the wall."

"What are you going to do?" Pima said quietly.

Laura Bell was quiet, looking at the blood on her hands. She'd tried to wipe it off, but had only smeared it. There was no water in the trailer, so she had no hope of washing it off.

Laura Bell sniffed and stared vacantly at the floor. "You know, I used to want to be a nurse. Imagine that shit, a girl like me."

Pima didn't say anything.

"When I got out of high school a couple years back, I went to this community college for a couple semesters. There was this program, you started out getting your CNA, then you kept going up from there."

Pima scrunched her face up.

"Certified Nursing Assistant. They do all the dirty work at hospitals, cleaning up puke and wiping asses and stuff. I did a couple weekends of it and I didn't care, I thought it was great.

"Then you did more training and you became an LPN. Just a little different than CNA, that's all. Then you transfer from the community college and go to a big school like State and finish your degree and become an RN. The big time, good money, steady work..." She trailed off.

Laura Bell felt her eyes fill with tears and she blinked them away, but not before some fell down her cheeks.

She felt a small arm wrap around her shoulder.

"I wouldn't have had to do none of this. But then Daddy went to prison, and my brothers needed me. If it weren't for Richie, I wouldn't have left school. Nope, I'd have stayed and got my degree."

Pima nodded along.

Laura Bell exhaled and shook her head. "Now look at me. Everyone knows I killed a cop."

"You didn't kill the cop. Dusty did."

"It doesn't matter. They got me on tape shooting at the man. It's all the same."

"I... I don't know," Pima said.

Laura Bell leaned back against the couch, blood-stained hands on her lap. "You know, I hate Seth. I've always hated him. He used to hurt me, you know, when we were kids. Said since we didn't have the same momma that we weren't really family, and he could do whatever he wanted to me."

Pima raised her eyebrows.

"Right? And here I am helping the bastard. All because he's barely family. Hell, I like that big idiot Dusty more than Seth."

There was silence in the trailer and Laura Bell could hear Seth outside, speaking loudly to someone on the phone. Big Man, setting the meeting place and time.

She looked down at Pima. "What you want to be when you grow up?"

"Huh?" Pima said.

"When you get big. What you want to do?"

"I'm not really sure," Pima said.

"Don't give me that. Every kid at least thinks about it. You probably got a hundred ideas. Like, a vet or something?"

Pima closed her eyes for a moment. "I like to take pictures."

"Any money in that?"

"I'm not sure," Pima said.

"Well," Laura Bell said as she stood, "I'm sure you can figure out a way to make it big. You seem like a smart girl. Don't never let nobody make you do something you don't want to do. You hear me?"

Pima nodded.

Seth came back into the trailer, leaving Dusty outside.

"Big Man said we can meet tonight at the Teddy Bear."

Laura Bell thought for a minute. "It's a trap. You know that, right?"

"What the hell you talking about?" Seth said.

"Why else would we meet at that shithole in the middle of nowhere? There are fifty other places we could go. We're meeting at the Teddy Bear for a reason, Seth, think about it."

"Don't know. Don't care. All I know is we're going and those cartel boys are going to regret ever coming to town."

Laura Bell chewed her lip. "Maybe we should leave now? We can get there early and check the place out. Figure out the best place to set up and all that."

"What the hell for? We know the Teddy Bear like the back of our hands."

"Any idea how many the Mexicans are bringing?"

Seth raised his good arm, a gesture for her to shut up. "Stop asking so many damn questions. It's gonna be what it's gonna be."

Laura Bell crossed her arms and shook her head, but didn't say anything further. She watched her brother find his pipe again and blow smoke across the trailer. Then he motioned for her to follow him into the kitchen.

Laura Bell followed, afraid of what he was going to say, knowing in her heart what it would be.

Seth eyed Pima for a moment, then turned his back so no one could see them talk. "You know what I'm about to say, right? You're a smart girl."

"Not gonna happen, Seth. I already told you," Laura Bell said.

"I know you did and I respected that. I let you play house for this long, making pretend you had a little sister or something. But now? Now it's time to be serious. We both know we can't keep her around."

"We ain't gonna kill her," Laura Bell said. "She hasn't done anything wrong."

"She knows who we are."

"So does everyone else, remember? Our names are everywhere. Pima can't hurt us now."

"Yes, she can. We let her go, she tells the cops I took her, they add kidnapping charges to the mix."

"We get caught, we're already going to fry for killing the trooper, Seth. Who gives a shit about the kidnapping charges?"

"I do. And I don't like loose ends," Seth said as he pulled his pistol from his waistband.

"I said no." Laura Bell stood in the doorway from the kitchen to the living room. Seth pushed her out of the way.

Laura Bell pushed back, standing in front of her brother. "No, Seth, I said no."

He pushed her again, his eye focused on the living room, his gun up near his head. Laura Bell pushed him back, what little success she had due to Seth's bad arm.

As he began to walk, Laura Bell started slapping him. Over and over she hit him, until Seth reached back and slammed his pistol into her face.

Laura Bell collapsed on the dirty floor, hands held to her

face. She felt and tasted the warm flow of blood into her sinuses. "Big man, hitting a girl."

Seth kicked her in the side. Laura Bell knew the pain was a cracked rib. She crawled backward, trying to get away from him. "You're a rotten pussy. You big—"

Through watery eyes she saw Seth's face go red. "You call me a pussy? I'll show you pussy."

He raised the pistol high, to bring it crashing down on top of her, and Laura Bell saw him lifted off his feet and hauled away.

It was Dusty.

"Don't," he said.

"Don't what, you big idiot?" Seth said.

"Don't hit her."

"You gonna stop me?" Seth raised the pistol toward Dusty.

Dusty reached out and grabbed the pistol, wrenching it from Seth's hands. "Yes."

Seth stood there for a moment, looking down at Laura Bell then up at Dusty. "Then my sister better remember who she's dealing with." He walked toward the trailer door and paused in the living room. "We have a couple hours till we meet. You two bitches better be ready to go."

He kicked the door and rushed out into the front lawn.

Dusty sat the revolver on the counter, then reached down and lifted Laura Bell off the ground. He carried her over to the couch, sitting her next to Pima.

"You don't have to do this," Laura Bell said weakly.

Dusty smiled, then went out the door.

Moments later, Laura Bell heard the car start and drive away.

She leaned her head into Pima and sobbed until she was out of tears.

# FORTY-THREE

FRESH OUT OF THE SHOWER, Porter checked the inventory of his ever-expanding list of injuries. He'd managed to keep the arrow wounds in his arm and leg clean and covered, and now he dressed them again. Then he checked the lump on the side of his head. He swore as he probed it.

Porter kept his head shaved, a result of most of his hair deciding to take a permanent vacation. He found if he didn't keep up on it, he looked homeless a week into the growth process. He'd never minded low hair, and in this case, it made it easy to see the wound.

Two of the ridges of the brass knuckles had connected behind his right ear. The area was pooling blood and there was a nasty bruise forming. He poked at it. "Damn it."

On the counter next to him, the phone rang. He answered it and put it on speaker.

"What do you want, G-man?"

"'G-man'? Who talks like that anymore?" Joe said.

"I figured you were so old that I'd use terminology you understood. I think I'm going to the soda fountain later, and tonight I might hit the sock hop," Porter said, wincing again as he probed his wound. At least it didn't feel like anything was broken in there.

"You know you aren't as funny as you think you are, don't you?"

"Probably depends on who you ask," Porter said, sitting on the bed.

"I'm sure it doesn't. What the hell are you doing?"

"Just sitting around. You?"

"I wanted to check in," Joe said. "Somebody has to keep an eye on you."

"If you're going to call, you could at least make yourself useful. Got anything to give me? Any news on Seth Rollins or his pet gorilla?"

"Nothing. Every cop in the state is looking for them, not to mention the marshals and a bunch of my guys. Still no luck."

"That's not what I wanted to hear," Porter said.

"I know, but it's all I got. Hopefully with all these eyes, someone can find him soon."

"Then he can take us to Pima's body," Porter said.

"Why would you say that?"

Porter measured his next words carefully. "She might be better off, Joe."

"What the hell does that mean?"

"Pretend like you don't know the Newtons. Pretend like this was just another case. It's been days since she was taken. We both know the people who took her, right? Not just them, but a dozen assholes like them. What do you think they've done to her? Unless she has a guardian angel over her shoulder, she's probably in rough shape. I don't hope she's dead, Joe, but she may wish she was."

There was silence on the other end of the phone. "Well, that's what we're going to hope hasn't happened. She's just a little girl. We need to get to her first."

"I'm trying," Porter said.

"Well, try harder, kid. Try harder." The phone disconnected and Joe was gone.

Porter threw the phone on the bed and stared at himself in the mirror for a few moments. The nagging feeling was still in the back of his head, like he'd missed something along the way. He thought about it for a minute, then it was gone. He let it escape and dressed, then left his room.

The diner lunch had long since worn off, and he decided looking desperate wasn't the worst thing. He needed to figure out what he was missing, and he'd never be able to do that if he were starving.

The Yukon almost drove itself to the Burger Hut. The parking lot was empty, except for Claudette's car.

Porter parked three spaces away.

He found her leaned over the counter, face inches away from a menu. She didn't look up at the clank of the cowbell. "You're really into that menu."

"There are some idiots in the world, you know? I send off to get some new menus printed and these morons can't even spell 'burger' right. They forgot an R," she said, handing Porter a copy of the new menu without looking up. "Now it reads like a food only kids would like."

"I don't know about that," Porter said. "I think at this point, I'd eat a 'buger' if you gave it to me."

She looked up from the menu with a smile. "That was really bad."

"I'm here all week," he said.

"I hope so," she said, dark eyes fixed on Porter for a few moments before going back to the menu. "Listen, I have an ethical dilemma and I hope you can help me figure it out."

"I'll try, but my moral compass is skewed," Porter said. "You might not get the best advice from me."

Claudette looked up from the menu and leaned across the counter toward him. "I assume you are about to order something to eat, right?"

"No doubt."

"There's my problem. See, given our... new friendship, my gut reaction would be to comp your food. I mean, after last night, I feel like the least I can do is give you a burger. I figure I owe you for the beating I gave you."

"Glad to any time," Porter said.

"But if you step back and look at it, it looks like I'm desperate and bribing you. Like I'm trading food for sex, like we're in some type of prison society." She smiled at Porter. "I'm not sure if I can live with myself if I've turned you into a burger gigolo."

"I think that's a job I could get used to."

"You sure? I'd hate for you to be unhappy with your new life as a prostitute. How will you sleep at night?"

"Not by myself, I hope," Porter said. He watched the red creep across her face and down her chest again. Before he could speak, the cowbell clanged. Porter didn't bother turning around.

"Afternoon, Sheriff," Claudette said.

"Miss Claudette."

Porter lingered on her face for a moment, before turning to face Spaulding. "Sheriff."

"Porter." Spaulding leaned on the counter next to Porter, the three of them arranged in a triangle. "I see you found your way back to the Hut. Best damn food around."

"You're too kind," Claudette said, standing up from the counter and straightening the neckline of her shirt.

"No, I am not. It is the best." He looked at Porter. "Have you tried the fried chicken sandwich? May be the best damn thing I've ever eaten."

"Nope. More of a red-meat guy, myself," Porter said, looking at Spaulding. The nagging feeling was back, jumping to the forefront of his mind. He tried to ignore it, but it was strong. He knew he was missing something.

"Oh, come on, you gotta give it a shot."

"I can make you one instead of the usual," Claudette said helpfully.

"Tell you what, Porter, my treat. You give the chicken a shot and if you don't like it, you're not out anything. Call it a 'welcome to my town' treat."

"I think I've already had a few of those," Porter said, eyeing Spaulding. "Beggars can't be choosers. Let's do it."

"You won't be disappointed," Claudette said. "Tell you what, Sheriff, settle up, then you guys go find a seat and I'll bring it out when it's ready."

"I could use a seat," Porter said, the feeling scratching at the front of his head.

"Hell, sitting and waiting is what I do best. At least that's what my Martha always says." Spaulding patted the pockets of his uniform as if he were looking for his wallet, then his hand went to his front pocket and pulled out his cash. "How much was it?"

Claudette gave Spaulding the total.

"That's damn reasonable." The sheriff pulled a twenty off a folded stack of money that was completely unremarkable.

Except for the fact that it was held together by a rainbow-colored rubber band.

# FORTY-FOUR

"NO CHANGE, sweetheart. You keep it for being you."

"Very kind of you," she said.

"What happened to your head, Porter?" Spaulding said.

Porter's attention was fixed on the rubber-banded wad, remembering where he'd seen that before. The nagging, scratching feeling in his head went away. He finally knew. "What?"

"I said your head. It looks like hell."

"Let me see," Claudette said, reaching over the counter and turning his head. "Ouch."

"Would you believe I hit it on the door frame getting into the car?"

"No, I would not," Sheriff Spaulding said.

"True story," Porter lied.

"Need some ice for that?" Claudette said, genuine worry on her face.

"Nah. I got a hard head," Porter said.

"Seems like it," Spaulding said, his smile replaced by a blank look.

"Fine, but if you change your mind, let me know. Got it?" she said.

Spaulding gestured to the dining room and Porter went first, sitting at the little table he always chose.

"Mind if I ask you a question, Porter?"

"You just did."

"Then can I ask you at least two more?" Spaulding said.

"It's your dime," Porter said, eyes fixed on the sheriff.

"This car door you banged your head on? Did it happen to be parked at a shitty little bar out on I40?"

Porter was quiet for a few moments. "I don't think so, but I could be wrong. I hit my head pretty hard."

"Just wondering, because Sheriff Upton from the next county over called me just a little bit ago. He said he got a complaint about some vandalism from some of his constituents that run a bar. They said some big black guy popped all their tires and they're pretty pissed about it."

"Big black guy?"

"Well... Upton used some more colorful language, but I won't repeat it. It offends my Northeastern sensibilities."

"Nice of you," Porter said. "Good thing they aren't talking about me." His mind was racing to try to knit everything together with the pieces he had.

"They aren't? That was the bar I gave you directions to a few hours ago."

"Yeah, but I'm not black. If they had said a big brown guy, they might have been talking about me. They seem confused."

Spaulding frowned. "In any event, they aren't looking to press charges, but I imagine they are looking for said big black guy. Things would probably go bad for him if the club found him."

"Then I'm in the clear," Porter said. "That's a load off my shoulders."

There was silence. Both men were looking at each other, neither speaking.

The silence was interrupted by Claudette, coming with a glass of sweet tea for the sheriff and water for Porter. She dropped them off and went back to the kitchen, but not before rubbing Porter's back on her way back to the kitchen.

Porter watched Spaulding look at the two of them, then his eyes followed her as she walked away.

"That is a hell of a woman. But I'll assume you already know that," Spaulding said.

"What was your other question?" Porter said. "You asked me about the bar and a bunch of little follow-ups. Did you need something else?"

"I was just wondering when you were planning to move on," Spaulding said.

Porter took a sip of his water, eyes never leaving the sheriff. "I may stay for a while. I think the fresh air is doing me good. Besides, I have a few loose ends to tie up."

"Relating to the Newton girl?"

"And some other things. I feel like I haven't been getting the whole story and I don't like being lied to."

"You don't say."

"I do say." Porter sipped his water again.

"We've had people looking for her. Agencies all over the place are in on the manhunt. The Rollins boy and his sister are on the run. Even if they took Pima Newton, you can't imagine she's still alive, can you?"

"At this point, I don't know what to think. All I'm sure of is that you've been lying to me."

The sheriff carefully regarded Porter, then broke out into a smile. "How long have you known?"

"Not very long. I've been trying to figure it out, but sometimes I'm a little slow on the uptake."

"You seem pretty perceptive," Spaulding said.

"It was after my motel room got broken into. When we met up in the parking lot, you said the two guys who kicked in my door were gone when you got there. How would you have known how many there were unless you sent them?" Porter said.

"You want to know something funny? I knew as soon as I said it I screwed up. But I figured you wouldn't have caught it. It's the little things that trip us up, you know?"

"Yeah, that's been bothering me for a couple days, I just couldn't put my finger on it. But you know what the icing on the cake was?"

"I'd love to," Spaulding said, crossing his arms and leaning back in his chair.

"That rubber band on that money wad in your pocket. I saw one in the Rollins trailer and again in the trunk of the cartel guys' Honda."

"So that *was* you at their trailer? I should be pissed that we're having this conversation, but I'm actually impressed. That was three hitmen you took out. Not to mention you catching me on the rubber band. Like I said, I'm impressed."

"Don't be. You're pretty sloppy."

"In this little shit town, I can afford to be," Spaulding said.

"How are you involved with the Rollinses and the cartel?"

Spaulding looked around. The Burger Hut was empty and Claudette was nowhere to be seen.

Porter clenched his jaw watching the sheriff.

"We have an arrangement. It lines my pockets."

"Why did you have them take Pima?" Porter said.

"I didn't. That was the dumbest thing they did, bringing all that heat down on us. Those damn fools thought the kid was spying on them in the woods and grabbed her. Morons."

"Is she still alive?" Porter said.

Spaulding looked at Porter for a few moments. "I think. Last I heard they were still dragging the kid around with them. I stay out of that side, since it's not really my problem. All I care about is the product. "

Porter felt his heart speed up and there was a tingle running through his shoulders. "Where?"

"You don't need to know that yet."

Porter had to stop himself from dragging Spaulding outside and beating him to death. His hand was trembling. "Okay. Why those guys? How'd you get wrapped up with them? Aren't you worried about them getting you pinched?"

Spaulding laughed. "Nah. No one can prove that I have anything to do with those losers. I never meet them in public. The only time we talk is on prepaid phones. The only one of them I ever met in person was their daddy; to the rest, I'm just a voice on the phone."

"Their dad got you into this?" Porter said.

"Hell, I got myself into this. When I first got elected, he was locked up in jail. I wanted the people around here to think I cared, so I went to him on the level, trying to see if he'd flip on some of his contacts so we could arrest them. By the time we were done talking, he had flipped me, so to speak. The amount he offered was too big to ignore."

"You're a hell of a cop, Spaulding."

The sheriff ignored Porter. "Then I told Papa Rollins that for a bigger cut, I'd introduce him to some potential big-time customers."

"The cartel? How'd you even meet with them? What were they doing around here?"

"It wasn't hard. A couple of their guys got arrested for DUI. I got them out and told them I had someone they could purchase product from. I made the introduction, played the middle, and made a little bit for myself."

Porter took another drink of his water. He hoped the sip would keep him from grinding his teeth into dust. "Cartels are in the import game. It's cheaper that way. Why buy from your rednecks?"

"They diversify. A load gets seized here or there, and they go looking for cheap product that's already in the States. Hell, last week the Feds seized one of their tractor-trailer loads somewhere out by the coast. The cartel wanted to replace their product, so they came calling. I guess they have deadlines, too."

"That why Richie Rollins got killed? He didn't meet their deadline?" Porter said.

"Sure. Don't promise a bunch of angry Los Primos hitmen you can give them a certain amount of meth if you don't have it. I wasn't going to save his dumb ass."

"So Richie's head in a bag was a warning to you, wasn't it? That's why they left it on your doorstep," Porter said.

Spaulding smiled. "I think they wanted to show me they weren't happy."

Claudette interrupted the tense conversation with the food—two plates of her fried chicken sandwiches and homemade curly fries. "Here you go, guys. Sheriff, I brought you some hot sauce. You guys need anything else?"

"No, sweetheart, I think that's everything for me," Sheriff Spaulding said.

"You good?" she said to Porter.

"I'm fine," he said, staring a hole through Spaulding.

"Okay..." she said, and headed off to the kitchen.

Spaulding began preparing his plate, getting the hot sauce and ketchup ready.

Porter left his plate untouched.

Spaulding noticed and said, "Just because we are about to have an unpleasant conversation doesn't mean you should let that go to waste."

"'About to'? From where I'm sitting, this has been a shit conversation already," Porter said.

Spaulding took a large bite and steam poured from the sandwich. He was shaking his head.

"No," he said, sipping his sweet tea to cool his mouth off. "It gets much worse for you."

# FORTY-FIVE

"REALLY? What, you gonna try to pin Pima on me? Maybe try to plant some of the meth on me and lock me up? Sound about right?"

Spaulding took another drink of his sweet tea. "Lock you up? Hell no. I'm sure you were a thousand miles away when she disappeared and can prove it."

"Then you sending some more guys after me? Might as well tell me and make it a fair fight."

Spaulding shook his head. "See, that was my first thought. That's why I sent my deputies after you when you first got here. I figured they'd rough you up and scare you off. Then I wouldn't have to worry about you fishing out the truth."

"They're in on it?"

"They don't know much, just that I grease their palms a little every month. I told them I'd pay them extra if they ran you off. Those clowns couldn't even do that right."

"Well, you were right," Porter said.

Spaulding looked at him expectantly.

"Good help is hard to find."

"Harder than I expected. So that's why I mentioned the biker bar to you. I figured if you're tough enough to smash my guys at your motel and to whack those Mexicans at the Rollins trailer, you'd probably be dumb enough to go out there and get your ass killed by some good old boys. Then I wouldn't have to deal with you poking your nigger-nose places it doesn't belong."

"You're learning new words, huh? What happened to your Northeastern sensibilities?"

"I'm from Boston, not heaven," Spaulding said.

Porter nodded along. "So if you won't try to set me up, and you're out of guys to try to kill me, what are you gonna do?"

"Who said I was out of guys to kill you? Fact is, I'd never tell you all this if I thought there was any chance you'd be alive come morning."

Reflexively, Porter's hand reached toward his waistband.

"Easy, easy. You kill me, you don't get what you want."

"What's that?"

Spaulding took another bite of his sandwich and took his time chewing. It was a power move.

Porter'd had enough. "Speak up before I put a hole in that weak little chin of yours."

"You want Pima, right? Well, I'll tell you where Rollins is going to be tonight. Go get her yourself."

Porter was quiet for a couple of moments. "Rollins and how many of the cartel guys?"

Spaulding shrugged. "I didn't say you were going to like it."

"You think I'll walk into a trap? You may overestimate my desire to get the kid back," Porter said. "I don't do suicide missions."

"Pima not enough? How about your little girlfriend in the back?"

Porter didn't say anything, convinced his molars were sawdust by now.

"Yeah, I saw her car at your motel last night. You two are pretty comfy. You were enough to fight my guys off, but do you think she is? What do you think Los Primos would do to her if I said she'd come to me as sheriff and knew something about their operation? She doesn't, but they don't know that.

"Claudette can disappear in a heartbeat. Have I overestimated your desire to make sure she stays alive?" Spaulding said.

Porter again suppressed the instinct to grab the sheriff and choke the life out of him. His head throbbed where the brass knuckles had smashed him earlier in the afternoon. He inhaled deeply and exhaled slowly. "Let's assume I go tonight and get Pima. What are you going to do when I come back and I'm pissed? Because I *will* come back, and I *will* be pissed."

"You won't make it back."

"Pretend," Porter said. "Make believe, the same way you do that you're a cop."

"Okay. Besides you, nobody knows I had anything to do with this. Pima goes back to her family none the wiser. You thank whoever you pray to that you survived, you keep your mouth shut, and you leave town. If you don't, Claudette's a dead woman. Simple enough for you?"

Porter didn't say anything.

"Either way, I don't have to see you again. I want you out of my hair, Porter."

"You'll see me again."

"That a threat?"

"Just count on it," Porter said.

As if on cue, Claudette came by again. "Everything still working out for you guys?"

"Everything is right as rain," Sheriff Spaulding said.

Porter nodded, not taking his eyes off the sheriff.

Claudette looked at Porter and patted him on the shoulder.

"Take it easy. The sandwich is supposed to be good; you look like you're lifting weights."

"I'm good," Porter said.

She gave him a strange look, then let her hand linger on his shoulder as she walked away again.

"Where's Rollins gonna be?"

"Nice to know you can be reasoned with," Spaulding said. "Got a pen?"

Porter pulled out his phone. "Just give me the address."

Spaulding did, then stood and adjusted his uniform. "This is the last time we speak. If you even think of being an idiot, remember Claudette." Spaulding turned on his heel and walked out of the Burger Hut.

Porter watched him go, breathing deeply to slow his racing heart down. Of all the things he'd done in his life, letting the man walk away might have been the most difficult.

He wasn't sure how long it was until Claudette came back to the table carrying two plates of sweet potato pie. "Is the sheriff coming back?"

"Hey, can you sit down for a minute?"

"I think I can break away from the mad rush," she said. "You don't look happy. Rough talk?"

"The roughest," Porter said. He looked at her soft cheeks and dark eyes, fighting the urge to tell her she was in danger. "Do you... uh... do you have your kids tonight?"

"No, my mom picked them up from school. She's retired and doesn't have a lot to do, so a couple days a week she has them spend the night." She reached out and held his hand. "Why? Are you trying to seduce me again?"

"I'm not too good at the seduction game."

"Good enough for me. Why do you ask?"

"I was thinking... you want to get out of town tonight?"

She squinted her eyes. "What do you mean? Go where?"

"I don't know, you're the local. Where would you go if you wanted to get away for a night?"

Claudette rubbed his hand as she thought. "They just expanded the casino on the reservation. It's supposed to have some nice new rooms now."

"How far away is that?"

"About an hour," she said.

"Perfect. Let's go."

"Really?"

"Sure. Tell you what, after you close up tonight, meet me out there."

"You don't want to ride together?"

"I have a couple things I have to handle first, but I'll meet you," Porter said.

"This have anything to do with the sheriff?"

"No," he lied, "but I won't be long. I'll even pay for the room."

"But if I buy you lunch and you pay for a hotel room, are you still a gigolo? Or am I the hooker now? The lines are starting to get very blurry," she said with a smile.

"I think we can figure that out later." He fished a couple of bills from his pocket and slid them across the table.

Her smile dimmed. "Actually, think we can go Dutch on the room? I was mostly joking—I don't feel right about taking money from you. It makes me a little uncomfortable."

"How about I'll pay for the room, you pay for dinner. Fair?"

"Okay, but just so you know, if I buy you dinner, you're putting out. I figure you should know what you're getting into," she said, a smile plastered to her face once again.

"Fair deal," Porter said. "I have to go. Call you later?"

"Works for me."

He leaned over and kissed her on the cheek and was almost out the front door when her voice caught up with him.

"You forgot your pie."

"Bring it," Porter said. "We might need the energy."

"Well, aren't *you* feeling frisky," she said.

Porter nodded. "Yeah. Yeah, I am."

# FORTY-SIX

"THE SHERIFF? ARE YOU SURE?"

"Of course I'm sure, Joe. The asshole admitted it over a chicken sandwich. He doesn't give a damn."

"We'll build a case on him so big, they'll stuff his ass under the prison."

"How?" Porter said. "The only reason he told me everything is because there's no proof. No reliable witnesses. They never meet face-to-face; he gets cash, so no bank records to trace; and they use burner phones. I've been out of the cop game a while, but how do you make a case on that?" Porter said. He pulled into a parking lot as he spoke, slammed the car into park, and rubbed his face.

"There are ways. Just come back to Charlotte and let's figure this thing out. We'll take that son of a bitch out, if it's the last thing I do," Joe said.

"You know as well as I do there's no time. If Spaulding is telling the truth, Pima's going to be there tonight. I can't pass up the chance to get eyes on her."

Joe was quiet for a few moments. "You know this is a setup,

right? You haven't taken so many shots to the head that you can't see that, have you?"

"I've gotten pretty dinged up, but I'm thinking clearly enough. You called me out here to find this kid, and that's what I'm going to do."

"This doesn't have anything to do with Spaulding threatening... whatever her name is, does it? Your waitress friend?"

"Nope," Porter lied. "Nothing to do with her."

"Look, kid, when I asked you to come up here, it wasn't to go on a suicide mission. I figured you could beat the bushes, and if you got lucky and found Pima, you'd get yourself a nice chunk of change. I can't ask you to do this alone."

"You damn sure can't send me help—deniability, remember? Not to mention it takes you guys at the Bureau twelve hours to plan anything out, bunch of slow-moving prima donnas. No, I'm good. Besides, it's like that saying about outrunning the bear."

"What the hell are you talking about? Is that some mountain wisdom you picked up since you've been out there?" Joe said.

"If you're in the woods and there's a bear, you don't have to outrun the bear; you just have to outrun the next slowest guy," Porter said.

"And in this example, the next slowest guy is...?"

"It's a metaphor, but I don't know. It just seemed like the right thing to say," Porter said.

"That's real dumb, kid. So is this whole thing. I... you know... I like you. I wouldn't want you to get hurt on my account."

"It's a little late for that," Porter said. "Besides, I owe you."

"You don't owe me shit."

"Says you. How's the leg? You gone on many runs lately? Of course you haven't. That's my fault. I have to watch you gimping around, the least you can do is quiet down and let me have a chance to help Pima."

"I can't talk you out of this, can I?"

"Not a chance," Porter said.

There was silence for a couple of seconds. Porter looked out the windshield at the sun, still hanging strong in the sky before starting its nightly dip behind the mountains.

"So I changed my mind. I guess you can ask Amanda out. You wouldn't be so bad to have around."

Porter laughed. "Well, right now my dance card is a little full, but I'll keep her in mind if I get an opening."

"Fair enough. Call me when you have the girl?" Joe said.

"Will do."

"And Porter?"

"Yeah?"

"What did I tell you the first day I met you? What did I tell you every day we ever worked together?" Joe said.

"Do whatever it takes to go home."

"Whatever it takes." Joe hung up the phone.

Porter took a deep breath and punched the address Spaulding had given him into his GPS. It would take almost an hour to get to the location, and he couldn't afford to be the last person to show up.

It would be like walking into the middle of a firefight.

Porter did a quick Google search, then put the address into his GPS and followed the robotic voice until it spat him into the parking lot of just what he was looking for.

A gun shop.

The place was in a strip mall and was fairly nondescript, if you didn't count the Confederate and Gadsden flags in the windows, the flashing red light on the windowsill, and the thick bars that covered the entry door.

Porter pulled the heavy door open, stepping into a place that smelled of rubber and gunpowder. Two men were speaking to each other across the store counter; the man behind it had a bald head and a full Gandalf-style beard.

Porter smiled at the Tolkien reference that popped into his head. Claudette's favorite. He hated having to stand her up, but didn't see any other choice. Depending on how the night went, he hoped he would get a chance to apologize to her.

"Anything I can find for you?" Gandalf said to Porter. The other man, wearing a black Vietnam veteran hat, turned toward Porter as well.

"No, I think I have a good idea what I need," Porter said.

"A man on a mission," Gandalf said. "Do your thing. If you need me, I'm gonna be holding this counter up."

Porter nodded and let his eyes wander. In truth, he didn't need a gun. He had everything he needed in the trunk of his Yukon. He was looking for something more specific, something that was the right tool for the job.

He found it on an end cap, a clear plastic jug with a label on it that read "Quickee-Boom."

The basic product went by many names, and was easy enough to purchase. Some intrepid souls even ventured to the internet to order ammonium nitrate and aluminum shavings in bulk, to mix it themselves. As much as Porter loved the stuff, he wasn't keen to get on a DHS watch list for importing mass quantities of it.

People would think he was planning the next Oklahoma City.

It was billed as an exploding target. The basic components were inert and shipped together in a clean, plastic canister for use. In this state, they were impossible to detonate. The product was a binary explosive. The components of the target, when mixed properly, became volatile and could be set off with an influx of kinetic energy. In short, when shot with the right-sized projectile, moving at the right velocity, the mixture would explode.

It was this bomb-like quality that Porter was interested in. This particular model of Quickee-Boom could be detonated with a round from his AR-15. He picked up the three remaining canisters and carried them to the counter, interrupting the two jaw-jacking men.

"You got a good range day planned," Gandalf said.

"I hope so. I cleaned your shelf out, got any more in the back?" Porter said.

"I damn sure might." Gandalf stepped around the counter and disappeared into the back of the store.

"I just love that stuff," Vietnam Hat said.

"Big fan," Porter agreed.

"Tell you what, I saw on the interwebs the other day where some farmer was having trouble with the feral pigs on his land."

"Like big rats," Porter said.

"They sure are. So this crazy son of a bitch mixes up a bunch of that stuff you got there, then hides the canister in a bunch of food. Corn scraps and the like. Them damn pigs come out at dusk to eat, farmer's about fifty yards away with his rifle. He shoots the canister and *boom*. Pig parts everywhere." Vietnam Hat started laughing hysterically.

"Good way to take care of pests," Porter said.

"Hell yeah. Damn expensive, though. Wish I could find it cheaper."

The shop employee stepped back through the door with four additional canisters in his arms. "All we got left, friend, but it's yours if you want it."

"Lucky for me, that's exactly how much I wanted," Porter said, and slid the cash across the counter.

Gandalf made change, while resuming his conversation about foreign policy.

Vietnam Hat reached behind the counter and started bagging the Quickee-Boom for Porter.

"I mean, we was just for asking ISIS to take over, you know?" Gandalf said.

"Hey, I've been in war," Vietnam Hat said. "I don't want them boys over there any longer than they need to be."

"Yeah, yeah," Gandalf said.

Porter didn't join in the conversation, waiting instead until all the canisters were bagged up and then accepting the bags from the men. "Thanks, guys."

"If you do some cool shit with all that, put it online. Maybe I can find your video someday."

Porter shook his head. "I think there are enough videos of people taking care of pests already," he said as he backed against the front door and stepped out to the parking lot.

# FORTY-SEVEN

THE NEXT STOP was the big box store. Porter checked the time on his phone and resolved to be in and out as fast as he could.

He kept his word. A quick trip to menswear for a pack of socks, a stop in the spray paint section, and then to electronics for the last item. He surveyed the choice in prepaid cell phones and grabbed two of them, paying at the in-department register and jogging out of the store with all his items in one bag.

His phone showed he'd only been inside for eight minutes.

Porter reconnected the GPS and let its robot voice guide him to the main highway, which he followed for nearly an hour. During the drive, he went past the Peaks MC clubhouse.

The lynch mob he'd imagined forming wasn't there. The bar's parking lot was light on people and only a couple of the vehicles from Porter's visit remained.

He could see the still-flat tires.

The blue line on his phone's screen pointed him off the interstate, followed closely by the voice telling him to turn right. He obeyed and turned onto a much smaller surface street, choked on both sides with thick kudzu vines and the power lines and poles they were enveloping.

Porter followed along the two-lane road for ten minutes without seeing another soul. Eventually, as Jimi was wailing about a watchtower, Porter came to a T intersection.

The GPS seemed stuck, pausing for a long moment, before recalculating and telling Porter to take another right.

The thick vegetation continued on the left, but on the right the forest opened up and was replaced by a wide but shallow river. Porter tried to sneak a closer look, but the embankment leading to the river was steep and there was no guardrail, so he pulled his eyes back to the front.

Almost twenty minutes later, he saw a structure peeking out of the overgrown trees and vines. Porter slowed his truck as he passed.

It was an abandoned motel. He couldn't make out any of the signage, and the windows were all busted out. He feathered the gas again, chasing the blue line on his navigation.

Minutes later, there was another structure—not as decrepit as the last, but Mother Nature was still doing her best to take her land back.

Once upon a time, these motels had been part of a great number that littered the area. They had been on the main road cutting through western North Carolina. Largely rendered obsolete by the advent of Interstate 40, they had now fallen into disrepair.

As he went along, the motels grew in frequency. Sometimes they were to Porter's left, fighting their way out of the forest, struggling for recognition. Other times, they were on the right, in a spot where the river took a bend outward and allowed for just enough space to put a building.

Many of the signs were still intact, if dingy and overrun by shrubbery. The signs evoked a strange nostalgia in Porter, making him wistful for a time period before he had even been alive.

Porter passed the Ramblers Inn, the Hide Away Stay-Place and the Starlight Motel. The Starlight had a façade that screamed "space race," with a very Sputnik-esque geometrical pattern on the road-front sign.

The next motel on the left had the sign Porter had been looking for: the Teddy Bear Motel. It actually read "Teddy ear M t l," as much of the signage had been lost to time.

The Teddy Bear had a wide front and a big parking lot that wasn't nearly as overrun with vines as some of its contemporaries. It was two stories, with a white façade and a smattering of staircases.

Just like Porter's motel back in town, every door on the Teddy Bear was front-facing and opened out to the sidewalk or the balcony of the second floor.

He pulled into the parking lot, confident he was the first party to arrive.

A hill rose up behind the big old building, connecting the motel to the mountain above it. Through one of the stairwells, Porter saw a rusted old playset, sitting on an overgrown plateau.

He drove closer, looking at the destroyed rooms, their windows open and doors smashed in. He blared the horn, checking for squatters. There were clothes and trash and barbeque grills littered all over the place. There was even a stack of mattresses against the door to the check-in area.

Porter laid on the horn again and rolled this window down. "Police. If you're in there, you gotta go."

Nothing moved. Satisfied there were no homeless people trying to escape the cold afternoon, he put the truck in park and reached into his back seat, grabbing the bag of Quickee-Boom.

The Teddy Bear was unique among the motels he'd driven past in that there was a small overflow parking lot opposite the motel. There was a bend in the road, not quite big enough for another motel to have been planted there, but there was plenty of space for a parking pad.

He eyeballed the distance, happy with what he saw.

Porter ripped into the bag from the gun store and mixed four individual canisters of the Quickee-Boom. Then, using duct tape from his trunk, he taped them all together by their sides, ending up with one big square of ready and mixed explosive.

He took the big improvised bomb and double-wrapped it in the bags from the big box store. He left it on his lap while he fumbled with the prepaid cell phone, ensuring it was activated properly, that the phone got enough reception to ring out there in the sticks, and that the volume was up. Porter used the rest of the duct tape to secure the bag closed, with multiple lashings of tape for good measure.

He pulled back to the road. There was no other traffic, so he went across the street. Porter grabbed the spray paint and his bundle of Quickee-Boom, and hopped out of the truck.

Placing the big package on the ground in the middle of the parking lot, he shook the can of spray paint and put a softball-sized dot of yellow paint on each side of the bundle. He set it down and looked back across the road at the Teddy Bear and the parking lot. Porter moved the bundle a foot to the right, looked back at the motel, and nodded.

He pulled out of the overflow parking, driving slowly away, opposite the way he'd come in. A few hundred feet around the next bend he found another motel, next in line of the forgotten. This one was in much worse shape than the Teddy Bear; Porter couldn't read the sign any longer, but could just make out the remnants of a graphic Cherokee Indian brave, more cartoon than realistic.

There were willow trees in front of the Cherokee, and they'd long since overrun the parking lot. Porter circled in and out, then backed into a spot, willow branches almost completely covering the Yukon, rendering it virtually invisible from the road.

He ripped into the bag of wool socks from the store and put a double pair on each of his feet, tying his Chucks tight. Then he dug through the pile of clothing in his trunk, pulling on his thickest long-sleeve shirt and pulling his dark hoodie on last.

His gloves were sticky with the blood of the Los Primos hitman from the trailer. Porter paused for a moment, but pulled them on anyway, sighing in disgust. Then he opened his lock-box, sliding on his magazine carrier with two extra mags for his pistol, and pulling his AR from its resting place.

It was simple and no-frills: sixteen inches with a light attached to the end and a sling to hold the entire thing to his body. He slid an extra thirty-round magazine into his back pocket and slammed the trunk. He got back into the running truck, thankful for the warmth of the heater. It was getting colder as the sun dropped, and now there were places its rays weren't reaching, blocked out by the surrounding mountains.

He closed his eyes for a moment, wondering if there was anything else he could do to give himself a chance. There was no doubt that this was the worst-case scenario—himself against an unknown number of people, all of whom had murderous intent. He hoped Pima was alive. He hoped he could help her. He hoped he'd get a chance to eat another burger sometime.

That last thought made Porter laugh and he slid out of the truck, turning the engine off but leaving the keys on the seat.

The plan wasn't ideal, but nothing ever was. There was an old saying, "No battle plan survives contact with the enemy."

Too many times in his life these words had been right. His only hope was that this particular enemy had no clue they were even in a battle until it was too late.

Porter cupped his hands and blew into them. He adjusted the sling to cinch the rifle tight to his chest and pushed his way behind the Cherokee brave hotel, into the woods and up the hill, back toward the Teddy Bear Motel.

# FORTY-EIGHT

"WE COULD, YOU KNOW..." Pima said. "Just go. Leave."

Laura Bell was sitting on the edge of the chair, gauze stuffed into the nostrils of her badly broken nose. "You want a little tip?"

Pima nodded. "Sure."

Laura Bell touched her nose and felt a jolt of pain across her face. "If you have a broken nose, you aren't supposed to blow it."

"Why not?"

"There's a membrane in your head. If your nose is broken, it could be punctured. You blow your nose, then air leaks into your eye socket and other weird places. It hurts like a bitch until it goes away," Laura Bell said.

"Did you learn that in school? When you wanted to be a nurse, I mean?" Pima asked.

Laura Bell laughed. "No. That's from experience."

Pima reached out and touched Laura Bell on the shoulder. "You know we can make it. Let's just go, right now. Don't wait for those guys to get back here. All they're gonna do is hurt us. Let's run."

"You can, but I can't," Laura Bell said. "I can drop you off anywhere and you'll go back to your family. I run, all I'm going to do is get arrested somewhere. I'm broke; I need money to get away."

"But—"

"No buts, baby girl. I'm going to go with Seth and Dusty. Once I get mine, I'm gone, you understand? Gone. Nobody will ever see me again."

Pima was quiet for a few minutes. "My family can help you."

Laura Bell laughed. "Them nice folks don't want any part of a murderer. Trust me. Once I get through this, I'll find my way. But until then, I promise I'll stay with you, got it?"

Pima nodded. "Thanks for—"

The door of the trailer swung open, slamming into the siding with a *bang*. Seth walked in, unsteady on his feet. "The hell is this, nap time? We gotta go, come on. Teddy Bear's waiting."

Laura Bell stood, eyeing her brother. "How much you had to drink?"

"Not as much as I wished I did. Why?"

"You need to sober up."

"Like hell I do. I'm fine, come on," Seth said.

Laura Bell took a step backward. "You sure you even need me? You and Dusty should be able to handle it. I could stay here and watch the girl, wait for you guys to get back."

"Of course I need you. Only three of us and we need to watch each other's back. You still got that wheel gun you shot the cop with?"

Laura Bell nodded.

"Good. Tell you what, I'll set you up in your own room. Me and Dusty will do the talking. Any kind of double-cross, you waste anyone that comes into that room that ain't one of us."

"What about the girl? Let's just leave her here. We don't need her in the way," Laura Bell said.

"I'm sick of hearing about this girl. She's coming too, the hell with it. You wanted her around, now she stays," Seth said.

"It's just—"

Seth reached out and grabbed Laura Bell by her dirty blonde hair and yanked her close. He swayed back and forth in front of her face.

"Let go of me."

"Now you need to listen here."

Laura Bell pulled her pistol out and stuck it to his chin. "I. Said. Let. Go."

Seth smiled and let go of his sister's hair, taking a couple of steps backward. "What, you gonna shoot me, Sis? You don't have the balls."

Laura Bell pointed the revolver at Seth. "You don't know what I have. Out. Now."

Seth rocked back and forth, then stumbled out of the trailer without another word.

"Laura Bell, let's just go. We can sneak out the back. They'll never find us."

"No," Laura Bell said, stuffing her pistol back into her pants.

"But why can't we—"

"I said no. Come on."

Laura Bell led Pima outside by the wrist. Dusty was waiting at the back of the Lumina with the trunk open.

"She ain't going in there."

"But Seth said—"

"I don't give a damn what Seth said. Nobody's gonna see her sitting in the back with me. Hell, nobody even on these roads this time of evening," Laura Bell said.

"Let's go already," Seth said from the passenger's seat.

"Okay, Laura Bell." Dusty closed the old car's trunk and

opened up the back door. Pima climbed in and slid across to the passenger's side. Laura Bell sat behind Dusty.

The old car lurched into action, out on the road and toward its destination.

Laura Bell struggled to breathe the entire trip, and it wasn't just her shattered nose. She was wishing Pima was right and that they could have left. Wishing she'd saved some money that she could have run with. Wishing she was anywhere but the back seat of the Lumina.

# FORTY-NINE

PORTER'S TREK through the woods had been quicker than expected; however, he'd huffed and puffed the entire way up the mountainside. There'd been a game trail, something for him to follow through the thick vegetation, but the steep hills and elevation taxed his oxygen supply. He resolved fewer burgers and more trips to the gym if he got back to Tampa.

His climb had paid off, and he was able to approach the Teddy Bear from the rear, coming down off the mountain and onto the plateau near the rusted playground. There was a walkway from the playground to the second floor of the Teddy Bear, which connected to the balcony that ran along the front of the building.

He walked the pathway, peeking in the back windows of the rooms on the second floor. Moments later, he was thanking himself for showing up early and still having a modicum of daylight to see by.

One of the windows he looked in revealed a disaster zone. As he'd descended the mountain behind the Teddy Bear, he'd failed to notice that a sizeable amount of the roof had fallen in.

He reached up and hoisted himself over the roofline, seeing

exposed rafters and support beams. Porter picked his way past the collapsed area to the roof that was still laid as intended. He stepped gently as he walked up the roof toward the top, sure he'd hit a rotten patch and fall through.

That never happened, and soon Porter was flat on his stomach, rifle resting on the ridge of the roof, barrel just sticking over. He looked through the ACOG sight on top. Manufactured by a company named Trijicon, the ACOG had seen battle atop the rifles of US servicemen for years. Its four-power magnification was a boon to his situation. As the light was fading, the ACOG managed to magnify the entire area, as well as the increasingly minimal light, and gave Porter a good view of the parking lots and road below him.

Listening to the last chirping of the last birds of fall in the last light of the day, Porter was glad he'd doubled up on his socks. It was chilly, but he imagined he was clothed enough to stay warm. He settled in, waiting for the rest of the party's guest list to show up.

# FIFTY

"WHEN'S EVERYBODY else supposed to get here?" Laura Bell said, seeing the empty parking lot of the Teddy Bear as Dusty pulled in, then reversed his way into a spot.

"No clue. Big Man just said sometime after ten."

"He couldn't do any better than that?" Laura Bell said.

"I didn't ask. What am I gonna do, argue with Big Man?"

"Never mind. How do you want to set up?"

Seth stepped out of the car and Laura Bell joined him. "I reckon you two girls can go right upstairs into a room with our little bit of product. Once we get the money, we'll send them up to you, that way we divide them up a little bit. You blast whoever comes upstairs, and me and Dusty will handle the rest down here."

"That's it?" Laura Bell said. "That's your plan?"

"Yep." Seth reached into the trunk and pulled out three camping lanterns. The lamps gave the area underneath the second-floor walkway an eerie glow. "All you have to do is keep your eyes peeled, make sure there's no funny business."

"Like chopping Richie's head off?" Laura Bell muttered.

"You think I ain't still sore about that? Of course I am. But right now, I gotta make sure everything runs smooth. I'm being real pragmatical."

"Pragmatic," Laura Bell said.

"That's what I said, isn't it?"

Laura Bell shook her head and followed her brother's lead. He walked up the crumbling staircase and onto the upper walkway. The group moved from room to room, Seth sticking his head and lantern inside to look each one over.

The roof was collapsed into one of the rooms, and the other two reeked of mildew and of something recently dead.

Laura Bell was glad her nose was broken, so the smell wasn't as bad.

Seth poked his head into one of the motel rooms and came back out. "This'll do."

Laura Bell let Pima walk in ahead of her, and held up her lantern to look around.

The room was intact, with moth-eaten drapes and blinds. At least it was dry enough. There were two twin beds with the sheets torn off, and a small dresser opposite them. Laura Bell set her lamp down, its blue glow enough to light the entire room.

"You two wait here until one of us comes and gets you. Remember, anybody comes in here that ain't us, you ambush 'em. Got it?"

"I'm not an idiot. I understand," Laura Bell said.

She pulled the revolver from her pants and set it on the bed next to her.

"Look," Dusty said, pointing out the window.

A bright set of headlights approached from the left.

"It's them," Seth said. "Game time, big boy. You ready?"

Dusty nodded.

"Then let's go."

The two disappeared from the room.

Laura Bell patted Pima on the leg. "We're going to be okay. Don't worry. I won't let anything happen to us. It'll all be over soon."

# FIFTY-ONE

PORTER'S LEGS had grown stiff and he couldn't feel his toes. Up on the roof, wind whirling and swirling past him, he realized his Tampa tolerance wasn't ready for a dark night in the Appalachian woods. He wished he'd brought some hand warmers to thaw his fingers.

Or maybe a blast furnace.

By his own estimation, confirmed by a check of his smartphone, he had been lying on the roof of the Teddy Bear motel for nearly four hours. No one had shown up and he was beginning to wonder if Spaulding had played him. Shined him off to a location where he knew nothing was happening just to keep him out of the way. He lost himself in thought for nearly ten minutes, dreaming of the things he'd do to Spaulding when he got back to town.

His phone vibrated in his pocket. He lowered the brightness and checked the text.

It was Claudette. *The new rooms at the casino are nice.*

He blew onto his fingers. *Real question is, how big is the shower?*

Porter stole a glance at the empty road until he felt the vibration in his hand again.

*Big enough for you. I already checked.*

He smiled and slipped his phone into the back pocket of his jeans not occupied by a rifle magazine.

The night had settled in completely. Despite there being a large moon out, he could barely make out the fluorescent haze of the large dots he had sprayed on the bundle of Quickee-Boom. He settled his eye back into the ACOG, which helped to magnify the moonlight. He could see well enough.

His pocket vibrated.

*You going to be long?*

Porter tapped at the screen, his hands cold and stiff, having a tough time hitting the correct keys.

*Not if I can help it.*

He put his phone away and looked over the roofline again. This time, he heard a noise off to the right. Porter flattened himself as much as he could to the roof and strained his eyes to see what was coming.

A noisy, silver car with dim yellow headlights came barreling off the road, around the bank of trees that bordered it.

Porter watched as the car bumped its way through the parking lot, shocks a mess, until it pulled so close to the building that Porter could only see the trunk sticking out.

"Asshole," he muttered to himself.

Then the silver car lurched to life, pulling backward and doing a one-eighty before backing into a space in front of the motel.

"That's a little better," Porter said.

Eye straining through the ACOG, he saw two men get out of the silver car. He couldn't make out their faces, but one was small and the other, even from far away, was much, much larger.

"Dusty and Seth," he said quietly. Then, "Why the hell am

I talking to myself?"

He shook his head and strained his ears at the sound of muted and muffled speaking. He couldn't make out what was being said. He looked again, but only saw glimpses of the two men as they ducked in and out of the car's back seat.

Unsure if they'd even brought Pima, Porter was considering moving off the roof to try for a better angle to get the information he needed, when a bright white pair of headlights appeared from the left. He snapped his eye back into the ACOG and followed a Honda Civic off the road and onto the parking lot of the Teddy Bear.

The driver of the Civic had the good grace to park halfway across the parking lot, and its aftermarket halogen headlights lit up the area below Porter like a Christmas tree.

Two figures walked out from underneath Porter's field of view, into the middle of the parking lot. In the bright headlights, it wasn't hard to tell that these two were definitely Rollins and his muscle, so Porter looked over the new arrivals.

Porter's elevation gave him certain advantages, one of which was that he wasn't blinded by the Civic's headlights, like he would have been on the ground. He could see over the wall of light to the vehicle behind it, and counted five men standing around the Civic. There were three rifles pointed at Seth and Dusty.

Porter was sure the men couldn't see the weapons, their wielders front-lit by the lights and protected from view. Seth had his baseball hat pulled low and Dusty had his big mitts in front of his eyes. If they could see the rifles, they were moving as if they weren't concerned that the Los Primos cartel hitmen were aiming at them.

Seth stopped and there was a conversation. Porter was too far away to hear it, but Seth was talking animatedly, gesticulating with his hands and moving back and forth as he did.

A large bag came hurtling into the field of light, obviously thrown by someone in the Honda. Dusty stepped up and held the bag up while Seth rifled through it.

"Payment," Porter muttered. "Once they get the meth, everyone's in the wind and I'll have to start from square one." That wasn't going to happen if Porter could help it.

He pulled his phone from his pocket, then went to the recent calls and clicked the top number on the list. He looked back toward the men on the ground, and saw two of the gunmen line up next to each other.

He realized this wasn't going to be a transaction—it was going to be an execution. The cartel was just distracting Seth and Dusty with the money. Then they'd kill them and take all the drugs and money. Porter would have no clue where to find the girl.

Porter clenched his jaw, ready for the gunfire. Instead, he heard the distinct sound of his prepaid phone ringing. Everyone in the parking lot below him stopped moving. Porter watched as, after some back and forth, the three men with the rifles turned and walked off toward the ringing bundle Porter had left across the street.

Porter pulled the rifle stock to his shoulder and sank his eye into his sight.

He watched the men cross the road. The three of them huddled together as they looked down at the ringing plastic bag. One of them bent and picked it up, holding it at chest level while the rest of his men looked at the bundle with him. The entire group turned and started walking back to the Civic.

Realizing his opportunity might disappear as quickly as it had materialized, Porter put the crosshair on the fluorescent dot bouncing with the man's steps. He concentrated, waiting for the perfect shot.

# FIFTY-TWO

SETH DESCENDED THE STAIRS, looking hard at the vehicle approaching. The lights were too bright to make it out clearly, but he figured it was a Honda. "All these beaners drive Hondas."

"What?" Dusty said from behind him.

"Nothing. Just be ready. They're gonna try something, I know it."

Seth continued down the stairs until he was on the ground level. He walked out into the parking lot, standing in the wash of the halogen bulb and wondering if he'd get some sort of suntan from the beam.

"You got our money?" he said into the brightness.

A rough voice from the vehicle called out, "You got our product?"

"What am I, a thief? Of course I have your product." He stepped forward, pulling down his baseball hat to shield his eyes from the withering glare.

"Well?"

"This is weird, like I'm not even talking to a person. It's like talking to the sun."

"What?" the voice said.

"It's just, you know, bright. What's your name, Sunny?" Seth laughed.

"You high?" the voice said.

"No," Seth said, and cleared his throat. "What's your name?"

"It doesn't matter."

"It does if we're gonna do business together," Seth said.

"Chuy."

"Chewy what?" Seth said. He felt Dusty step closer to him.

"My name, *cabrón*."

"Got it," Seth said, turning his face to the side. "Look, Chewy, you give us the money and you'll get your crystal. Simple transaction."

"It doesn't work like that, *cabrón*. You know better."

"Yeah, well, usually I don't have interrogation lights in my eyeballs, either. We all make sacrifices."

Chuy laughed. "How do I know you aren't ripping me off?"

"How do I know you aren't?" Seth said. "Listen, you can be Billy Badass if you want to, I'll just take my crystal and go home. Simple as that."

Chuy laughed again. "Like you have a choice. Remember your brother?"

There was a quick conversation in Spanish between Chuy and his men. Seth couldn't see them speaking and he damn sure had no idea what they were saying. He figured if he was going on the run to Mexico, he'd have to meet a girl down there to shack up with so she could teach him.

"No matter, we can show first," Chuy said as a large rolling suitcase was thrown out into the parking lot.

Dusty stepped past Seth and picked it up. He held it while Seth opened it up and saw a sizeable sum of cash. He wasn't sure how much it was and he wasn't going to try to count it.

"Okay, this is good business, *amigo*," Seth said, heavy emphasis on one of the few Spanish words he knew.

"Where's our shit?" Chuy said.

"It's all upstairs," Seth said. "You may want to send a couple guys, it's pretty heavy. Also, you want a girl? She's pretty young, but she's cute. I figure you guys can find something to do with her."

"What? No, we don't want a kid."

"Suit yourself. I was just think—"

"*Cállate*," Chuy said.

"What the hell does th—"

"Shut up," Chuy said. "Do you hear that?"

Seth strained his ears. It sounded like one of the jingles from the old-school cell phone everyone had back in the day. He looked toward the direction of the noise, rewarded for that by the headlights burning his eyes.

"You expecting a call, *cabrón*?" Chuy said.

"It's not me, *amigo*," Seth replied.

"Go," Chuy said.

"What about—"

"Not you."

Seth watched as two men stepped from the bright lights. Each was pointing a pistol, one at him and one at Dusty.

"You playing some kind of game?" Chuy said.

Seth recognized his voice, and got his first look at the man. Chuy was tall and thin but heavily tattooed, including his face.

The man in front of Dusty was just as inked, but smaller and thick.

"Move," Chuy said. "Now."

He pushed Seth back toward the car, out of the bright lights. As his eyes adjusted, Seth could see by the light of the moon there were three men walking across the street to the other parking lot.

"Where are they—"

"Shut up," Chuy said. "You talk too much."

Dusty was several feet away, his hands up at the threat of the gun in his face. Seth looked at his friend, then back toward the men walking.

"Well?" Chuy called out. "What is it?"

For the first time, Seth noticed the rifles the men across the street were carrying.

"A package," a voice echoed back.

"*Mande*?"

"A package."

"Bring it here," Chuy said. He turned back to Seth and pressed the barrel of his pistol into the man's face.

"I told you that's not mine."

"Shut up, *cabrón*. When they get back, we'll see what it is. Then, it's lights out for you and your big friend over there."

Seth's jaw moved up and down, chewing on nothing, as he stared at the pistol in his face.

# FIFTY-THREE

PORTER WATCHED the trio of men pick up the bundle of Quickee-Boom and carry it, holding it out and away from their bodies. All that did was give him a better shot.

He took a deep breath then slowly exhaled, crosshair rising and falling in rhythm with the spray-painted bundle the entire way.

Then he thumbed the rifle's safety off and gently squeezed the trigger.

His rifle barked to life. The bright dot he'd been aiming at disappeared after the shot.

So did everything else around it.

# FIFTY-FOUR

JUST AS SETH was working up the courage to try to take the gun from Chuy, there was a flash of light from across the street and a deafening *boom*. The explosion went high into the air, and rather than being alarmed, Seth just stared at the big light show.

Chuy ducked his head and looked behind him, pistol dropping to his side as he looked at the group of men who were no longer there.

Seth realized he had an opening. He pulled his pistol and started pulling the trigger. Sound from the explosion still echoing off the mountain, Chuy didn't move until Seth's rounds found their mark.

"*Qué la chinga*?" Chuy said as he fell, then pulled himself to his feet and dived over the hood, taking cover behind the car.

Seth jumped against the car at the same time, the two men on opposite sides.

"You shoot at me, huh?" Chuy yelled out, his pistol firing back at Seth, who ducked his head behind the engine block. "Do you know who I am?"

"Fuck you," Seth said, looking under the car and seeing a pair of basketball shoes sticking out from behind the tire.

He pulled the trigger twice, hitting the shoe both times, then ran to the back of the car and leaned against the trunk.

Chuy howled in pain. "You son of a bitch. Get over here."

Seth looked around the trunk. Chuy was on his side, aiming under the car, pointing his pistol where Seth had been.

*Click. Click. Click.*

He stood up, walking over to the fallen hitman. "You out of bullets, *amigo*?"

Chuy looked up at Seth and tossed his pistol away. "You know you're a dead man, right?"

"I am?" Seth said. "From where I'm standing, it looks like you're the refried beans."

"Doesn't matter. We'll get you eventually. You can't run from us."

"Yeah? Well, who's running?" Seth said. He leaned down and stuck the gun into Chuy's face, then pulled the trigger.

He stood up and yelled at the top of his lungs, his head and hands tingling. He wasn't sure if it was the meth or the adrenaline that was making him fuzzy all over. He didn't care.

High was high.

He looked left and right. "Dusty? Dusty?"

Seth ran to the front of the car and found Dusty on top of the man who had, until moments ago, had a gun in his face. His hands were clamped around the man's throat and the cartel gunman's face was purple.

"You okay?"

Dusty looked at Seth, but didn't let of go of the man's neck.

"Finish up with that guy. They're all dead. Can you believe this shit?"

Dusty looked back to the man he was choking. "I don't like when people point guns at me."

Seth watched Dusty for a moment. "Yeah, I get it."

Seth jogged to the stairwell. "When you get done with him,

get all the shit they have and put it in our car. I'm gonna get Laura Bell and finally take care of that kid. She ain't coming with us."

Dusty nodded, fingers still embedded in the man's throat.

Seth ran up the stairs toward the second level. His shot-up arm was useless. It had slammed against the pavement when he dived and was bleeding again.

No matter. With the Mexicans gone, he could spend as long as he wanted rehabbing his shoulder.

An all-expenses paid vacation, courtesy of the cartel.

Without hesitation, Seth ran through the doorway of the room where Laura Bell was hiding.

"Holy shit," Laura Bell said. "It's you." She lowered her revolver once she saw it was her brother.

"They're all dead, Sis. All of 'em," Seth said, rocking back and forth as he talked.

"But how? What was that explosion?" she said.

"They're dead because they fucked with the wrong people, that's why."

"Wait, stop for a minute. What happened?" Laura Bell said.

Seth jumped on the empty bed and screamed, loud and long. He ripped his red hat off and threw it down to the floor triumphantly. "It don't matter. All you need to know is we're good now."

"Where's Dusty?" Laura Bell said.

"Wrist deep in some cholo." Seth jumped off the bed.

"What was that boom?"

"Hell if I know. Who cares?" Seth said. It felt like his blood was on fire.

"Was it the Mexicans?" Laura Bell said.

"I just said I don't know. Get your shit, we're leaving."

Laura Bell stood up and tucked the revolver into her waistband. She reached her hand out. "Come on, Pima."

Seth's brain was on fire now, his eyes feeling like they hadn't blinked in hours. "Uh-uh. That shit stops right now."

Pima stepped behind Laura Bell.

"We dragged her ass around enough. Perfect place to leave her. Everybody else is dead. Cops will think she was just part of them. Maybe think the Mexicans took her ass. This is where she stays."

"We can't just leave her here. She could talk. Remember the kidnapping charges?" Laura Bell said, grasping for anything she could to deter her brother.

Seth growled. He wanted to sprint and scream, and Laura Bell was stopping him. He needed to get out of the room. Seth pulled his pistol. "She's never gonna talk again."

Laura Bell was between him and Pima.

"Why are you always in the way?" Seth tried to push her out of the way, his arm not responding when he told it to.

Laura Bell grabbed him and pulled him. "You can't hurt her. Leave her alone."

"I said move, bitch," Seth said. He hit Laura Bell in the arm with the gun, knocking her out of the way. He stopped for a moment, trying to figure out why his arm felt like it was ten feet long and dragging on the floor. He blinked hard and looked at the other girl on the floor.

"You been nothing but problems. I should have done this a long time ago," he said, and raised his pistol toward her.

He blinked again, the young girl's face looking like a burst of light for a moment, then everything snapped back into place. "There you are."

When the gun went off, Pima's face was showered with blood. When she opened her eyes, Seth was missing half his head. He fell over, stiff as a board.

Laura Bell was standing behind him, holding her revolver protectively in front of her. Smoke was coming out of the barrel and the pistol was trembling in her hand. There were tears in her eyes and her nose was bleeding again.

"I said no. I said no. I said no. I said no," she repeated.

Pima stepped over Seth's body, which was now twitching, and wrapped her arms around Laura Bell. The pair of them sank to the floor together.

"Thank you."

# FIFTY-FIVE

IT ALL HAPPENED in quick succession: the recoil of the rifle into his shoulder, the deep *boom* of his homemade explosive, and the flash of light that followed. Porter had never set off that much of the Quickee-Boom at one time and was impressed at its potency.

The men who'd been huddled around the bundle were inert, in various stages of blown up and lying on the ground.

Porter fought the urge to jump off the roof, to go running down and see if he could find Pima. Instead, he flicked his rifle back to safe and watched the mayhem below him.

As the explosion happened, Dusty reached out and grabbed the cartel man closest to him and introduced his lunchbox-sized hands to the man's throat.

Seth shot a man and ran off somewhere Porter couldn't see. Things were about as fair as they were going to be. All the cartel men were dead and now only Dusty and Seth remained. Porter didn't like being outnumbered, but this was as good as it would get. He rolled onto his back and carefully slid his way down the rotten roof, pausing to shine his flashlight in front of him to make sure he wasn't going to end up an involuntary guest of the room below.

He got to the edge and pushed off, dropping the eight or nine feet and landing softly in the grass. He quickly stepped over to the first window, hoping he'd see Seth.

It was dark.

The next room was dark as well, and Porter moved on to a third.

The snap of a gunshot rang out from the room directly ahead of him. He moved faster, rifle on his shoulder, and paused for a moment just to the side of the window. He heard crying and took a quick look, sticking his face in front of the window.

The room was brightly lit, a camping lantern on the table by the wall. There were two people on the floor, holding each other.

"Who the hell is that?" he muttered to himself.

Porter passed the window and moved to the walkway, which would lead to the staircase down and the balcony, where he could gain access to the rooms he'd been peeking in.

Before he walked around the corner, he stuck his head out, checking to see if the coast was clear.

Dusty Walker came ambling up the stairs and turned right, onto the walkway, then disappeared in front of the building.

Porter waited several seconds for the man to move away, then hurried through the walkway to the front of the building. He didn't peek around the corner this time, hoping to see Dusty's large back as it walked away, and let his rifle put the massive man down quickly.

As his muzzle cleared the corner, a bear paw grabbed it and pinned it to the wall to Porter's left.

"I saw you hiding. I don't like it when people point guns at me."

Porter's rifle was nowhere near Dusty, but he fired it

anyway, trying to frighten the man into letting go. It didn't work —Dusty still held the muzzle pointed toward the wall as the round tore through the siding of the Teddy Bear, kicking up wood shavings and splinters.

"You another one of them Mexicans? You the biggest I ever seen."

"You're one to talk, Bubba," Porter said. Dusty was easily four inches taller than Porter, and probably had a hundred pounds on him.

"I'm not Bubba," Dusty said, trying to yank the rifle from Porter's hands.

Porter took a step backward, trying to use his weight to pull the rifle into position to shoot Dusty.

It didn't work. Dusty grabbed Porter's arm and, with his other hand still on the barrel, slammed Porter and the rifle into the wall. Porter pushed back, heaving Dusty off him, but the drug trafficker responded by slamming Porter into the hard side of the motel half a dozen more times.

There was a *crunch* and Porter glanced down at his rifle, the barrel now bent askew. It was worthless to him, even if he had a shot. He didn't want to take the chance; pulling the trigger could result in the top end of the weapon blowing up in his own face.

He hammer-fisted Dusty's hand, breaking the grip on his arm and giving him a bit of space. While Porter believed every rifle needed a sling, the only drawback was a situation like this. With the sling attached to his body, he couldn't just let go of the rifle.

"Let go," Porter growled. He slammed a punch into Dusty's collarbone. The man took it without flinching.

Porter changed tactics. Instead of trying to get away, he bulled into Dusty, which was like trying to move a tree. Porter let go of his useless rifle and grabbed Dusty by the back of the head, smashing a head-butt into his nose. The man's nose opened up, blood freely flowing down his face.

"Shit!" Dusty yelled as he let go of the rifle.

"I told you to let go." Porter's back was against the front wall of the motel and he couldn't move far, so he wasted no time reaching for his pistol, which was waiting patiently in its holster.

Dusty looked up, lower face covered in blood and charged into Porter again. He grabbed Porter in a bear hug and trapped his arms by his side. Porter couldn't get his gun free.

Then Dusty slammed him to the ground.

Porter felt the air driven from his lungs by the impact. The big man's bulk landed on top of him, leaving tiny pinpricks of light dancing in front of his face.

Dusty released the bear hug, now content to introduce his hands to Porter's throat. Porter's newly released hands did him no good—his head was swimming from the impact of the slam. Dusty was straddling him, and squeezed.

The pressure was incredible. Porter felt like an eye might pop out, like the top of his head would spurt out like a geyser. He first went to Dusty's hands, trying to move them, but quickly realized that was impossible. The man's size and strength made him impossible to move.

As the darkness closed in around his face, Porter reached down and felt the grip of his pistol. He closed his hand around it and pulled as hard as he could, ripping it past Dusty's thigh where it was trapped.

With no way to see where he was aiming, Porter pointed the pistol up and into the big man, squeezing the trigger three times.

There was a howl of pain from on top of him. At the same time, the vise on his neck was released and fresh, cool air came rushing into his lungs.

He'd hit Dusty in the armpit, rendering his left arm useless. His arm hung limply at his side as he rose, trying to get away from Porter. For his part, Porter lifted the pistol, trying to aim it at the man on top of him.

Dusty must have seen what Porter was doing, and he reached out with his good arm to grab the pistol. The two men silently struggled for the gun. Dusty's reach left him off balance and Porter grabbed him by the collar, pulling him down toward the ground while he pushed up with his gun hand.

The two men rolled and now Porter was on top.

Dusty's left arm flopped uselessly by his side, and he used his good hand to try to push Porter's gun away from him. Now that he was in control, Porter grabbed Dusty's hand and, using two arms against the drug man's one, wrenched the pistol back into position.

Dusty was definitely bigger than Porter, and he was stronger. Probably. But there was no way he could stop Porter from moving the gun now. Porter yanked and yanked the pistol, turning and torquing, until it was hovering in the space above Dusty's body.

His face covered in blood, his arm dead weight, Dusty spoke out. "Wait, wait, wai—"

Porter pulled the trigger over and over, until Dusty stopped moving and struggling underneath him. Then he stood up, coughing and sputtering, trying to catch his breath.

"I... told you... to let go."

# FIFTY-SIX

PORTER SUCKED wind as he leaned against the motel wall. Below him, Dusty was a bloody mess, Porter's rounds having torn through his upper torso. He adjusted his rifle, now useless, and tightened it to his back. He couldn't use it, but he didn't want to leave it behind. A few fixes and it would be good as new.

When his head was mostly clear, Porter leveled the pistol in front of him and moved down the walkway in front of the rooms, trying to remember which room held the two people sitting on the floor.

The curtains were shut tightly on a room several doors down, but the light of the lantern was still spilling through the holes and rips. Porter walked to the front door, swung it open and stepped in behind the barrel of his gun.

"Who the hell are you?" he said, lowering his pistol. "Huh? Speak up."

The two girls looked up, their arms wrapped tightly around each other. One, with dark hair, had her head buried in the chest of the one who was blonder and bigger.

Porter looked on the floor at a motionless body. There was

enough of the face left to identify the body as Seth Rollins. "What the hell happened to him?"

"Same thing that'll happen to you," the bigger woman said. Porter saw her go for a revolver on the floor. As she reached for it, he stepped forward and kicked her in the chest, flipping her onto her back and knocking her cold.

The raven-haired girl looked at him, and for the first time, he could see her striking blue eyes. "Please don't kill us."

"Pima?" Porter said.

"Huh?"

"Damn it, listen to me. Are you Pima Newton?"

"Y...yes."

"Good. Come on, we're leaving," Porter said.

Pima's eyes went wide and she started to run, but Porter caught her by the arm.

"No, no, let me go!"

"Stop it," Porter said, holding the girl tightly by the arms. "Look at me."

The struggling girl didn't.

"Your dad is Mike, right? Your mom's Terri? They sent me. I'm here to help."

"Huh?"

"I'm here to help. Come on, we have to leave," Porter said.

"My dad?" Pima said softly.

"Yeah, FBI agent. Ring any bells?"

Pima nodded her head. For the first time, Porter saw a glimmer of coherence.

"Good. Now we have to go. There are dangerous men around."

Pima pointed toward the woman on the floor as Porter dragged her from the room. "Wait, what about her? She helped me."

Porter paused in the doorway and looked at the unconscious woman. "Did she get taken or is she one of them?"

"She's one of them, but—"

"Then I don't care. Let's go."

"But—"

"Let's go!" Porter said. "Grab my belt and stick close to me, got it?"

Pima nodded, taking one last look at the woman on the floor. She grabbed Porter's belt.

"Good. Now keep up," he said.

Porter moved quickly down the hall. Cognizant that Pima had shorter legs, he slowed down enough for her to keep up. They walked past Dusty's lifeless body and Porter heard the girl retch. "Come on, we don't have time for that now."

She held tight to his belt as he led her down the stairs and into the parking lot. Porter's head was constantly moving, back and forth, again and again, eyes moving to find any hidden assailants.

The pair crossed into the bright beams of the Civic's headlights and Porter looked at the bodies of the cartel men Seth and Dusty had left in their wake.

He opened the passenger door and let Pima into the idling Honda. Porter shut the door tightly behind her and stepped out into the field of light, reaching down and grabbing the rolling suitcase of money that the cartel had tossed to Seth. It was lying there in need of a new owner, and Porter was happy to oblige.

He tossed the rolling suitcase into the back seat and slid the driver's as far back as it could go, then dropped heavily into the vehicle. He listened to the whine of the four-cylinder as he slammed the gas and pointed the car out of the parking lot and away from the Teddy Bear Motel.

Pima had her hands on her head. "Who are you?"

"Wait a minute."

"I mean, where did you come from, how did you—"

"I said wait a damn minute," Porter said.

Moments later, he pulled into the Cherokee Brave motel, leaving the Honda running with Pima in the car.

He ducked underneath the willow tree and fired up the Yukon, pulling it out in front of the Honda. Porter got out and opened Pima's door. "This is our ride. Get in."

Pima followed Porter's orders, half-stumbling over to the passenger's seat.

Porter made sure she was in, then reached back into the Honda to grab the surprisingly heavy suitcase of money, and threw it into the Yukon.

Taking advantage of the Yukon's larger engine, Porter stomped the gas and the engine roared to life as he pulled back onto the main road. The Teddy Bear Motel went flying by on his right and Porter adjusted the rearview mirror and watched as it grew smaller and smaller, glad to see its broken sign disappear into the night.

# FIFTY-SEVEN

TEDDY BEAR FIRMLY BEHIND HIM, Porter took care to slow down on the winding roads. It seemed unlikely that anyone was following him. Now it mattered more that he had arrived alive with the precious cargo he'd managed to grab. The last thing he wanted to do was end up in a ravine because he drove like an idiot.

There was silence in the car. Porter was trying to come down from the events of the last half-hour and Pima was looking out the side window into the darkness.

He swallowed hard, and felt like his Adam's apple wouldn't go the entire trip up and down his throat. He swallowed again and forced it, then cleared his throat.

Dusty had a hell of a grip.

He looked over at the back of Pima's head. "You want to listen to something?"

There was no answer, just the small shake of her head.

Porter looked at the road. "You feel okay? Do I need to get you some help?"

Another shake of the head.

"I mean, if they hurt you, we should get you checked out."

Pima turned and faced Porter. "I'm okay."

He looked at her small face, unable to see her eyes by the glow of the dashboard. "You sure? Because if one of those guys... you know... you should see a doctor."

Pima looked at Porter for a minute. "You mean... eww, no. I'm fine."

"Okay, good," Porter said, glad to change the subject. "Food?"

"No thanks," Pima said, looking out the window again.

There was a long silence. Porter turned onto the main highway, which he'd follow for a long while.

He pulled out his phone. He thumbed it and the screen glowed to life.

"What are you doing?"

"Calling your parents. They should know you're all right."

"No," Pima said. "No, don't."

Porter looked over at her for a few moments, then turned the phone off. "Something the matter with your folks?"

The girl looked out the window for a few moments, then it was like a dam burst open. "They're gonna be so mad at me, I shouldn't have even been in the woods and I didn't listen, I should have been at home. Dusty tried to kill me and my neck still hurts and my dad's gonna kill me. Seth got shot in the face and I never seen a dead body before and they shot that trooper, he was just trying to help me. I was so scared and they kept putting me in a trunk and, oh my God, Laura Bell is dead too." Pima was silent again.

Porter looked over at her, his eyebrows raised. "Uh... there's a lot to unpack there."

She went back to looking out the window.

"If it makes you feel any better, Dusty tried to strangle me, too. So we're kind of like strangle twins."

Pima didn't say anything.

"Yeah, that was dumb. It's been a long time since I was thirteen. Trust me, all this is not as bad as you think."

"People are dead," Pima said. "It doesn't get any worse."

Porter nodded. "Yeah, but except for the trooper, they were all shitty people. Don't feel bad for them."

"Laura Bell wasn't... that."

"Who's she?" Porter asked.

"We should have helped her. She's probably dead by now."

"Who are you talking about?"

"The girl you killed."

"I didn't kill a girl."

Pima turned in her seat, facing Porter. "The girl you kicked in the hotel. She's not dead?"

"Look, I'm strong, but I'm not Pele."

"Who?" Pima said.

"Never mind. She's okay, trust me."

Pima looked at him for a few moments. Porter didn't meet her gaze, but was aware that she was staring at him in the dark. "The rest of it... it's bad. I feel bad."

"Your parents just want you home. They don't care about the rest of it. Trust me, they'll be cool."

"I just keep thinking about Seth's head." She mimed an explosion by her head.

Porter turned the heat down and lowered the blower a level. "Want to know something? It's never going to go away. I know that's not what you want to hear, but it's the truth."

Pima didn't say anything.

"When I was a kid, my family moved around a lot. We didn't stay many places too long, and it was hard for me to fit in. So when I had a friend, they were like my best friend ever, you know what I mean?"

Pima nodded in the darkness.

"We'd just moved to Tampa, and I met this kid named Tommy who lived down the block from me. Tommy Thomas."

"His name was Thomas Thomas?" Pima said.

"That's the part you're worried about?" Porter said. "Can I finish?"

"Sorry."

"Me and Tommy hung out all summer long. It was great—his parents both worked and they were never home. So we'd go to his house and eat all the food and get into stuff we shouldn't. His parents had the dirty channels on cable and we thought we were all grown up, but we had no clue what the hell we were even watching. We'd get tired of that and watch dumb action movies, the whole nine. We had a great time, me and Tommy."

"What's so bad about that?" Pima said.

"One day, Tommy manages to find the key to his dad's gun safe. He gets this little pistol out and starts pretending to be the Terminator or something like that. I'm laughing along like an asshole, because Tommy's funny, right? Then, he pulled the trigger."

Porter turned off the highway and slowed as he came off the ramp. "He blew his own head off and I watched the whole thing. I remember thinking, 'How can blood be that red?' It was surreal. I just stood there for a few minutes, frozen, not sure what to do. Then I ran home, and you know what I did?"

"What?"

"Nothing. Not a thing. I walked in the house like nothing happened. My dad asked me where I'd been and I lied and told him at the park, then I went into my room and read comic books for the rest of the day. But I couldn't shake the picture of Tommy in my mind, no matter what I did."

"Did they ever find Tommy?" Pima said.

"Of course they did; he was dead in the middle of his living room. When his parents came home they freaked out and called the cops. Eventually they came to my house, because everyone knew I was tight with Tommy. The cops asked me what happened and I was scared. So, I lied. I told them I wasn't there."

Pima was silent.

"My father believed me and told them to leave, to stop bothering me with their questions. I thought everything was done. But I couldn't sleep that night. I kept seeing Tommy's head blow off, over and over again. All night I laid in bed, petrified. So, I got up right as the sun was coming up, I went into my parents' room and woke them up. Then I told them everything that happened. All of it. I didn't leave anything out."

"How did they take it?" Pima said.

"Honestly? Better than I thought. They called Tommy's parents and the cops, and they still stuck up for me about the whole thing. Because that's what your parents do. Don't be scared to tell them. Just do it."

"Do you still think about it?"

"No, not really. This is the first time I've told the story in twenty years. I told you it would never go away, and it doesn't. It's always somewhere there, waiting for you to pick at the scab and think about it again. But eventually, you won't pick at the scab as much. Then you'll wake up and realize you haven't thought about it for a while. Then the time between you thinking about it gets longer and longer. Trust me, you won't see it every time you close your eyes. Not forever, anyway."

"You think so?" Pima said.

"Yeah, I do. And if there's something else I know, your parents are cooler than mine were. You'll be all right—just tell them everything. Get it off your chest and be done with it."

Porter pulled up to the gatehouse in front of the Newtons' neighborhood. The omnipresent guard was in the gatehouse, his face illuminated by the soft glow of a square television on the table.

"Does that guy live in there?" Porter muttered to himself.

"Huh?"

"Never mind."

The guard opened the gate and waved the Yukon on. Porter slowly drove the streets to Pima's house, careful not to speed in the neighborhood in the dark. He took the last few turns and pulled into the driveway, careful to avoid the bicycle half in the grass. He killed the lights.

"You're going to be okay."

"Think I'm going to have to see a shrink or something?"

"Nothing wrong with that. Just tell your parents the truth, got it?"

Pima rested her hand on the door handle.

The lights outside the garage clicked on, then the lights on the porch. Mike Newton's head came around the corner, followed by his wife's. She had a thick robe on; he wore a jacket on top of pajama pants.

It was dark in the driveway, and with Porter's tint, they had no way to see into the truck.

"You should get out. They probably think I found your body or something."

Pima nodded, then pulled the handle and slowly pushed her door open.

The sidewalk exploded in motion. Terri pushed past her husband, screaming "Pima?" the entire time. She slammed into her daughter, squeezing her tightly, showering her with kisses. Mike was hot on her heels, wrapping them both up in an enormous bear hug.

Porter rolled the window down and watched the reunion. Moments later, the youngest Newton, Bryce, came outside barefoot, wearing a pair of shorts and a tank top. The whole family stayed in one big bundle for several minutes.

As if she were snapping out of a trance, Terri spoke up. "Bryce! Where are your shoes? It's too cold out here. Come on, let's go inside." She led the two children back to the warmth of the home, and Mike Newton stepped over to the open passenger window.

"How did you... I mean, where did she come from?"

"Long story," Porter said.

"Well, get in here, I need to know."

"Later. I don't want to interrupt family time. I'll be in touch."

Mike nodded. "Okay. Okay, well, let's talk tomorrow, got it?"

"Sure, tomorrow. Go inside and see your girl."

Mike Newton turned away and was halfway up the sidewalk when Porter called out. "Mike?"

He turned back toward the Yukon.

"Take it easy on her."

Mike gave Porter a thumbs up and turned back toward his front door.

Porter never saw any of the Newtons again.

# FIFTY-EIGHT

ON THE WAY back to his motel, Porter pulled his phone out and saw three texts and a missed call from Claudette. His finger hovered over the callback button, but he wavered, instead scrolling down to one of the recently called numbers. The phone picked up on the first ring.

"What happened?"

"I figured you'd be asleep, old man," Porter said.

"I don't sleep much anymore. I think my body has gotten so used to running on caffeine and hate that sleep is irrelevant. I'm very efficient now."

"Sure you are. Why does it sound like you just got out of a grave?"

"I may have nodded off," Joe said.

"I'll bet. Hey, listen, that thing with Pima is handled."

"Pima Newton? You found Pima Newton?"

"Who else would I be calling you about? You sure you aren't asleep?" Porter said.

"Are you shitting me? Is she okay?"

"I think so. She's seen some shit, but physically, she's fine."

"What happened? I need details," Joe said.

"It's a long, cold story," Porter said.

"I have time."

"I don't," Porter said. "Sorry man, I'll fill you in later."

"Deniability?"

"Something like that. But I do have a quick question. Does your office cover the county next to Mike Newton's?" Porter said.

"The western half of the state is ours, so yeah, we got it. Why?"

"Something may come across your desk. A hotel incident," Porter said.

"Is this related to the trailer incident?"

"It's definitely a sibling. Don't pay too much attention to it, you tracking? It doesn't need an FBI investigation."

"More deniability?"

"Yeah. It was the universe sorting itself out. Nothing to see here, folks; move along," Porter said.

"I'm following. You all right?"

"Peachy. I'll be even better when I get that reward money," Porter said.

"I'll make sure Mike sends it on. He won't drag his feet."

"Good," Porter said.

"Look, kid, I want to say thanks for helping. I want to tell you how much I appreciate you and that I owe you the world for this. But I'm not going to," Joe said.

"Good. I don't want you turning into a pussy on me," Porter said. "Especially with that new mustache you have. It's unsettling to think about."

"Never. Still, I wasn't kidding. If you ever did ask Amanda out, I could think of worse guys for her to spend time with. Not many, but some."

"I'll take that as a compliment."

"You should." Joe hung up the phone.

Porter drove the rest of the way to his motel in silence.

He opened the room cautiously and found no one lying in wait for him.

No cartel thugs, no crooked cops, and no giants with base-ball-glove-sized hands.

No pretty diner owner, either.

He dragged the rolling suitcase full of drug money into his room, pushed the dresser across the door, and was asleep in his clothes in seconds.

# FIFTY-NINE

LAURA BELL PULLED Seth's red hat low on her head. It wasn't just to hide the terrific colors her face was turning from the beatings she'd taken.

It wasn't just to shield her eyes against the bright light from the big windows beaming right into her face.

She pulled the hat down to hide who she was.

The news playing on the small television above the vending machine had been running nonstop since she'd gotten there. It seemed that every few minutes, there was a segment on her family, still wanted for killing the trooper.

Every time the old high school yearbook photo of her splashed across the screen, she sank a little lower in her chair.

The news had flashed a picture of Pima a few times, breaking the news that the young girl had been found alive, with no mention of where she'd come from or been.

"Good for her," Laura Bell muttered.

She coughed gently into her elbow. If her ribs had been broken from Seth kicking her, they'd been shattered when the big guy at the hotel did the same. She didn't know who he was, but he kicked like a mule.

When she came to, Pima was gone and everyone else was dead.

At first, there had been a moment of panic. The need to run. Laura Bell had suppressed that quickly and realized she was alone. And while being alone was scary, it beat being dead, or following her family around trying to keep them out of trouble.

"Excuse me," said a young man with dirty jeans and ratty shoes.

Laura Bell pulled in her legs to let him by, her face tilted down.

Once she'd calmed down, Laura Bell had paced around the room her brother's dead body was in. Gave herself time to think. There was no telling when anyone would stumble on the massacre at the Teddy Bear, if they ever did. Laura Bell told herself she was in charge now, and she could make the plan that made the best sense.

So she did.

Wiping off the revolver with which she'd shot both the trooper and Seth, she'd dropped it to the floor. Then, she painstakingly went through every dead man's pants, looking for money.

She wouldn't get far without money.

Her brother had the most, followed by one of the Mexicans who had tattoos all over his face.

Dusty didn't have a dime.

All told, she'd scraped together almost nine thousand dollars. Nine thousand dollars wasn't much compared to the amounts they used to keep around, when they'd sell off some of the product, but it was a hell of a lot better than nothing.

She'd picked up Seth's hat from the floor, something to help hide her, and to keep anyone from recognizing her face. Laura Bell had pulled her hair back with her rainbow rubber band and stuffed it underneath the hat.

The Lumina was the only car left in the lot, and she'd driven it as far as she thought was safe, ditching it before she got to one of the more traveled main roads. Then she'd walked and thumbed a ride to get to where she was.

The bus station.

Ever since she'd arrived, she'd been frozen, a new strain of fear gripping her. Her face was on all the news broadcasts. Everyone was looking for her. The ticket seller would want her ID. If she bought a ticket, they'd know who she was, call the cops, and arrest her.

So she sat. For hours.

Her leg was bouncing as she watched the people move around her, everyone going their own way. Everyone with a plan on who they were seeing. Everyone with someplace or someone to go to.

The gnawing in her stomach finally getting the better of her, she walked over to the vending machine and examined her options.

"It's not easy, is it?" a voice behind her said.

Laura Bell wheeled around and saw a plump woman wearing a bus employee uniform.

"There are a lot of choices," Laura Bell said as she turned back to the vending machine and bent over to look closely.

"That's not what I mean."

Laura Bell straightened up and turned around again. The lanyard around the woman's neck had an ID that read *Sharon Simpson*. "I'm sorry?"

Sharon looked around, then stepped closer to Laura Bell. "I know."

"You know what?"

"Who you are."

Laura Bell looked at her for a moment, then pulled her hat

low again. "You must have me confused with someone else," she said as she started to walk away.

Sharon gently hooked her arm. "I know who you are because it was me once."

Laura Bell turned around and raised her eyebrows.

"Once upon a time, when I wasn't much older than you, I had a husband who beat me, too."

"You think my hus—"

"I mean, look at your face, honey. You're so swollen and black and blue, I can tell you don't even look like you anymore. No pretty girl gets beat on like that, ain't a man involved."

Laura Bell didn't say anything.

"See? I can tell. I recognize the signs. I've been watching you for hours, sitting over in that little corner. Scared, watching everyone that goes by. You trying to work up the courage to leave, aren't you?"

Laura Bell hesitated for a moment. "Something like that."

Sharon nodded her head. "It's a look you girls have. Time to time, someone shows up, looking like they need to get away. Sometimes, they get up, get on a bus and go who knows where. And I'm happy for them. Sometimes, they walk right out the front door, and I'm sad for them. Because I know what they're going back to."

Laura Bell didn't say anything.

"You got any kids, honey?"

She shook her head.

"It's even easier if you got no kids. I had two when I walked out the door. It was hard, but the best thing I ever did."

"I think I should—"

"Go. Yeah—yeah, you should. You should go wherever you want. And tell you what, since I work here, I get a few free bus passes to use. I never have time; I'm too busy working. I always try to give them away. Give them to people who look like they need them. Would you like one?"

"I'm not sure if I should."

"Why not? What do you have to lose?"

"I don't even know where to go."

Sharon nodded. "Tell you what, you come with me right now and I'll set you right."

"Right now?"

"Yep. Come on."

Sharon gently pulled Laura Bell's arm and met with no resistance.

The pair walked out the front, to the large asphalt parking lot where several buses were idling. The bus station employee looked at the destination placards in a couple of the windows and walked Laura Bell to the third one.

"But I don't... I don't have my ID or anything."

"That ain't no problem."

Sharon banged her fist on the bus's bi-fold glass door. It opened with a squeak.

"Hey, Sharon. How you been, baby?"

"Better than I deserve, Gus," Sharon said, pulling Laura Bell in front of the open doorway.

Laura Bell looked up the stairs at the driver's bushy white beard and thick glasses.

"Gus, this is a friend of mine who needs a ride. Can you use one of my vouchers?"

"No need. Hell, we leaving in a few minutes and we only half full. Just go find you a seat."

Laura Bell looked at Sharon, then to Gus, then back to Sharon. "Where's the bus going?"

"If you have nowhere to go, does it matter?"

Laura Bell looked down for a moment, then reached out and squeezed Sharon tightly. "Thank you."

“No need. You just help someone else that needs it someday.”

Laura Bell nodded and started up the stairs. She paused halfway up, then stepped back down to the asphalt.

“Forget something?” Sharon said.

“Yeah.” Laura Bell took her red hat off and handed it to Sharon. “Could you please throw this away for me? I don’t need it anymore.”

# SIXTY

THE COWBELL CLANKED its usual welcome and Porter stood for a moment in the entryway, looking across the counter.

"Are you colorblind?" a voice called out from the kitchen.

"My dad was," Porter said. "Fun fact about me. Well, him, I guess."

Claudette came out of the kitchen holding a spray bottle of blue cleaning liquid and a rag. "Then you should have been able to find the little green button on your phone—the one that says 'talk'—and call me. Or am I missing something?"

"I know. I'm sorry. How was the casino?" Porter said, a hopeful lilt in his voice.

"You mean despite getting stood up?"

"Naturally," Porter said.

"It was actually great. I won seventeen hundred dollars. Go me."

Porter smiled. "Then you should really be thanking me."

"How's that?"

"If I'd been there, you would have been too busy to gamble."

Claudette blushed. Porter hadn't tired of watching the flush of color move around her chest, neck, and face. "Says you."

They each leaned on the counter, an easy silence between them, which Claudette soon broke. "It was because of Pima Newton, right?"

"I'm not sure what you mean," Porter said.

"Please. I told you this was a small town. A couple of our big-mouthed crones saw her going to breakfast with her parents. I'm sure she didn't come home accidentally."

"Definitely no accident," Porter said.

"So it was you, then? Look, you don't have to tell me, it's okay. I'm probably better off not knowing. But if you stood me up to find her, or help her or something, how can I be mad?"

Porter stared at the woman. "I am sorry, though."

"I know. It's okay." She broke away from his eyes and looked down at the floor beside him. "Nice suitcase."

"You like it? I got it for you," Porter said.

"Pretty random to give somebody one piece of luggage, but I could use a new roller."

"Glad you like it," Porter said.

"How can I say thanks?"

"You know what I want," Porter said.

"Since we're in public, I'll assume you mean something to eat."

"Well, that too," Porter said with a smile.

"Go sit," she said and disappeared to the kitchen.

Porter sat at his table and looked out the picture window at the small street. People walking up and down; parents with their children, pushing strollers. The setting was picturesque, with the last of the leaves still dangling from their branches.

It seemed nice.

Claudette came back after some time and handed Porter a brown paper bag.

"What's this?"

"Your usual. And although I will never bless that concoction you put on my masterpieces, I gave you a few handfuls of ketchup and mayo packets," Claudette said.

"No tray? I really am in the doghouse, huh?"

She smiled. "I'm not stupid, Porter. I know you're leaving."

Porter looked at her and didn't say anything.

"And that's okay. Honestly. Don't get me wrong, I like you and you seem like a great guy. But I knew you were leaving when you were done doing what you came for. Now that Pima's back, I don't think you'll stay much longer."

"Claudette, I'm—"

"It's fine. Seriously. I'm not some delusional schoolgirl stalker who thought you were staying forever. That thought never crossed my mind," she said.

"Never say you aren't a schoolgirl. I bet if we dress you up in a little skirt—"

"Oh, shut up. I had a great time with you. I know I would again. If you're out this way in the future, look me up. Deal?"

"I will," Porter promised. He fished in his pocket and pulled out the copy of *The Graveyard Book* that she'd loaned him. "I wanted to give this back to you."

"Did you read it yet?"

"No. I was a little busy the last few days," Porter said.

"Keep it. When you come back, tell me what you thought about it."

"I can't take your favorite book."

"I can find another one if I need to," she said. "I'm sure we have it at the library."

"Just make sure you turn it in on time. I've met Lonnie the librarian," Porter said. "I think he'd hunt you down."

They laughed and held each other's eyes for a moment.

"Come here." Claudette motioned for Porter to stand and he did. They hugged for several moments and ended the embrace with a small kiss.

Porter picked up his bag of food, then tapped the handle of the rolling suitcase.

"Let me put this in your car for you," Porter said.

"Just leave it. I'll get it in a few."

"It's kind of heavy," Porter said.

"What am I, feeble?"

"I'm only good at a couple of things, and lifting stuff is one of them. If you take that away from me, what else will I have? You wouldn't want me to feel unfulfilled, would you?"

Claudette flashed her crooked smile. "Fine, just put it on the passenger seat."

"I will."

After one last hug, Porter was out the door without another look behind him. The cowbell was the last thing he heard from his new favorite restaurant.

The only thing keeping him from leaving the little town and heading home was the small matter of keeping his word.

And Porter was a man of his word.

# EPILOGUE

SHERIFF DENNIS SPAULDING'S stomach turned at the thought of another sip of bourbon. The stupid country hicks he'd surrounded himself with worshipped the stuff. He tried to pretend, so they didn't accuse him of being any more of a Yankee than they already thought he was, but he couldn't stomach another mouthful.

Deep down, he dreaded every sip he took. He knew he needed to drink it, as the most influential of the men in the area seemed to worship the stuff. If it wasn't the mayor, it was the district attorney; if it wasn't the county manager, it was the head of the local political party. Everyone trying to be so much more important than they were with the old bourbon and cigars.

"Silly rednecks," he muttered to himself.

He pulled another microbrew from his refrigerator. It was from a small brewery based in his neck of the woods, just outside Boston. He missed the Northeast, and wanted to go back. In fact, his Martha was there for the next couple weeks, visiting friends and family.

He was supposed to be with his wife right now, but this Pima Newton business had popped up.

He couldn't believe the mess the Rollins clan had managed to make. Not only kidnapping the daughter of an FBI agent, but then not having the good sense to kill her like professionals.

When he'd gone to the county next door, to help work the crime scene at the Teddy Bear Motel, he hadn't shed a tear for the idiots who'd died there. Why should he? They'd brought it on themselves. In fact, if each group had been a little smarter, none of this would have ever happened.

Still, the incident wasn't a total loss. Now that Pima Newton had been rescued, that big son of a bitch Porter was out of his hair. That alone was worth his losses at the Teddy Bear.

Sure, he'd have to find a new crew to split their profits with him, but it shouldn't be hard. The jail was full of local idiots who were looking for a quick buck. Spaulding didn't think he could broker a new deal with the cartel, though; they would be pretty sore about losing so many men in one small town in only a few days.

That was the only part Spaulding was concerned about. The Los Primos cartel had a way of carrying a grudge. But this was America, not Mexico. People didn't just kill police here. Elected officials didn't get kidnapped and executed as a warning to stay out of things.

This wasn't Juárez; no one killed the town sheriff here.

Even if he'd been inclined to worry, he'd positioned himself as a hard target. His big pension plus the salary the county paid him had afforded him the luxury of living in the nicest neighborhood in the area, with a gate and twenty-four-hour watchmen. There were two guards on at all times, and they even got into a little golf cart once an hour and checked things out. It was a better neighborhood than Pima's father could afford on his fat federal salary.

No, there was no easy way to get at him, and Spaulding knew it.

Spaulding drained the last of the beer, then padded across the wide, hardwood planks and went to the kitchen in search of another one.

He passed the massive granite island that took up the middle of the kitchen and dug through the fridge. It took a bit of a contortionist act, but Spaulding found the last one, way in the back.

He'd have to order more from the brewery. He cursed at the thought of having to leave and go get a lesser local brew, but smiled because there was no one to arrest him for drunk driving.

As he popped the top off, he heard a faint ringing noise. He stood still for a moment, then brushed it off.

On his way back to his leather sectional, he heard it again. Spaulding paused once more, this time holding still for much longer. About the time he convinced himself that he was imagining things, he heard it a third time.

Spaulding moved toward the direction he thought the noise had come from. He stood still, waiting to hear it again. It wasn't any noise he remembered hearing in his home before.

The noise came once more.

Spaulding went to the laundry room, thinking maybe his sweet Martha had changed the ring alert on their double-capacity washing machine.

The machine was off.

Walking around the kitchen hunting the noise, Spaulding heard it again and got a bead on it. He walked to his front door. Putting his ear against it, he stood frozen, trying to verify his hunch.

Through the door, yet another ring.

Spaulding retrieved his pistol from the countertop and slowly opened the door, coming face-to-face with nothing. His nearest neighbor in either direction was over a hundred yards away. There was a conservation green space across from him that would never be built on. That was one of the things he liked best about the lot he had chosen to build his home on. Privacy.

Looking around for a few moments, Spaulding heard the ring again. This time, he turned and saw a large box on his porch swing.

He frowned, stuck his pistol in his waistband, and walked over to the box. It was for a low-priced bourbon, more of the stuff he hated. He wondered why whoever had dropped it off hadn't waited and shared some with him. He had come to expect that from these idiot locals.

Resolving to figure out who the gift-giver was later, he lifted the box up, noticing an odd splash of spray paint on either side of the box.

The last thought Sheriff Dennis Spaulding ever had was to lament having to drink the contents of this box with someone. More bourbon—he just couldn't get away from the stuff.

The last sound Sheriff Dennis Spaulding ever heard was the crack of a rifle, sending the right-sized round, with the right velocity, piercing through the package.

And then *boom.*

## LIKE MOVING TARGET? GET READY FOR ROUGH COMPANY!

**To reunite a father and missing son, there's no telling how many laws—and bones—he'll break.**

Porter isn't above breaking the law in the name of justice. So when his cousin pleads for his help in reuniting a military friend with his young son, the former federal agent suits up to settle matters outside of court. But with a vindictive ex and her crooked fiancée thwarting his every move, the custody battle may just end in bloodshed...

And if tracking down an endangered child wasn't enough of a challenge, Porter finds himself roped into a turf war that threatens to drive his cousin's bar out of business. With brawling Armenian gangsters, a growing pile of dead bodies, and a prying journalist on Porter's case, his retaliation comes up two fists shy of law and order.

When the justice system fails the most vulnerable, how much pain is Porter willing to inflict to set it straight?

*Rough Company* is the third novel in a razor-sharp series of crime thrillers. If you like bone-shattering action, gripping suspense, and quick-witted heroes with nerves of steel, then you'll love R.A. McGee's unflinching tale.

Buy *Rough Company* to join a brutal hunt for justice today!

You can find all of R.A. McGee's books on Amazon.com

# WANT FREE BOOKS?

# ABOUT THE AUTHOR

R.A. McGee is the best-selling author of gritty mystery and thriller novels, including the Porter series and the Blackthorn Thrillers.

He lives in the mountains with his wife and small tribe of children.

He can be reached at: info@ramcgee.com